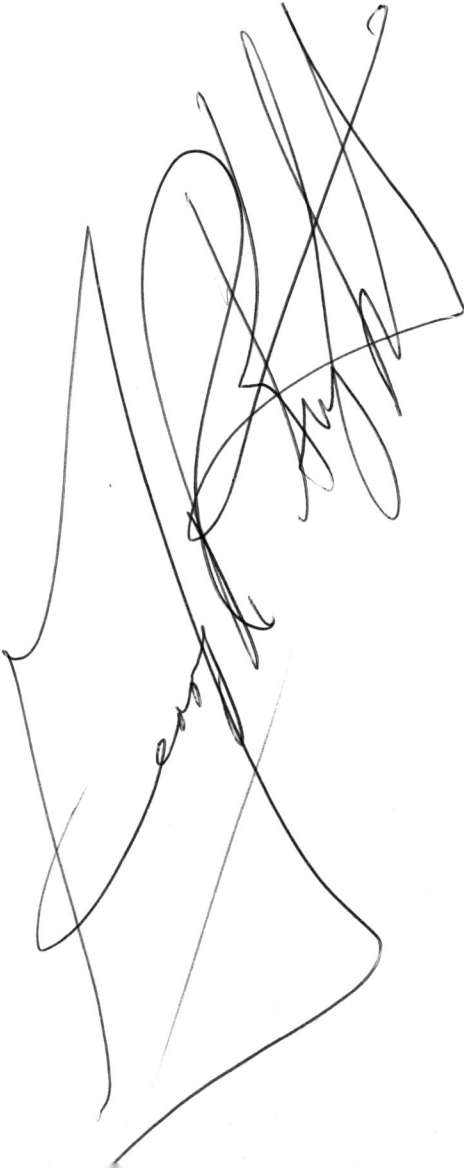

WEST
by Bullwhip

by George Richard Knight

IP

ITHACA PRESS

NEW YORK

Ithaca Press
3 Kimberly Drive, Suite B
Dryden, New York 13053 USA
www.IthacaPress.com

This book is a work of fiction.

Cover Design	Gary Hoffman
Book Design	Gary Hoffman
Cover art	Original oil painting by Lindy Johnson

Manufactured in the United States of America

9 8 7 6 5 4 3 2 1

Library of Congress Cataloging-in-Data Available
Knight/George Richard/ U S Western history/Historical Fiction/Adventure/

ISBN 978-0-9819746-0-6

First Edition

Printed in the United States of America

www.GeorgeRichardKnight.com

WEST

by Bullwhip

by George Richard Knight

DEDICATION

I dedicate this story to my many grandchildren and great grandchildren to give them some background of their heritage.

—George Richard Knight

ACKNOWLEDGEMENTS

To have written a novel is a satisfying task. But knowing what was ahead and all the people to be involved was an experience beyond my original expectations.

First of all, I would like to thank my publisher, Joan Mayor of Ithaca Press for publishing this first writing called *West by Bullwhip*. Also, Liz Muse, Joan's editor for taking me through the changes necessary for the reader's enjoyment of the story I wish to portray.

My wife, Yvonne, gave support beyond belief. She accepted the fact I felt the need to travel to some of the areas covered in my story for my own satisfaction and gratification as well as getting a feel for the areas that my great grandfather and grandfather had traveled.

My appreciation goes to my sister-in-law, Betsy Knight, for her first editing of spelling and grammar as I wrote my story and to my brother, Donald, for his historical facts of the family and his research back to Ireland. Also my sister, Mary Lou Barnes, for the help she contributed about railroading.

Not to be overlooked, I received much encouragement from a writing teacher, Margaret Park, here in Green Valley, Arizona at Pima Community College.

Last but not least, I wish to thank Sheila O'Hare with the Western History Department of the Denver City Library for help with my research of the Colorado territory during the time period taking place within the story.

FOREWORD

My brother asked me to write this foreword and I feel extremely honored to do so. *West by Bullwhip* is a fictionalized story, cracking with action and based on some of our Irish Grandfather's life and exploits between the ages of 10 and 24. It follows the journey of the Knight family from Kansas City, Missouri in 1863 to Denver City, Colorado and beyond. Our Grandfather, James Alburn Knight, called Jack, led a very colorful life and his parents, Richard and Elisabeth, were among those who helped settle and establish the town that would grow into the Rocky Mountain capitol of Denver located in the state of Colorado.

George researched, in depth, the history that is presented in this story and I am aware of how much time and dedication he put into it. So many of the natural sites were visited and the man-made histories of the Colorado and Kansas Territories were authenticated. As you travel along with our Irish family, you will share a real sense of being right there with Richard and Elisabeth and Jack and his younger sister, Mary Alice. You will experience the Knight family's journey along with other early western frontiersmen and settlers.

Some of the actual locations have been laid out for you in so much detail that you will be able to follow the story with map in hand if you wish. It is one of the author's hopes that you also may want to trace your family history in settling this great country called the United State of America.

How the west was won was not by larger than life heroes or legends but by hard working, self driven down to earth decent people. This was a time when a man's future had infinite possibilities, when a frontiersman like Andrew Jackson could become President and when the country was welding a solid work ethic. Each of our subsequent generations was imprinted with this fortitude and the drive to succeed and endure. We are all indebted to those who have preceded us and we owe them much respect and gratitude. *West by Bullwhip* is a tribute to rugged pioneers everywhere.

Respectively,
Donald G. Knight
Diamond Bar, California

AUTHOR'S NOTE

West by Bullwhip is taken from many stories I have heard from childhood to adulthood from my parents, siblings, and other relatives about my grandfather, James Alburn Knight. In putting these life stories into readable print, I had to bring into being fictitious characters and situations that were not part of any real facts but contributed to the realism of the times, places and adventures. Jack and his family were real people and lived a lot of the adventures. Some events were taken from a great uncle's scribbled writings; information gleaned from my brother's, Donald Knight, genealogy searches; and many of the tales told to me when I was very young.

Most of the times and dates coincide with history as recorded in various history books and on Internet sites. Many historical accounts have been altered over time and some of my research showed the same story has two different outcomes.

James Alburn Knight lived during a time of expansion and growth in America and he had a spirit of adventure that took him into many avenues within that expansion, bringing him into close contact with colorful figures of the day.

My hope is that the story will jog one's memory of some of history's great figures, events and legends or instill an interest in these happenings when our country was still in its formative years.

George Richard Knight

Green Valley, AZ

2009

CHAPTER 1

For a boy of 11, Kansas City, Missouri in 1860 was a daunting and mystic place to grow up. My imagination tended to run away with itself and I saw myself as an adventurer and an explorer, with the West as my personal playground.

My father, Richard Knight, was a blacksmith with a shop across the street from Boone's Trading Post in town. I spent time with him and heard the stories of adventure and riches that lay in the mountains, canyons, and plains of the West, told by men that brought wagons for repair and horses to be shod.

I had three half-brothers: Edwin, Charles and Jay, and a sister, Mary Alice. Edwin was 22 and training to be a lawyer. Charles, 19, was learning the blacksmith trade; Jay was just 16 and had no idea what he would accomplish other than being a gunfighter. Mary Alice was five and the greatest thing ever to happen to our family.

Going to school is mandatory since my mother, Elizabeth, was a teacher and was very strict about education and reading the proper books for boys my age. I collected books about adventure and anything about the West that was available, but I found the stories told by the mountain men and hunters at father's shop much more exciting.

At school I have a friend, Buddin Jeanette, and we have become what our parents called "inseparable." Buddin had an uncle, William Cody, and we heard of his adventures, even at his young age, and can't wait to be like him. Buddin had a flare for acting and putting on a grand display. He also had to be in charge of our adventures. That did not bother me because my passion was at my father's shop.

One day Buddin had an idea that we both needed code names or names that we could use for one another to confuse other kids. We both had known an Arapahoe Indian that used the word *Saki*, meaning friend. Buddin liked that word and so he was Saki. I searched for one word I liked, but found nothing. Buddin said, "Look your name is James Alburn Knight. Let's use J.A.K and call you Jack." My name, after that, was Jack. As we grew up, we drifted apart, as boys do, and went our separate ways. Buddin took up acting and I began learning to be a gunsmith. Guns were not my passion, since my father had taught me at a very young age to use the bullwhip for protection and sport. But father felt a gunsmith could survive quite well in the West. Besides, when a person needed a blacksmith, he might also need a gunsmith so we could be in the same building. That was his simple order of thinking.

We lived only four blocks from the river so much of any playtime with Saki was close to the water. I always had my nine-foot bullwhip with me and found we could get bullfrog legs with my whip to take home for dinner. Saki's father is French so frog legs are his favorite meat on Friday.

We spent most of that day getting Saki's father a large mess of frog legs. I stunned them with the popper on the business end of my bullwhip and Saki skinned the legs to take home. Lying on the banks of the Missouri River, and watching the boats coming from the north, we could just feel the adventure and excitement the people on the decks of those boats had experienced. I would run to the docks to listen to their tales of adventure. The fur trade had dwindled in the last 10 years but we still had a few trappers that had been as far up the Missouri as you could go bring their pelts to market in Kansas City. They liked to brag about their adventures and I tried to get two or more of them together and just listen to their tall tales.

My favorite mountain man was Jim Bridger. He would come down the river to do business with father since he needed support for his own ventures and had father do work for the miners up in Montana. He loved to tell me about the geysers at Yellowstone, the animals that roamed, the tall trees, and about the time he discovered the Great Salt Lake. These were the stories that made the West so enticing to me and were the things that told me I had to follow my dream.

My father also had a dream; he talked about moving to Colorado and the gold country around Denver City. I listened to the conversations he had with the men who come from that area and found out that they are working on him to move his business and family to their area because of the need for his services. I knew father still looked ahead for adventure, but he and mother were very happy here in Kansas City and had made many friends so he was reluctant to push mother to pick up and trek to an unknown part of the country. Father, Charles, and I talked among ourselves at the shop about moving but never discussed the subject at home around mother. Father said, "Mary Alice is too young to travel, but in a year or so she will be older and may be able to stand a short trip to possibly, Denver City, Colorado and the gold fields."

I continued with school and with my apprenticeship with Diego DeLacruse who was the only gunsmith in Western Missouri and Northeastern Kansas. I was getting quite handy with the tools of the trade. Diego said, "You be one fine fixer one day." Diego was trained in Spain by Old World craftsmen and makes gun parts that are better than the original parts that come into his shop. He also made knives for a hobby and some said they were the finest blades made in the West.

Diego was showing me how to work with leather and how to make scabbards, holsters, and belts. He produced fine-tooled sheaths for his knives and customers came long distances to purchase his handcrafted items.

A lot of the tools of his trade and hobby were similar to those father uses only on a smaller scale

When Diego agreed with father to apprentice me, the first project he gave me was to turn a one-inch steel ball into a half-inch square cube that was perfect on all sides. It was a six-week program and I worked on it every day of those six weeks and when I completed the cube I told father, "I am not sure this is what I want to do with my life." But when Diego told me it took him nine weeks to accomplish the same thing when he was a boy, I felt maybe I will succeed with Diego's training.

1860 was coming to a close and my birthday, December 24, was only a week away. The year had been a disaster for Kansas and the plains states. Drought and prairie fires had devastated the area. Crops were short and markets like Boone's Trading Post had been low on product all year. We could only hope for better conditions in the coming years.

I continued my self taught use of the bullwhip and spent an hour or so every night after school learning the uses and ways people could defend themselves with the whip and was amazed at the accuracy I was able to attain with practice.

CHAPTER 2

We had a new President, Abraham Lincoln. He would be inaugurated in March. I was sure President Buchanan would be glad when his term was up. His presidency had been plagued with discontent and threat by some southern states to secede from the Union. Father said a war among some states is a sure thing.

Diego had given me the task of making a new firing pin for a Henry rim fire rifle that a buffalo hunter brought in to be repaired. I had to cut and file the new piece and also harden the finished product. What a great feeling it was to accomplish this. My first complete repair by myself!

My brother, Edwin, had also accomplished part of his dream. He had moved across the river to Kansas City, Kansas and was now with a law firm working as an intern. March had come upon us like a lion as my father says. It was cold and snowing in the hill country. The river was rising every day and would flood down stream if it continued. I hoped last year's drought was over and farmers and cattlemen would have a good year. Last season several farmers picked up and went west to Colorado to start over again because there was no rain for the crops.

On April 13, 1861, the Kansas City Enterprise announced the Civil War had begun yesterday at Fort Sumter, South Carolina where Confederate forces attacked the Union Army. Robert Anderson, commander of the fort, surrendered only after he had exhausted all his supplies.

Missouri, despite the acceptance of slavery, did not join the Confederacy. A combination of political maneuvering and Union pressure kept us from seceding. I met the man who brought the Henry rifle in for repair. He was no buffalo hunter; he was George Catlin, the artist who painted all the great pictures we saw of the buffalo, roaming wild, and being hunted by Indians. He told me there are 50 million buffalo on the plains, but as the white man moves west we would see the great herds disappear. George said when the railroads take over the prairie the buffalo would have to be thinned to make room for the trains.

The Enterprise front-page story today told us that after three months of being in charge of Union troops, General Irvin McDowell, had been replaced by General George B. McClellan, due to his chaotic retreat at Bull Run. President Lincoln, with the threat of a protracted war, was aware of the army's need of better organization and training. General McClellan graduated second in his class at the U.S. Military Academy in 1846. General McClellan served in the Mexican-American War, and was sent to observe the Crimean War in Europe and watched the siege of Sevastopol in 1856. He wrote the manual on cavalry tactics and developed the McClellan Saddle now in use by the cavalry. His past experience had influenced President Lincoln to appoint him to organize the Army of the Potomac to defend Washington, D.C.

The war seemed so far away. We talked about it and saw some of the young men leave to serve. Some went to the Union and some went south to join the Confederate Army, dependent upon on their allegiance.

Father had a friend in Illinois with two sons in the Union Army and his brother, who lives in Atlanta, Georgia, had two sons in the Confederate Army. I would not like to know I might have a cousin rushing at me during a cavalry charge and would want my only concern at the time to be to survive the charge.

It was a gorgeous day and I needed to relax from the grind of school, work with Diego and helping father. Buddin had gone away to a military school so my daily life was very boring. I got my whip and headed for the river. About a block from the river, I saw something out of the corner of my eye move. There was a vacant lot that ran all the way to the water and had tree stumps washed up in several places. I focused on the movement by a stump and then it moved again.

As I let my whip lay limp in case I needed it, a large black dog jumped from behind a stump and charged at me. I reacted and looped the whip around the neck and jaws of the dog and pinned it to the ground. She was wet and hurt. I tried to check out what was wrong but she wouldn't let me close without trying to bite me. She was bleeding a lot and I could see there was a large wound across her back. I continued to try to calm her and finally she became still. She had bled to death.

I unwound my bullwhip from around her and stood up to leave when I heard a whimper from under the same stump. There in the grass were two little balls of fur, one pure black and one gray. The gray one was not moving so I picked up the black one. The eyes were not even open yet. I picked up the gray one but it was dead.

What was I going to do with this little thing? I cradled it in my arms and headed for home. Mother was home and I told her the story about how I found the puppy. She got some cream from the cooler in the basement and wiped it on his lips. Yes, I checked. It was a boy dog. Mother said, "James! You have to feed him every two hours for a couple of days".

"What are you talking about? He's not mine. I just found him."

"James, this poor little thing will die if you don't take charge of him."

Well Mother prevailed so this was how I came to have Thor. I got a shovel and went back to the lot and buried Thor's mother and sister.

After I buried the dogs, I was curious why they were where I had found them. Tracking back to the river I find where the big dog came out of the water. There was some blood on the trail so she was hurt in the water. The only thing that could have done the damage to her back would have been the paddles on a river boat or someone who hit her with something sharp and threw her over-board.

Well, thanks to whatever happened to momma dog and thanks to my sister, Mary Alice, who became a surrogate mother to the puppy I now had a companion named Thor. If the size of his paws was any indication of his stature when grown, he would be larger than his mother.

As 1861 was coming to a close, the Enterprise lead stories were about General Thomas W. Sherman and his occupation of Port Royal and the Sea Islands of South Carolina.

Buddin's uncle, William F. Cody, was at father's shop. He was having two horses shod. The Pony Express that he was riding for had been discontinued since the telegraph lines were now complete to San Francisco. He rode the routes out of Denver City, Colorado. He said, "I used to ride 75 to 90 miles in a day changing horses every 10 or 15 miles." Cody was only 16 and had more time in the saddle than most 30 year old cowboys. He wanted to become a scout for the army next year so he had his life all planned out.

Bill saw me in the backyard working with my whip. He came out from the shop, and showed me a side arm position I had not been aware of.

"Sometimes," Bill said, "you need that whip to come around from the side when you are driving a wagon, or a stage."

As Cody turned to go into father's shop, Thor, being still a young pup, grabbed Bill at his ankle. Bill reached down picked the dog up and looked like he was blowing in his ear. I could hear him saying something but didn't understand what he was talking to Thor about. "That will be a fine animal when he grows up. What kind of a name did you hang on him, James?"

"Thor. I think it was a Greek, or Roman name I picked up in a school book sometime."

Bill said, "No, James, Thor was a protector of the Germanic Tribes in Europe and was their protector from evil."

As Bill continued into father's shop, I had to wonder why he knew so much about history.

CHAPTER 3

Thor was growing every day. It was time to train him and father showed me how to use a horse as the best way to teach Thor about guns and bullwhip noise so these weapons were not something to bark or balk at. He learned fast and surprised both father and me at how comfortable he was at the hooves of a horse.

I went hunting rabbits and chased one on horseback, stunned it with the bullwhip and was happy to find Thor would retrieve the rabbit and brought it straight to me. We learned to hunt quail in the same manner, which was great for mother as she no longer had to search for the lead shot from the ammunition.

In early April, General Ulysses S. Grant forced the retreat of Confederate forces at Shilo, Tennessee. Thirteen thousand out of 63,000 Union soldiers died and 11,000 of 40,000 Confederate troops were killed. This all happened in less than three days.

We had a detachment of Union soldiers in Kansas City but otherwise the war still seemed a long way off. The one part of the war that my family had become involved with is the so-called Underground Railroad. My father had helped hide and move southern Negroes on their way north to safety. Father had taught us all that the shade of skin, black, brown, or yellow in no way has any bearing on your status in the chain of life. We were all created equal.

Father was getting worried about the war. He was talking about moving west to Denver City, Colorado more seriously. Mary Alice was going to be eight later this year. She was healthy and growing wise beyond her years. Mother felt if the war continued it could come to this area, so she agreed that a move might be good for us all. We had to make a decision soon as father felt that if our departure was the middle of April next year we would arrive in the Denver area about the 1st of June.

Father said, "We need two wagons, eight oxen, eight head of cattle, and 10 horses to make the trip. One wagon is for the forge and blacksmith tools, one is for mother's furniture and household goods." We had two Conestoga wagons at the blacksmith shop that were used to haul equipment for customers. A Conestoga wagon was 16.5 feet in length and 4.5 feet wide and could carry seven tons of freight.

Charles asked me to come see what he had built for the trip. In the back of the barn he had put together a small kitchen that would attach to the rear of the household wagon. It was as wide as a wagon, about four feet tall, and had a table that folded down when not covering the sectioned off shelving. That would make mother's job on the trail a lot easier when she had to cook for us all.

Fall had come and father had planned a trip to the lake country east of us to hunt deer. Father, Charles, Jay, Thor and I took a three day holiday for winter meat. Thor learned fast to flush game our way and by the end of the second day we had three nice white-tailed bucks to take home.

The next morning, as we were loading the pack horses and gear to head home, the sky opened up and we got a fall storm. It rained, and hail the size of quail eggs fell from the sky. The trip home took us two days. Our three day holiday turned into two wonderful days and two of the coldest, water soaked days I had ever experienced.

We got to the barn and skinned our three deer, and carefully hung them to cure before butchering them for mother to dry some of the meat, and to can most of it in Mason jars. She would make pemmican out of the tough portions and bake a couple of mincemeat pies after the canning is finished. Father found he could put calcium chloride salt in the boiling water to make it hotter and cook the meat that mother has canned in three hours instead of five hours.

This meat would last all winter and gave us some preserved stock for our trip next year. Mother would can some fruit. She also canned vegetables to make venison stew on the trail to Denver City. The box Charles made for the back of one of the wagons would sure help us all eat well.

The Enterprise had photographs of the Antietam battlefield and a great picture of President Lincoln's visit to General McClellan's headquarters. In October, the Union Army reoccupied Harper's Ferry.

In November, President Lincoln, replaced General McClellan, due to his slow troop movements, with Major General Ambrose Burnside. Then Burnside was defeated in a series of attacks against Confederate forces at Fredericksburg, Virginia, and Lincoln replaced him with General Joseph Hooker.

Winter has set in for good and father was getting the wagons and tack ready for next year. I would be 14 in two weeks and father gave me a new 12 foot bullwhip from a whip maker in Santa Fe, New Mexico. The extra three feet made me make some adjustments in my aim and timing. I needed a lot of practice to get proficient with this weapon.

Diego had expressed a desire to make the trip to Colorado with us. He had four mules and a new Studebaker wagon. He had never been west of the Missouri River so this would be an adventure for him, also. Father said, "His talents will be of great value in the area we plan on settling and another hand on the trail is always a good thing when entering new territory."

Diego had dropped the Adams .49 caliber revolver line and now handled the Colt Manufacturing Company's six shot .36 caliber Navy revolver. The Adams was hand made and each one had to have parts made for replacement. The Colt was produced on an assembly line and spare parts were available for replacement by ordering from Colt. Colt agreed that Diego would carry their line in the northern half of Colorado and had given him a three year contract to that effect.

Now all Diego needed was a good brand of rifle to sell and his line would be complete.

CHAPTER 4

Thor weighed in at 125 pounds with no fat anywhere on his trim body. He loved to run along side my gray line back horse, Powder. I named him Powder the day his momma dropped him in the dusty part of the barn and fine powder dust flew all over when he scrambled to get to his feet.

The Kansas City Enterprise had printed President Lincoln's Emancipation Proclamation. This declared that in the eyes of the federal government, all slaves in areas still in rebellion are free. Father, being a staunch Republican and abolitionist, felt this was a step in the right direction.

April was getting closer. Father had sold the home place, and found a blacksmith from Ohio that wanted to take over the lease on his shop in town. Mother had sold or gave away the large pieces of furniture too big to put in the wagon. She had purchased two large trunks for clothes and dishes she said had to go with us. Jay had made a small box with leather hinges on the top for Mary Alice to keep her dolls and doll clothes in one place. Now that she has her own trunk she is looking forward to our trip. She had not been happy about leaving all her friends that she had known growing up. Mother had explained to her how she would continue her schoolwork with mother as the teacher.

Father is concerned about the Conscription Act. He is 51 so not a problem for him but Charles is 20 and next year Jay is 18. The Conscription Act passed by Congress the first week in March required all males 20 to 45 to register for possible draft. Father hoped that he and Charles could get to Colorado before Charles was called to serve. Jay will be getting close so both father and mother were concerned. Charles had been doing the research for our trip and had picked the Overland Trail to start. We would go north to Atchison, Kansas, and follow the Oregon Trail west to the Oketo Cutoff in Kansas, north into Nebraska and the Platte River, west to Latham, Colorado and south to Cherry Creek where Denver City is located. This was the east and west route for Ben Holladay's Overland Stage Company.

Ben Holladay had brought six shot guns to Diego DeLacruse for repair. He came to see father and told him, "Richard you need to come to the Denver City area as soon as possible. The opportunities are unlimited. I am moving my office and headquarters there to the Planter's Hotel. Denver City is growing fast. We have four churches, a school, five brick stores, a private Mint, two banks, and three daily newspapers."

Father said, "Ben, we plan to be there the last week in May of this year. Diego is coming, too, so we will need to find locations for both businesses."

"Well, that is great news. You both are needed and will be an asset to our growing community. One of our daily papers printed a story about Denver City and said we have a population of over 5,000."

I walked back to Diego's shop with Ben and asked him how long it took to ride one of his stagecoaches to Denver City from Atchison. He said the trip was about 7 to ten days depending on weather and Indians. I want to know what he means about Indians. He said, "At times, some of the tribes still try to frighten the white man's advance into his country and we have to hold our coaches until the army gives us the go ahead."

He said the trip from Kansas City would be about 700 miles of every kind of land you would ever see, prairie, rivers, valleys, and mountains like you read about in school but they would be even more impressive when you see them right in front of you.

Ben said, "Your father said he figures it will take 50 days but I'll bet you make it in 45 days or less. You have good equipment and great animals that are the most important ingredients for success on a trip like yours."

It took us three days to load all of the shop and household goods into the two wagons. Diego had been ready to go since yesterday. He had a traveling gunsmith shop in his wagon; he built shelves and a bench inside, along with his bed. What a sight we must have been. Father was driving the lead wagon with mother beside him. Diego was in the second wagon and Charles, with Mary Alice riding in the shotgun seat next to him, was in the back wagon. Jay, Thor, and I were herding 10 cows, a bull, and six horses down Main Street, Kansas City on a beautiful day in the middle of April 1863.

We past the wagon train outside of town. Jay and I herded the livestock well ahead of the wagons and tried to stay off of the trail. Ben Holladay had explained that the livestock should stay off the trail as much as possible as the trails are for wagons and stagecoaches.

CHAPTER 5

The three day trip to Atchison, Kansas was exciting. Thor was learning to herd the livestock, making Jay's and my job less stressful giving us time to scout ahead for grazing, water, and a place to stop for the night.

The first night after leaving Kansas City we camped on the east side of the Missouri River across from Leavenworth, Kansas. Brother Edwin came up to spend the night. He had to stay in Leavenworth for the next week for a trial about someone trying to steal firearms from the Union Army Depot in town. This worked out well since the family would be many miles away for some time to come and would not see Edwin again for a couple of years.

Edwin told us, "I hope to move to San Francisco, California by 1866. I will have gained the experience needed to compete in the financial market by then and I feel that is my calling. I know California sounds a long way from you, but two or three years from now you watch, the railroads will make distances a lot shorter and bring a greater prosperity to our nation than we have ever seen. We just need to get this war over."

Next morning, very early, father had negotiated a ferry to move us across the river to Leavenworth, Kansas. This took three trips as the ferry was only 40 feet long and 18 feet wide. We took one wagon and some livestock on each trip across the river. Thor and I rode all the trips helping the ferry operator watch for floating objects that need to be deflected from the hull of the ferry with pike poles.

We had taken a half of a day for the crossing but father wants to push on toward Atchison and Fort Leavenworth that was only 10 miles away and he knew a good spot for the animals just past the Fort.

On our third day, during our travel through Atchison, Father stopped at a granary and purchased 500 pounds of grain to feed the oxen to keep them fit on the trail since they were pulling the heavy wagons. Father picked up the Atchison Daily Champion newspaper. Several stories about raids in the area by rebel jayhawkers gave father an uneasy feeling. He destroyed the paper so mother will not read about the problems, but he told Diego and us brothers to be alert on the trail.

We were finally heading directly west and it felt good. Father's warning about the jayhawkers had a lot of dialog going between Jay and me, but we realized our main objective was to keep the livestock moving ahead of the wagons and find water and feed for a nightly stopover.

As Thor and I returned from a scouting trip, and as we were walking with Powder and enjoying the smell of the prairie, we came over a rise to see Jay on his horse with his hands high in the air and two men on horseback, both with rifles in hand, looking over our livestock. Thor and I were about 200 yards from them. I mounted up and walked Powder about 75 yards from them. I spurred my horse and yelled, "Thor go get him." I rode to the closest rider and jerked the Sharps rifle out of his hands with my bullwhip. At the same time Thor jumped and knocked the other man off his horse. Jay pulled his gun on the one still on his horse and Thor was standing over the one on the ground.

"What should we do with these Jayhawkers?" asked Jay as we dismounted and pulled the one on his horse down to the ground.

"We could string them up by their feet and let them hang till father comes by with the wagons."

"Wait a minute. We're not Jayhawkers. We saw a guy alone with all these cattle and horses and figured it was an easy score. That's the truth, boys."

"Well, today is your lucky day. Unload their guns, Jay. Check their saddle bags for all the ammunition. Take the boots, tie them on their horses and send them down the trail."

"What names do you guys go by?"

"I'm Harry Logan, and that's Josh Bean."

"If I ever see you again my dog will get his time with you and he has a good memory for guys like you. Smell them good, Thor."

That night when we related our story to the family, Father and Diego felt we might have been too soft on both the men, but agreed we did the right thing because when they passed the wagons on the trail both had a hangdog look in all four eyes. Mother said, "I wondered why they didn't have any boots on when they passed us."

CHAPTER 6

We woke early and found two more wagons pulling off the trail to camp the night. Jay and I found nice grass for the livestock and a nice stream for good water. Someone had built a corral from poles brought from some other area because there sure weren't any trees large enough to make a corral in this place. We herded all our stock in the corral after they grazed for an hour.

Father said, "We're about 15 miles out of Atchison, so the corral was built to hold horses that the army moves at times." Made sense to me since there was water and plenty of knee high grass for stock to feed on.

Mother was cooking breakfast for us. Father was inviting the people from the other wagons to stand with us for the Lord's Prayer after we eat. It is Sunday and since there was no church for mother to enjoy. Father was trying to help her make it through her day of worship.

After our prayer, the two ladies from the other wagons started singing "Amazing Grace." Mother's face lit up and we all sang along. Diego was getting his mules traced up and the rest of us fell into line getting the other two wagons set to roll.

Jay and I rounded up the livestock and made tracks well ahead of the wagons trying to make, at best, 15 miles even though it would be a short day of travel. The farther we traveled, the more buffalo signs we encountered. We were seeing a single buffalo now and then. Later small herds of four to six were showing up on the prairie as we moved away from civilization. Driving our livestock off the trail as we do, we crossed "buffalo trails," as they are called. As buffalo leave their feeding grounds, they usually walk in single file heading for water and a place to bed down. At times, the lead bull would stop and roll himself on a grassy spot (probably to clear the dust and vermin from his hide). When the next bull got to that spot he rolled just like the leader. This is why the holes, or "buffalo wallows" are found on the prairie.

Thor had spotted the little "prairie dogs." He and I had to work this out as I didn't need him off chasing these varmints when the cattle started wandering away from our bunch. We also had to make sure our horses didn't walk in a dog hole as some are very deep. Most of the time you could avoid the critters as they liked to live in areas just like people do in a town. So if you saw their town, you just go around it. So far, we had found water not to be a problem. I assumed the wagons traveled this route because there were a lot of creeks that are flowing south toward the Republican River. The ones flowing north ran into the Platte River. We would be traveling on the north side of the Republican River for about 60 miles before we turned north to Fort Kearney, Nebraska, and the Platte River. Father said, "We should be at the Republican River on our 15th day out of Kansas City, and when we get there I will have to re-shoe the oxen, and possibly Diego's mules."

About the time we were crossing out of Kansas and into Nebraska, father and Diego wanted to get off the wagons for a day, so Jay took the mule wagon and I drove the wagon loaded with the shop in it. Mother and Mary Alice found it easier to walk most of the time since the seats, even though they have cushions, were hard to ride for too many miles.

Father and Diego cut their own horses out of the herd and saddled up with a couple of biscuits and bacon. Both had a rifle and a pistol. Father said "Yesterday four men rode this trail from Fort Kearney, and said they saw Indians about 20 miles beyond here. I feel Diego and I will have a better chance negotiating with them than you boys. I'm sure all they want is a cow or two to let us pass on their land."

"What do you mean their land? I thought this trail belonged to Ben Holladay and he had the say about its use."

"Son, the Indian was here long before any of us and they still want to believe it belongs to them. Sometimes we can humor them, avoid a lot of trouble and, at times, make a friend we might need later. Remember Blue Feather, the Arapaho? I befriended him many years ago.

He has become a true and loyal friend to us and many whites just because of a favor that we happen to do for one another."

"What was that favor, Father?"

"Some day when we have more time I will tell you the whole story. It would take too long now to do justice to that time in history. Just remember Blue Feather as a special man in our family history. And if it were not for his love and understanding of all people, my older brother John, and me would not be here today."

As we continued on the trail, we were passing wagons every day. Ben Holladay must have been right when he told me 20,000 people use the trail every year. Father was probably right about the Indians. I could see why he would think the white man was always trying to take his land. They had the use of it for many years at anytime they needed it and then they moved on. The white man took an area and settled down and ran the Indians off when he tried to hunt or set his village close to the white man's home. With the amount of whites moving in the Indians' territory, I agreed he would have to see us as a threat to his existence.

CHAPTER 7

When we camped that night, I counted the cows. Somewhere father and Diego had lost two fresh cows. During supper I said, "Father we didn't see any Indians today. They must be farther up the trail."

Diego slowly got up from the flour barrel he was setting on, walked to the center of our circle and said, "You guys missed the party. Richard was riding point and 12 big bucks with paint on their bodies surrounded your father, brought him back to the herd, held rifles on me and said they were going to take all the livestock and leave us for the buzzards."

"Your father started talking to them in sign language, even though two of them spoke a little English. They all backed up a little and one walked his horse forward and talked to Richard with his signs. Your father got off his horse, reached into his saddle bag and brought out this pouch of tobacco and gave it to the Indian. I never knew you smoked, Richard. They talked some more with their hands, Richard asked me to cut two fresh cows out of the herd, put ropes on them and hand them the ropes.

They all put their guns away and lead the two cows across the creek, into the poplar trees and we never saw any more Indians all day."

Father said, "They really wanted the bull and cow to have milk for the young children. I gave the two cows and the pouch of tobacco, telling them the cows were with young, and would give milk for a year. They said, 'We can get a bull later.' So someone coming this way is going to lose a bull before the year is over. "

Mother asked Father if he was frightened when they surrounded him like that. "No," he said, "I remembered a story Blue Feather told me about the difference in war paint and hunting paint on the body. They were a hunting party and wanted to see how far they could go to scare me. They really did not want trouble."

The next two days were rainy and wet. The wagons were soaking wet, even the canvas leaked where the hoops touched the material. It was cold and windy. Mother had a hard time making breakfast and supper. We had to make a lean-to to keep a fire going and there was wet ground where ever we lit.

If we were making 15 miles a day, I thought we were lucky. The livestock were hard to control. They wanted to wander all over trying to take the high ground as it was easier to walk out of the streams of water running down every gully on the prairie. Thor was even irritable trying to keep them in line. I never gave any thought to an animal having a bad day, but as I watched my dog, you could see the frustration in his actions.

We were seeing larger herds of buffalo now as we got farther into Nebraska. I understood what George Catlin, the artist, was telling me now about buffalo being so prevalent on the prairie. I could see it would be a problem for the railroad when they made it to this open country. The rain had gone and I felt we were only two or three days from the bend in the Republican River where we would camp for a day and father could put new shoes on the oxen and Diego's mules. I looked at the mule shoes and was amazed at the wear on them. I really had no idea the trail is that hard on metal, but they are pulling a lot of weight with the wagon.

Sun and a slight breeze dried the prairie rapidly. We were making good time again and everybody was comfortable, with dry clothing and a lot less mud to walk in. Even the cattle were talking to one another as Thor rushed around like a momma quail watching her young. Thor stayed with me when father met with the Indians, so I think he still looks for the two cows that father gave to them. As I watch him he looks back once in a while like he is looking for the other cows.

The land was getting to be more like rolling hills than flat prairie the closer we get to the Republican River. Father was having a hard time with his wagon as it carries much more weight than the one Charles is driving. The ground was soft and has a lot of sand mixed in letting the wheels run deep and father's oxen have to overcome this danger of getting stuck.

When we get to Fort Kearney, Nebraska, on the Platte River, Father was going to increase the oxen to six on each wagon because we would start our climb in altitude all the way to Denver City, Colorado. Our trail map showed 400 miles to Denver City from Fort Kearney. We had good equipment, and stock pulling our wagons as we were passing three or four wagon groups with some times five wagons in a group.

CHAPTER 8

The weather had been horrible for five days with wind blowing straight east like a gale storm. That made us ride right into the wind. Mother was passing out her pemmican because trying to make a fire to cook with was out of the question. All her preparation last year was paying off. We could have survived on this type of food very well as it is made from venison so it has a lot of protein. The previous night we had found out we would get to the Republican River that next day while father had been talking to an Overland Stage driver at our camp and he said we were only 18 miles from a good camp site just off the bend in the river.

Well, we would be getting to Fort Kearney five days later than Father's original plan. Weather and the hold up of other travelers on the trail had caused our delay so mother said, "Life goes on. We do the best we can."

Diego talked to a man on the stage who gave the newspaper he got at Fort Kearney to him. News from the war was not good. The last week in April, General Hooker was defeated when he crossed the Rappahannock River at Chancellorsville. General Lee split his army in three places and trounced the Union good. Hooker withdrew his forces back across the river, giving the South a victory. It was the Confederate's victory that was the most costly in casualties so far in the war.

We had circled our wagons for the night, picketed the horses on great grass, got the cattle to bed down and looked forward to a hot supper and a good night's sleep. And then the Cavalry arrived to let us know about Indian trouble between here and Fort Kearney. The Lieutenant with his 20 men was on a scouting trip because two different wagon groups had been attacked and lost horses and cattle. The Indian party had kidnapped a 14-year-old girl, but her father had chased them and they had let her go after he wounded one of the party and killed one of their horses. The troop was camping in the area tonight, but was heading back to Fort Kearney the next day, going straight north to the Platte River and west to the fort.

"We expect to arrive at Fort Kearney in four days with no trouble from Indians," Father told the Lieutenant.

"Well you must be vigilant day and night. I am not sure we have them on the run even though we did chase them north for a little while yesterday."

Diego and father had a talk with all of us to make sure we understood the severity of our situation. Father began by telling the group, "We might want to join up with three or four more wagons on the way to Fort Kearney. More people in the group may make the Indians think they would have less chance of success on a raid.

What about that, Diego? Think that might be a wise solution to our problem?"

"There should be safety in numbers." Diego replied. "We will no doubt have company before we finish with the shoeing of the animals and we can talk to them about it."

By early afternoon all the stock that needed to be shod were shod. Father had made extra shoes for all the animals so all he and Diego had to do was bend some just a little to make them fit. Charles and I helped by pulling the old shoes and trimming some of the hoofs making the animal ready for new shoes. Two wagons pulled in for the night and father talked to them about joining with us to give us both more protection with larger numbers. Both parties agreed, so we will be a party of five wagons with five more men to help, if we need it.

Father told mother, "Elizabeth, we want you to drive Diego's wagon and take Mary Alice with you. Diego will handle the freight wagon so I can ride with the boys and the herd of livestock. Three of the men from the other wagons will ride with us even though they have no livestock to add to the herd. You drove our wagon when we came down from Ohio. Do you have any problem with what I just put on the table?"

"No, Richard, I can handle Diego's wagon just fine. I like your plan. I want all of you to be careful. We are not sure what tribe we are up against, so watch all the signs you know to look for. These other men with you have never had Indian experience before, so you need to look out for them, too."

The next morning with a beautiful sunrise behind us, we headed for the Platte River country. Jay and father started the herd; I stayed back as father wanted me to have Thor stay with mother and the mules. As I was telling Thor what to do, he shook his head just like he knows what I am trying to get him to do. We lined the wagons with Diego driving father's wagon first, mother second, the two joiners (with a woman driving one of them), and Charles bringing up the rear. I had everybody moving so I headed for the herd to help train Carl, Art, and Harvey as they had never handled cattle and horses and they needed a little learning to help them relax and enjoy the experience. Father had Harvey, the father of Art and Carl with him. Jay was working with Art. Carl was bringing up the last of the cows. I went to help Carl, but he was doing a great job so all I could do was compliment him.

Carl asked a few questions about cattle but seemed to be a natural at handling a herd. Carl was 18 so he had a couple of years on me. He was easy to talk to and treated me like I was his age. I supposed I had a new friend that I felt comfortable with. The sun was straight above us now and there was not a sign of a redskin anywhere. We watched the hills to the north as that usually was their direction of travel. We were about a half mile ahead of the wagons. Father rode around the herd to where we were and headed to check on the train. Hopefully he would bring some biscuits and cheese back for all of us.

It would have been nice to have some bacon mother had cooked ahead the night before also.

Jay rode back to the rear of the herd. "Look straight north. Does that look like a dust cloud or am I seeing things?"

"Looks about three miles off. I hope father gets back right away with the glass so we can see what it really is. In the meantime, let's get the herd over there toward that grove of trees way down on the left, on the other side of the trail." By the time father returned, we had the livestock rounded up close to the tree line and he hurried to our spot wondering why we came here.

"We have a situation, I think. Look straight north with the glass and see what you think is making the dust cloud." Father used the glass for several seconds said it was a band of Indians then sent Carl and me to speed the wagons up and get them to the herd and circled. He wanted to be stopped and ready if they spot us and attack before dark.

"I am sure they know we are here or they would not be coming in so fast. Looks like maybe 25 braves, can't tell what tribe yet," Father said. Father made sure all the stock was inside the circle of wagons and everyone had a gun that could help repel the charge. By the time we got the wagons set, we could hear the hoof beats of their horses as they crossed the trail headed straight for us.

Diego yelled, "Make sure they are in your range before you fire. Every round is important in a case like this." My heart was pounding like I had never remembered. Thor was standing beside me and watching between the spokes in my wagon wheel. His tail was swishing as fast as my heart is beating.

CHAPTER 9

The attack was swift with heavy fire from rifles. Some of the braves had only bow and arrows. There were about 40 braves altogether. One chieftain, having a full headdress to his hips, stood out from the rest.

Father said, "These are Cheyenne," as he pulled an arrow from the side of Diego's wagon. "I was not aware of the Cheyenne so far south of the Platte River."

The Indians were not able to circle us as we have everything backed up to a large grove of trees. They rode by, all going the same way and fired whatever weapon they had. One brave jumped one of the wagon tongues and Charles shot him off his horse. The brave was shot in his right arm, lost his rifle, and ran out of our circle and was helped by another brave onto his horse. We continued to fight for about 45 dreadful minutes when we heard a bugle sound from the south. Sure enough it was the Cavalry.

When the Cheyenne heard the bugle they took off west across the Little Blue River, leaving two injured braves for the army to take care of and three dead horses to bury. Colonel Robert Furnas of the Second Nebraska Cavalry said, "We have been chasing that bunch of renegade Cheyenne from way up north and this is as close as we have gotten to them yet. We can help you get squared away first and then get on their trail again before dark."

We were lucky. Jay had lost a small piece of his right ear and Harvey had taken an arrow in his left leg, but only in the flesh above his knee. Mother cut the arrow and pulled it on through the skin. He would have a good scar but no permanent damage. We had gained an Indian pony from the brave that had jumped into our circle. We decided it belonged to Harvey, since he was the most severely wounded of the group.

It was late in the evening. We had taken the livestock to the Little Blue for water and returned to camp for a supper of mother's great venison stew and biscuits, with all the hot tea we could drink.

Jay, lamenting about his ear, remarked, "I guess I can honestly say I took a bullet in a gunfight for the rest of my life and be telling the truth."

"We were all very fortunate today. Most attacks like this are a disaster, Jack. Your idea to put those trees to our back was a stroke of good luck for us. We always had the enemy right in front of us. He could not circle and be all around us with some of us having our backsides open to their fire," Father said.

Well now, that's the first time father had ever addressed me as Jack. He and mother had always called me James. My brothers and Mary Alice all called me Jack because all the school started calling me Jack. Was this a sign of respect or a slip?

Nebraska was Union Territory. Harvey had a paper from Omaha called *The Nebraska City News*. It told all about the remarkable fact that Nebraska had contributed 3,300 troops to the Union forces in the south. The forts in Nebraska were all under the protection of the State of Nebraska Militia, volunteers who garrison at Fort Kearney and Fort Randall. Major General John M. Thayer was in charge of the State Militia.

Nebraska was being settled by the Homestead Act set in place by President Lincoln. The first homestead in the United States was recorded in Gage County, Nebraska on January 1, 1863, by Daniel Freeman according to the Omaha newspaper. The paper related that for a small fee a family can homestead a quarter section of government land, live on it for five years and if the head of the house was a United States citizen, 21 years old or older, the land was deeded to him. Let's see now, there were 640 acres in a section, so a quarter section would be 160 acres. That was a large piece of land.

Daylight was earlier now so we had more hours to travel. Everyone was ready to travel before the sun is over the hills to the east. Carl and I lead the livestock to the north side of the trail, with Jay and Art bringing up the rear. Harvey's new pony had not figured out what is happening to him and ran wild a couple of times, but Art was getting the hang of keeping him in line. The farther we went west in Nebraska, the better the feed was for the animals. The land between the Republican River and the Platte River was great for grasses that the buffalo feed on so we were seeing more and larger herds of the big critters. We made over 35 miles today. I needed father to show me how he figures the amount of miles we go. I knew he used his watch for part of the equation, but was not sure what he used for the rest of the calculation.

CHAPTER 10

We woke to a wind coming from the north. It was very cold but with not much velocity so it shouldn't have kept us from making Fort Kearney before nightfall.

Father needed to buy four more oxen at the fort. He had put Jay in charge of driving mother's wagon so Charles could ride ahead and deal with the animals. Charles cut out two of the best stock and saddles; one to ride for 10 or 12 miles and the other to change to for 10 or so more miles.

He was expected to make it back to the fort way before dark to find four oxen we needed to increase the two teams to six each for the climb on up the Platte River and into Colorado. Carl and I split our duty with Jay gone. I took the lead for two hours and let him lead for a couple. The land was rolling hills and all we did was keep the herd moving with the trail in sight on our left.

As the sun went above us, I heard the most deafening roar off to the north. Looking that way, I could see a big cloud of dust coming our way. I rode to a hilltop to our north and saw the largest herd of buffalo I had ever encountered stampeding just west of us. I rode back to Carl's position and explained that we needed to back our herd up and hope the buffalo stay west of us.

As we turned the herd and headed east, we ran into the wagon train. Father yelled and wanted to know what had happened. He couldn't hear the buffalo herd yet. He stopped the wagons and ran over to me and asked me to let him have Powder because he heard the buffalo now. Father rode to the same hill I saw the herd from. He watched for a couple of minutes, turned Powder around and rode back to the wagons. He said, "They have turned west and only a stray or two will come this way. I have no idea why they veered off that way, but we are better off for it. Let's give them a half an hour and have some of those biscuits your mother made last night."

By the time we started up again, the roar of the buffalo had left our area. When we got the wagons to the spot where the herd had crossed the trail, there was no trail to follow. It was hard to pick a route to find the trail on the other side. Carl rode ahead and found the trail; then came back and got father headed in the right direction.

Once we got our herd headed west, we were making around three miles an hour. Father said he counted the times his oxen picked their feet up and put them down, then figured what that distance is and divided by two. Whatever he thought worked.

I was leading the herd and spotted the fort. What a sight. We had now traveled over 300 miles from Kansas City. We found a corral behind the fort and ran the livestock into it. Carl, Art, and I milked the cows before the wagons arrived at the fort. The oxen and mules would get oats with cow's milk mixed in for supper tonight. Charles was nowhere to be found. We know he made it because both horses are in the corral.

Father had the wagons circle just east of the corral to make camp as comfortable as possible before checking on Charles' whereabouts. We bought 200 pounds of oats from the Livery and fed the oxen and mules before putting them in with the other livestock. I gave Powder a bucket of oats without father seeing me.

Father had a chat with the Livery owner who said Charles came to see him three hours ago but he had no oxen to sell. He sent him to see Mr. Alley at the store on the other side of the fort. I had no idea why they called this a fort. There were no walls or a stockade, just a lot of sod huts with four or five wooden structures. Even the barracks where the soldiers live were sod.

There was a parade ground in front of the largest wood building. I figured this was the headquarters for the army. Father returned to the camp with Charles. "They say we have to go to Dobytown for more livestock. It is just a little to the west of the fort so tomorrow we can find oxen there. Bert Alley, the store owner, has some great looking bacon, Elizabeth. You might want to get another 50 pounds. Get us some sticks of horehound candy, also. I bought some tobacco to replace what I gave to the Indians with the two cows."

Charles spent a couple of hours with Bert and his family. He said, "Bert says we have been fortunate not to have had any more trouble than we have, as many of the wagons passing through have lost people to the Indians, along with several small herds of horses and cattle."

CHAPTER 11

The next morning, while father and Charles rode over to Dobytown to purchase the four oxen we needed, I went exploring this outpost called Fort Kearney.

I had my bullwhip and Thor. As we walked through the area of mud huts, a burly Sergeant came out of one of the huts, walked up to me and said, "That dog… where did you find such a magnificent looking creature?"

I told him the story about the momma dog and how I had to bury her and the other pup, about tracing her tracks back to the river and about finding the blood right at the river's edge.

"Well, boy, that's quite a story, but tell me how much will it take to buy the dog from you?"

"Thor is not for sale at any price. He won't know what to do if he's not with me. And I'm not a boy. My name is Jack."

"Okay Jack, I am Artimas York. You can't blame me for trying to buy your dog. He would make anyone proud to own him."

"You know how to use that whip on your side, there, Jack?"

"Yes, sir, I can pluck a cigar out of your mouth from 12 feet and you won't feel a thing. Watch that rat by the corner of your building."

A crack sounded loudly as I separated the rat from his head 10 feet behind Artimas.

"That's good Jack, how long you been working with the bullwhip?"

"I guess five years. My father started showing me when he thought I was tall enough to use a five-footer."

"What does your Pa do to know how to use a bull-whip?"

"He is a blacksmith. But when he was younger he lived in Ohio and he was a freight hauler and a mule skinner. He can handle an 18-foot whip better than I can work with a nine footer."

"Where are you and your family headed on your great adventure?"

"Somewhere in the Denver City, Colorado area. Father and Diego, the man teaching me to be a gunsmith, feel that area is going to grow and will need the trades they know."

"You seem to have your life planned out. I have 11 more months in this army and then I can retire. I would like to try the gold fields in Colorado when I am out of the army. Maybe I will see you there."

"Artimas, we have to get going. Look us up when you get to Colorado. Thor and I will be watching for you."

Heading back to our camp, I was amazed at the number of wagons passing the fort on the trail. As I walked past the trading post, a man standing on the board walk at the store was telling a soldier he had counted 160 wagons passing the fort just this morning. When Thor and I arrived back to camp, Father and Charles had returned with four big oxen and they were fitting them out with the new tack father brought for this purpose. Mother spent her morning with Mary Alice, baking biscuits in her large cast iron Dutch oven, enough for three or four days I think. Father, Harvey with his crew, and Diego were having a pow-wow about when we should join the wagons already on the trail.

They decided that we would load up for an early morning start, getting as far as possible before sunrise.

Carl and I fed the oxen along with Diego's mules with more oats and milk from the cows we milked earlier in the day. We fed the cows and horses fresh cut hay Father had bought from the livery stable.

We loaded another 300 pounds of oats from the livery onto Diego's wagon for later use up the trail.

After having an early supper, we all retired to our bed rolls for a good night's sleep. But the horses in the corral started an uproar that we could not ignore.

I think every man in camp was at the corral at the same time. Inside the corral three wolves had our youngest heifer on her side and one was just ready to go for her throat as Diego shot the critter. Someone got one other wolf, but one gets away.

We had 12 or 15 soldiers from the fort at the corral by then. One of the men from the fort says he saw a lone wolf by the river but had not seen any this close to the fort before.

Strange, that with deer and young buffalo all over the range, they would have came so close to a settlement to find a meal.

We dragged the wolves away from the livestock and headed again for the warmth of our bed rolls and a good night's rest.

CHAPTER 12

When the first hint of daylight came, father was getting the oxen ready on his wagon. Charles was lining his livestock up and Diego was all ready to get in line. Carl and Jay were getting saddled up. Thor had the cattle and horses ready to leave the corral while I overslept. "What are you guys going to do, leave me here with the wolves to starve with none of mother's biscuits and bacon to start my day?"

"I saw Thor licking your face half an hour ago," Jay says, "Thought you were up and hiding someplace."

Thor let Powder pass him and came to me. By the time I got him saddled and grabbed the biscuits and bacon mother left by my saddle, everyone was on the trail and the boys had the herd well ahead of the wagons. As I passed father's wagon, he said, "Well Jack, it's good to see you today. Are you going to be alright after all that sleep?"

Sometimes it was tough being the youngest boy among a bunch of wise guys like my brothers. That's okay, I waited my time and I'd get them back. Carl was great. He didn't even mention the morning ordeal. The day was on its way and we expected to make 25 miles. The cow that was attacked last night was keeping up well and had only a couple of tooth marks with blood on two legs. I thought, might have to dress them tonight to make sure she has no infection.

Once we got a few miles from Dobytown, the buffalo herds were back. Father said we needed to kill a young one some afternoon and cook it off for food for Thor and us. He said the meat was very good and until you had buffalo steak, you had not eaten the best the west has to offer. It was a good day. The trail was covered with fine gravel. The livestock had plenty to eat and lots of water.

Father said we made at least 25 miles. Everyone was in a great mood as we camped for the night. Mother had a surprise after our supper of venison stew and biscuits. She went to the wagon and brought out these bottles with a dark liquid in them. "Mr. Alley says he just got this in this week. I remember buying this in Kansas City, one time and you all liked it."

Jay got up and helped mother serve us all a cup of Sarsaparilla. I had forgotten how good it tasted. Some people used it as medicine, but mother said it tasted too good to be medicine. Mary Alice said, "It tastes like medicine to me so mother can have mine." I set my cup down and Thor was licking what remained in it. He had never bothered anyone's plates or cups before. Mother grabbed my cup away and scolded Thor for that little trick.

Time for bed. I made sure I was close enough to Charles so that when he got up the next morning he would wake me. I didn't need another morning like today. We all woke early and got things rolling. Father wanted to make camp at Plumb Creek crossing tonight. That meant we will be 45 miles west of Fort Kearny and we'd have a great start toward Denver City.

The weather was cold and looked like rain ahead. We were having trouble finding wood for mother's fire at night. There were lots of buffalo chips along our path so Mary Alice had been chosen to pick up dry chips to make the campfire tonight. She was careful to pick only the very dry ones. They burned hot and had no smell. Mother had a couple of flour sacks to give for the cause, so Mary Alice walked over the prairie about 100 yards from the wagon because the wagons in front of us had picked close to the trail for their fire fuel.

By the time the sun was straight above us, it had come out from behind the clouds and the day was warming. I was at the head of the herd and looking toward the river, I saw an animal unfamiliar to me. I had father's glass so I ride up on the next rise and had a closer look. There was a small herd of antelope grazing close to the river. Must be 10 to 12, all with their heads down eating the short grass. I was downwind from them so they didn't smell me or the livestock. Riding slow and straight at them, I got within 250 yards before one raised his head. Carefully I pulled my Sharpe's rifle out of the scabbard, sight on a medium-sized animal and squeezed the trigger. It dropped on the spot and the herd was gone in a flash. I rode over cut the animal's throat so it would bleed out on the way back to the wagons. I tied him on the saddle and away we went. One of the cleanest shots I ever had on an animal, right through the heart.

Father was watching me ride toward the wagons. I'm sure he had heard the rifle shot and wondered why any of us would have reason to shoot our guns. When he saw my kill he was impressed. "One shot and your first antelope, how did you get close enough for a shot like that?"

"Father, that shot was from over 250 yards away. The whole herd of antelope never saw me until they heard the rifle." We hung the antelope out the back of father's wagon, after he is gutted and cleaned. The five wagons made Plumb Creek well before dark. After crossing the creek, we made camp and built mother a great fire. We skinned and butchered my kill into steaks for everyone including Harvey's family and had a real party for the first time since leaving Edwin at Leavenworth, Kansas. Even Thor had a big steak just like the rest of us and fell asleep in front of our fire.

CHAPTER 13

The next 40 mile leg of our trip was to the point where the South Platte River joins the Platte. It would take us two days and we would pass two Indian villages and a large encampment of Union soldiers. Father said, "Those Indian camps are Pawnee. The soldiers are making scouts for the army out of Braves of that tribe." We passed two ranches that were set up for cattle. I was not sure how well that is going to set with the local Indians. It looked like the buffalo would be a problem too, as the herd grows and needs more grassland to feed on. I continued to be amazed at the width of the Platte River. Some places it looked a half mile wide and only a foot deep with nothing but sandy bottom. Diego said it looked harmless but had quicksand in many places.

As we continued up the Platte, I saw what Diego was talking about. We passed an area that had caught several buffalo in deep sand and as you watched they continued to sink into the sand and drown. Nature was strange to me but I continued to be fascinated and needed to learn the good and the bad if for nothing else but survival in this land called the west. The weather continued to threaten rain that we didn't need as the trail was soft anyway. When it did rain, the wagon wheels sank to the axles. We were traveling in the middle of the second day from Plumb Creek when the sky opened up with a vengeance and sure enough the oxen and mules could only slip and slide on the trail. Father, Harvey, and Diego found a mound to circle the wagons on and Diego mounted one of his mules, bareback, and rode with Carl and me to bring the livestock back toward camp and tethered them in case lightning hits the area.

When we got the herd settled down and got to camp, Father and Harvey had set up the large tent I had forgotten we had. Everyone was inside trying to stay warm without a fire. Harvey told Carl, "There is room between the tent and the wagon out there so you boys can set up the lean-to like we did the last time it rained. I think Mary Alice has collected enough buffalo chips to keep a fire going the rest of today and tomorrow if we need it."

Charles got the poles we made that were stored under mother's wagon. Carl and Jay set them and I got the 20 by 20 foot canvas from Diego's wagon. In less than 30 minutes, we had the lean-to up and a fire going so Mother and Harvey's wife could cook supper for us. Thor came from under a wagon somewhere and curled up under the lean-to, well out of the rain.

Up until we had the party at Plumb Creek, the two groups were kind of strangers to one another. Harvey and his sons worked with us, but his brother's family was quiet and kind of withdrawn. Now Carl's mother, Betsy, and her sister-in-law, Maggie wanted to help mother every time they have a chance. The three had bonded quite well and never stop talked among themselves. Mother had to make sure they include Mary Alice because she was the only girl in the mix and there was no way she wanted her to feel left out. Maggie had three sons, two are teenagers: Harry and Lewis. Freeman was only nine years old, like Mary Alice, but not anywhere as mature as she was. Maggie's husband, Hershel, was a likable chap but had no skills needed for this country. He was a bank teller from Leavenworth, Kansas. He hoped to get a job with the Clark and Gruber mint in Denver City. Harvey was a freight hauler and totally different than his brother. I expected he would have a good future in the Denver City area.

The tent would be full tonight with 16 people. Carl and I decided we would sleep in the lean-to and Diego had his bed in the wagon with his shop. That would leave 13 in the tent, out of the wind. It rained all night. It's was a good thing father put us on the mound like he did since there was water all around us when we woke up. The Platte River looked a mile wide across this morning and it was still raining. Father said we are probably lucky we did not get to the forks of the rivers the way the rain kept coming down. "It must be a lot worse where the two rivers come together. We can't move, anyway, so I guess we might as well relax and check all of the livestock. Jay, you and Jack check the hoof's on all the animals for rocks and pebbles."

CHAPTER 14

When daylight showed, the rain was letting up but the whole area was soaked. The livestock had made a mud basin in the area where we tethered them last night so father said we had to move and then feed them some oats to sustain them. We moved the herd, now swollen with 28 oxen and Diego's six mules to higher ground. We milked the cows and mixed the milk with oats to feed the oxen and mules. The grass was wet but when we moved the cows and horses to the grass they happily grazed on it. Other wagons were passing now but the extra effort needed by their animals to pull through the mud and soft sand makes the rush they were in seem futile. The ladies had prepared a biscuit and antelope gravy breakfast with all the hot coffee we could drink.

All the men, including Hershel's three boys, helped move the livestock and got them fed so now everyone was hungry and a little damp. After breakfast, I didn't see Diego and that was not like him. He usually sat by the fire and had some words of wisdom for us all. I went to his wagon and he was inside with the antelope hide, very carefully stripping away any fat on the skin. He said, "When I get all this fat trimmed away, I can salt this hide down and roll it very tightly and it will hold until we get to Denver City. Then I will tan it, strip the hair off, bleach it and make you and me two of the best leather jackets we ever will have."

"You know how to make that hide soft enough to make jackets?"

"Well, I will have to get me an Arapaho squaw to chew on the hide but that should be easy where we are going."

"Come on Diego. I been around you long enough to know when you're pulling my leg. You really can soft tan that hide?"

"Sure, and when it is finished it will be soft enough to use your mommas sewing machine to make the jackets on."

"Oh, yes, she would have to be asleep for that. She won't even let father sew a patch on a shirt, so how you going to talk her into letting you make jackets with it?"

"Well now, who do you think keeps that sewing machine tuned and running for your mother? Sure is not that big blacksmith over there."

"You never cease to amaze me with your talents. I suppose you used to build sewing machines before you worked with guns."

"Jack, as you work more with guns, you will find most things mechanical are related in some way and if you can fix a gun you can work on a steam engine or feel comfortable around a cotton gin. Eli Whitney invented the cotton gin, but what made him rich was in 1798 he developed machines to mass produce muskets that had interchangeable parts."

"Okay, thanks for the history lesson, Diego, but I better let the tent know where we are before they come looking for one of us."

"I heard father and Harvey talking about leaving at daylight tomorrow so we have a lot to get ready."

A nice breeze came up during the night and helped dry the country out, but the trail was soft and the wagons that went by the day before did not help the rut situation. We did get a good start and got to the fork of the South Platte River by high sun. The area was a mess. The river had left mud a foot thick over the trail and the wagons ahead of us were going southwest also. Father had Jay drive the wagon and he rode a horse leading the wagons off the trail on harder ground for couple of miles. We kept the livestock on the north side of the trail and Father had the wagons moving well 50 or so yards south of the trail. There would be fewer wagons going to Denver City since many we saw on the Platte were heading for Oregon, or California. The farther we went up the South Platte, the higher we climbed in altitude, but the sun was out and the mountains ahead were beautiful. Father rode up to the front of the herd and told me to take the livestock another two miles up on a rise we could see. He pointed to a spot just below where he was going to circle the wagons for the night. "Tomorrow is Sunday. We will have breakfast and a small prayer service for the ladies and be on our way."

I could see trees ahead. We would have plenty of wood for the fire tonight. As we got closer I looked across the river and just north of the spot but across the river was an Indian village of about 30 large teepees. Riding back to Carl, I told him where to head the herd and rode back to the wagons to let Father know about the Indian village.

"It's alright. That is an Arapaho village I know about it from talk at Fort Kearney. They said they are friendly and want no trouble from the whites. If we leave them alone, they have no reason to bother us. Ride back and let the other wagons know about them so they won't get excited when they see the tee-pees across the river."

"Maybe they are some of Blue Feather's people. Can we cross the river and see if they know of him?"

"Probably not a good idea, Son, just go and let the others know what I told you."

We made camp, had supper and Harvey got a banjo out of his wagon and played and sang for an hour. That was a surprise! That was the first time we knew he was an entertainer when he was a young man. After we went to bed, the Indians started beating drums and singing in their language. It was a little disturbing. Even Thor got up and paces while this is going on. The rhythm of the drums put me to sleep, when Thor lay down beside me I woke and all was quiet. All the clouds were gone from the sky and more stars than I had ever seen showed up at this altitude. What a great sight! It was easy to sleep when all was quiet and the roof over you was nothing but stars.

CHAPTER 15

We all seemed to wake at the same time. The men got the oxen and mules in their harnesses and close to the wagons, while the women cooked off bacon to make bacon biscuits to eat while we traveled.

It was daylight now and everyone was around the fire. Father was ready to lead us in a prayer and everyone had their head bowed when a dozen or so horses came right up to the wagons and stopped. We all look up and there were Indians dismounting. One of the Indians asked if they can come to the fire and pray with us.

As father invited them to the fire, the one Indian speaking good English said, "Most of our small tribe have been converted and many of us have been baptized by a priest that comes this way from Santa Fe, a couple of times a year. We saw you come in yesterday, heard your music at night and I know today is your day to worship."

Father asked, "What made you think we would have worship service this morning?"

"I hear the music you sing and know these are words and music of Christian people who mean no harm to our people and know you would not be offended if we come across the river."

"You and your people are more than welcome to pray with us. Please, everyone join hands and let's hear the Lord's Prayer."

Half of the Braves are able to recite the words and they smile the whole time we are repeating the Lord's Prayer.

"My name is Richard Knight," Father said as he walks over to the Indian doing all the talking.

"Me chief Eagle Claw and we are Arapaho. We live on this river in warm weather. We move south into what you call New Mexico in your winter."

"I am sorry we don't do the sacraments you are used to with the Father, but we only have them twice a year in our religion."

"It is our pleasure to have you and your braves with us this morning and hope we have time like this again later in our lives."

Chief Eagle Claw and father have a conversation in sign language as the braves mount their horses. The Chief mounts up and they ride off up the river for the place they ford in shallow water.

"Son, if you ever have to work with Arapahos always remember Chief Eagle Claw as he will never forget you."

"Father we were not introduced."

"Jack, the talk we had in sign was all about the young man with the bullwhip at his side. Believe me when I say he will always remember Jack Knight."

"Well, I like him too and will never forget the day he rode into our camp and had worship with us."

We hitched the wagons and got them lined up. The slight breeze all night really helped to dry the trail and the land we had to take the livestock over. The Indian village was about 10 miles from the fork where the South Platte ran into the Platte River. That meant we were about 80 miles from Julesburg, Colorado. We had to ford the river and the trail went on the north side of the South Fork of the Platte River, all the way to Julesburg. It was all up hill from this point on. Father said Julesburg has an altitude nearly 3,500 feet above sea level and Denver City was over 5,200 feet above sea level. Might be harder to breath up there. The mountains were getting closer every day and the weather was cold in the mornings.

The snow was melting but some of the high peaks we saw, father said, were more than 13,000 feet above sea level and might have snow all year. Having the chance to see the Rocky Mountains this time of the year was spectacular. I could see why they have magnetism for the Mountain Men, like my friend, Jim Bridger, and the fellows that used to come to this area to trap for beaver. On the fourth day up the South Fork of the Platte we arrived in Julesburg, Colorado. It couldn't be more than a mile or two from Nebraska's state line. Father rode ahead to find a corral for all our livestock and a place to camp as we all needed a rest before forging on to Denver City, 175 miles or so up hill. We needed grain for the livestock, also. Our supply was depleting rapidly as we climb and the strain on the oxen was evident.

CHAPTER 16

Today was Thursday, May 21, 1863. We had been on this trail 37 days. Ben Holladay was right; this had been the experience of a lifetime. I knew we still had about 10 days to go but the rest gave me time to reflect on the last month's adventures and I would not trade them for anything. Father had found a paper from Denver, *The Daily Rocky Mountain News*. It was two days old but had lots of news of the war.

Union General Grant had been busy in the Vicksburg, Mississippi area. He started May 7, at Big Black River on his campaign to open the Mississippi River to the Union. May 9, at the Battle of Raymond, Mississippi, he was victorious and went on to his second victory on May 14 at the Battle of Jackson, Mississippi. On May 16, General Grant defeated Confederate General Pemberton's army at the Battle of Champion Hill and continued to Black River, Mississippi and inflicted a second defeat on the remnants of General Pemberton's army on the 17th.

Father and I went hunting later in the morning and father killed a young buffalo with one shot from about 100 yards. After we skinned the animal, we took it back to camp to butcher into steaks for everyone. This would be a great change from the hardtack and pemmican we ate to speed our trip up to Julesburg. The ladies found some potatoes at a small market in Julesburg. They were going to bake these while father and Charles cooked the steaks from the buffalo. Father was right about the taste of buffalo. It was as tender and seemed to have more juices without the fat we found in beef. The cooks had the ribs on the fire and those would become feed for Thor for several days as we made our way to Latham, Colorado.

Latham was 4,700 feet above sea level and that meant we would go up 1,200 feet by the time we got there. The higher we went, the harder the animals had to work. Even Powder snorted more than he did in Kansas City. Diego said, "It will take you time to overcome the altitude so just take it easy at whatever you try. Remember animals have to adjust also so as you push the livestock herd they need time to get used to the thin air."

Friday, we started the trek up the trail. Everyone was in good spirits as the day of rest was great, not only the animals, but for us, too. We only made 15 miles Friday as father wanted the oxen and mules to get adjusted slowly and gain stamina without adverse effects. Mary Alice and mother preferred to walk and both said time went by faster than just sitting on a bumping wagon. We had saddled extra horses and I was trying to teach Harry and Lewis, not only to ride, but to handle a small herd of cows. Both boys were doing great and getting comfortable, not only with the animals but we now had something in common to talk about and I knew they feel like they contributed in some way instead of just being in the way.

Our second day out of Julesburg, we past a large ranch set up to raise cattle for the gold fields around the Denver City area. Harvey knew the two Morgan brothers that owned the ranch and had Jay drive his wagon while he rides over to see them. Harvey returned with the brothers to meet Father. "Richard Knight, this is Henry Morgan and his younger brother Frank. We all ran freight together in Illinois, back a few years ago."

"You fellows have a great piece of ground and should be very successful."

"Where will you winter your herd? The snow gets quite deep in this valley."

"We have an area over in Nebraska that has great grass and water, and can handle three or 400 head for about four months out of the year."

"Well, I sure wish you good luck because the Denver City area will need a continued supply of beef for a long time and as close as you are you can have an edge on beef coming in from Texas and Kansas."

"My brother can't take his eye off your bull, up there. You want to sell him before some Indians steal him from you?"

"We already had a tribe try that, but we had some great tobacco they liked better. No, we will keep him."

"Okay, Richard, we need to get back to work. It has been a pleasure to meet you and you come back anytime. We love company."

We moved another 10 miles and camped for the night. Mother had some potatoes and it was cool enough to keep parts of the buffalo for a stew with some of her carrots she canned last year. Tomorrow was Sunday so we would get a later start than on a weekday. May was almost over but at this altitude it sure was cold in the morning and it took time to get everything and everyone moving. I was getting used to dressing in layers as mother called it. You started with three shirts and a coat and by mid morning, you lost the wool shirt and with the sun straight above you the coat went away. I was not sure where mothers gained so much knowledge, but we were fortunate to have them around to learn from.

CHAPTER 17

As we gained altitude, the animals were showing signs of fatigue earlier each day so Father was pacing the forward progress and we were only making around 18 to 20 miles a day. The trail was narrow and some of the canyons forced the herd to walk the trail ahead of the wagons. We were now in mountain country with many creeks with run off water from the snow melting higher up. There was plenty of grass for the livestock so each night Carl and I found a small valley to hold the stock and a good site for the wagons to circle. We pass small Indian villages almost every day. Father said they are mostly Cheyenne and Arapaho. "The Cheyenne Chief, Black Kettle, and nine other Cheyenne Chiefs made a treaty with the government for money, of course, to settle down, plant and live like the white man. That was two years ago and so far it has been successful with Indians and whites getting along quite well in northern Colorado."

We were passing lakes now and tonight, after we camped, Carl, Jay, and I were going to see if there are fish in one of them. After we got the herd and the wagons set for the night, we rode up to a lake less than a mile from camp. All three of us had dug some worms out of the ground, baited our hooks and had our lines in the water when all three lines start pulling at the same time. We hooked them and get them to the bank. Wow, all three are half pound or larger trout. Thor went wild when he saw the three fish. He wasn't sure what to do with them as they jumped all around him. Just as fast as we put hooks in the water, we would get a bite. We continue to fish until we have 32 nice trout for tomorrow's breakfast, two for everyone.

I had caught a lot of fish in my young life, but never any that fought the hook like those cold water mountain trout. Mother was delighted with the catch, and said, "I think I can find some corn meal to fry those in and we can heat up the Dutch oven and make biscuits to have with them." The women did themselves proud with breakfast. Maggie had two pints of peach jam she was saving for their 4th of July supper but felt we all needed it now. We were in our 6th day out of Julesburg and expected to reach Latham, Colorado sometime to-morrow. The land had leveled and we were in an area like a prairie. It was all grassland and several ranches had been started for raising cattle. The river ran slow and shallow in this area. It looked ideal for a spot to homestead if that was your dream. We saw the moun-tains rise again about 20 miles ahead. That must be where Latham lied, closer to the mountains west of us. Harvey said he rode through this area when returning from Santa Fe in 1857 on his way to Kansas City. This area was called Jefferson Territory back then and there were very few white settlements then.

Carl had found a place just off the trail for the livestock and he said there was water and plenty of feed for all the animals with an area for the wagons to camp. We were eating supper when Harvey looked up and said, "Everyone be quiet. There is a large herd of buffalo all around us. I am not sure what to do but I know we sure don't need them to panic and stampede around our camp." Our animals were all tethered so they wouldn't wander away with the buffalo and so far none of the herd had come within the wagon circle. Diego got up and walked out to where his mules were tethered, and talked to them very quietly to keep them calm. The buffalo grazed around us for another hour as they made their way south. The moon came out and is full. Father climbed up on one of the wagons as they passed and said there were possibly 5,000 head in the herd that passed us. Mother said, "How do you know that, Richard. Did you count the legs and divide by four to get your answer?

"Now you know, Elizabeth, that's the only way I could tell for sure."

After all of the excitement had passed, the bed roll felt good and I got a good night's rest under the brightest sky I had ever seen. It must have been the altitude.

CHAPTER 18

Daylight came well before the sun was up and we were moving before the sun was on us today. We all wanted to make Latham early enough to see it in the daylight and maybe find a store or trading post open. Mother wanted to get some more sarsaparilla for the young ones, she said, but I knew she liked it too.

Father needed to buy grain of some kind for the oxen and Diego's mules. The last week had been hard on them and their ribs were starting to show. This bothers Father when livestock are not getting the feed they need. Powder had done well and looks good even though he has had me on his back, sometimes three days straight. Father said I should ride him two days and let him rest but when I go to get a mount in the morning, he nipped my shoulder if I pick an alternate mount too often. Jay rode on into Latham to scout us a camp and room for the livestock. When he returned, he rode right past me to the wagon train. He had some news for father and the wagons.

When Jay returns to the herd, he said, "Father sent me to see Frank Root, the Overland Stage agent for Ben Holladay. He has been waiting for us to show up since Ben told him we were coming and to telegraph him when we arrive. The livery stable is out of grain but Frank will sell father enough oats for one night, anyway."

"Did Frank tell you where we should take this herd of livestock for the night and where to camp?"

"Yes," Jay said, "Take the herd south of town and you will see a large corral the army uses when it's in the area. They will not be in this area till next week. I told father to follow us and circle the wagons behind the corral where there is water and fire wood for the night."

Jay continued, "Frank will load enough oats in a wagon and bring it out after the last stage comes through about 6:00 this evening."

We got to the corral by 4:30 p.m. and got the horses, and cattle in the corral. The cows were ready for milking when the wagons brought us the pails. The wagons showed up at 5:30 and Maggie and her sons got in the corral and started milking the cows so we could mix the milk with the oats to feed the oxen and mules. Harvey and Father had the animals in the corral ready for the feed bag before Frank Root arrived with the oats.

Mother and Betsy got Powder and another mount from the corral and rode into town to the trading post. When they returned with drinks, they also brought a large ham to cook for dinner since it was so early in the day. Out of nowhere, Mother and Maggie rounded up tables the army used and set a table for 16 before inviting Frank Root to stay for supper. Besides the ham, they had baked a potato for each of us, and prepared some of the string beans mother canned last year, adding bacon to the pot. We also had fresh biscuits with butter that Mary Alice churned from some of the cream she got from today's milking.

We ate hardtack and cheese on the trail a lot of the time but these women put together a fine meal when the men decided to stop and relax for a few hours. When you considered we are only 40 or so miles from our intended destination with two days travel left, we were all in fine shape after 46 days and over 660 miles of prairie, river crossings, Indians, and mountains. Jay lost a piece of one ear. Harvey has a great scar on his leg and we only lost two head of cattle. Oh yes, and we gained one nice Indian pony. All in all, that has to be considered a good and successful trip.

Today we are up with daylight. It was Saturday, May 30, and we were on our way to Denver City before the sun was up. After we had traveled 10 miles to another stage stop, Ben Holladay was waiting for father, riding the best looking sorrel and white horse I have ever seen. He rode up to me and said, "Hi, Jack, how far back is Richard?"

"Possibly a mile, he is in the lead wagon."

"I need him or one of you boys to ride on into Denver City with me and get you set up with a place to park your wagons and this herd."

"Good, Father will know which way will be best, If he wants me to drive the wagon so he is free, tell him I am ready."

"Why not cut his horse out and bring it with us. It could save some time and we can be on our way back to Denver City." Father was six-feet-three inches tall and weighed in at 225, too big a man for Powder. He had a large framed horse and rode him sitting tall in the saddle. I cut him out of the herd and followed Ben. Ben and I found the wagons and talked to Father. Father wanted to send Charles with Ben. I took the extra mount and got Charles to trade places and I took the reins of the wagon and sent him to see Ben and Father. Mary Alice wanted to ride for a while and Powder let her mount off the seat of the wagon. As Charles rode away, a wind comes up and it started raining. It was a cold rain but not hard, just enough to be uncomfortable and the wind caused the body to be cold. Mary Alice rode to the wagon that Mother was in and got a canvas serape to shed the rain but kept riding Powder. Thor walked under Diego's wagon to try and stay dry. I could see the sky a mile or so ahead and the sun was out. Looking past the wagons, I saw Art starting to circle the herd so he had found water and feed for the animals and our camp for the night.

CHAPTER 19

We camped in a small valley for the night. After we got all the livestock tethered and settled in, Father explained what was happening with Charles and Ben. "Ben has several acres just south of town on the South Platte River and is letting us use that along with Harvey and his brother, while we find more permanent quarters. Charles is to be shown a way to get there without taking the herd and wagons straight through downtown Denver City."

Ben told father about the April 19th fire that destroyed most of Blake Street and the main retail area because most of the buildings were wooden structures. He said they now had what they call the "Brick Ordinance" and if you build in the town area it must be brick. We got an early start on our last day and expected to get to our campsite well ahead of nightfall. We passed farms and saw homes being built in the area as we got closer to Denver City. As the sun went above me, I saw Charles riding toward me. "Jack, when you see the next stage stop, pass it and take the first trail west. It will take you a couple of miles west of town. Just stay on the trail until you cross the river. After you cross the river you are on Ben Holladay's place."

"Follow the river south and you will see a receiving corral to put the livestock in." Charles continued, "I have to see father as Ben said to take the wagons north off the trail and to the old line shack for a place to camp. Ben calls it a line shack but I slept there last night and it is bigger than our house in Kansas City and furnished very nicely too." He told me to remind Father it is for us until we can find a place in the area.

"See you whenever we get the wagons stopped and the oxen in the corral for the night," I responded.

Charles rode off to see the wagon train and now I had to find that stage stop because we were a half a mile off the trail, well to the east of where Charles was talking about. Thor was pacing the bull and his cows so I rode to tell Art and Carl where we were going to turn off. All of a sudden 30 or more Braves circled our herd and two of them ride up to where the three of us are.

"You there, boy with the whip. Where you taking these cows and horses?"

"I am not a boy and we are headed for Ben Holladay's place on the south side of town."

"These belong to Ben Holladay?"

"No, they belong with the wagon train behind us and we are all staying on Mr. Holladay's place."

"You bring more white men than you three?"

"Yep, there are 16 of us all the way from Kansas City."

"You come for gold in the mountains?"

"No, my father is a blacksmith and Harvey is a freighter and we have a gunsmith with us also."

"You have many guns with you?"

"No, just our personal ones. Diego just fixes them when they are broken."

As the wagons saw us, father changed places with Charles and rode over toward us.

"You, one big white man. Me Chief Walking Bear. We are Ute. Our village is across river and on that hill you see up there." The chief pointed west and on a rise about two miles away we saw several large tee-pees and a dozen small ones clustered on high ground.

"Well, Walking Bear why have you stopped our herd? I am Richard Knight and we are coming to this area to live and raise our family in peace."

"We see big bull cow and want to trade for him. We have horses or gold to trade with."

"Big bull not for trade, but if you have cows that need his services we can make some arrangements that will help you out."

"Richard Knight, we make deal some way."

"Good, you know Ben Holladay place south of town?"

"Me know place you speak of next to river."

"Let us get settled in and you come see me in three days and we bargain for use of big bull, okay, Walking Bear?"

"Okay, Richard Knight." With that, they all rode away after father and Walking Bear talked sign for a minute or two.

"Father, what do you talk about with sign to a chief like him?"

"Jack, if nothing else it makes him comfortable with me and also shows him that I respect him and his culture. Indians are people just like us and respect goes a long way when dealing with any group no matter their race, culture or color."

There is another lesson from father to his son so listen, Jack.

It took us four more hours to get to the river crossing and on to Ben Holladay's place. Mother checked the line shack out and approved. She couldn't believe there were five rooms and four beds in a line shack. After we get all the animals in the corral and fed, all 16 of us found chairs and sat on the porch that covered the whole front of Ben's shack. Father had a few kind words for everyone, including young Freeman, as he thanked him for helping milk the cows at night. Then he asked us all to pray a prayer of thanks for our safe journey. Diego, not to be outdone by Father, has to add his words of wisdom along with a speech about us all going separate ways, and enriching the country we have invaded.

CHAPTER 20

It was Monday, June 1, 1863. We were on the trail 47 days, passing some 60 stage stops, a dozen or so Indian villages, forded rivers and untold creeks. We avoided a buffalo stampede and fought off a band of Cheyenne Indians. What a story to tell my grandchildren, if I ever had any.

By sun up, Father, Diego and all three brothers were riding into town. Father was looking for where Cherry Creek came into the South Platte River. He had heard there was a building in the area suitable for a blacksmith shop. This area, as it turned out, had been burned out by the April fire. They were still in the process of cleaning up. We rode to Blake Street and see they have already started building brick structures to replace what was lost in the downtown area to the fire. With a population of over 4,000 just in the town area alone, they needed to get this town back in operation as quickly as possible. As we rode to Ben Holladay's office, we saw a place called The Stop. Father rode to the hitching post, got off his horse and said, "How would you boys like to have some bacon and eggs? Bet we can get some in here."

It was still early and none of us figured Ben would be in his office yet, so father had a very good idea. When we walked in, Ben was sitting at the back table, having his breakfast and coffee. Thor had to stay outside with the horses and looked at me as if to say, "why?"

Ben had the morning paper and put it down as we walk to his table. Standing up he says, "What a pleasant surprise to see you all this morning. Gentlemen have a seat. This is the largest table in the place. How about some breakfast? Best in Denver City. Richard, did you find the line shack large enough to accommodate your family? And I apologize about the name of the place, it was a line shack before I added to it for a place to live while building our home in town and we just continue to call it that."

Father and Diego continued a conversation about the town and what is needed for the area to grow. The Civil War was on the front page of the *Daily Rocky Mountain News*. There was a story about General Ulysses S. Grant and his assault on Vicksburg, Mississippi. His plan was to gain control, ever since May 22, and to put down the resistance made by Confederate General John Pemberton to defend that city. Ben had found a storefront for Diego to look at on 14th street, just out of the area the fire had burned. He told Diego his Colt contract could be a big deal here in the Denver City area but he also needed a rifle line to compete with a gun dealer up in Latham. Father wanted to know if the land on Cherry Creek and the confluence to South Platte River was available to develop.

Ben said, "I know where to start to find out. Hiram Wilson used to own the land on the south side of that creek early on. If he has sold he will know who has title now. His office is down the street from mine."

"Diego, I can send Albert, my bookkeeper, with you over to 14th street and you can have a look at that store front. If it is not right, don't feel you have to rent it. It is not my property, I just know about it."

"Richard, we need to go see Hiram. Why don't you boys meet us back here in three hours and you go roam our town and see what you think?"

Charles, Jay and I rode to the north end of town. We passed through the area of log cabins and homes that had been built in the previous four years, since all the miners started finding gold up the South Platte and farther up Cherry Creek. There must have been a brick plant in the area as some of these homes were made of brick and several, under construction, were being built with brick. We rode to the east side of town and found stands of big pine trees and a saw mill right in the middle of all those trees. Riding up to the mill, Thor has a problem with the noise from the big saws and stays behind us. The smell of the fresh cut wood is one I will never forget. Charles got out his sketch map of the area and found we should be coming up on Sand Creek and about the same time we see a large Indian village several miles to the south and east.

We didn't want to have a problem so we headed directly west hoping that would put us in the downtown area and close to The Spot. By the time we found the restaurant, we had been gone four hours and father was just a little upset because he needed to get home to talk to mother about buying the plot of ground on Cherry Creek. Diego was going to rent the store he looked at and said there was plenty of room for us both to have a bench with plenty of natural light. The shop area had high ceilings so we could have the small forge inside, not out in the alley like it was in Kansas City. Father had agreed that I could devote all the time Diego needed in order to get his shop set up and in order.

As we rode back to the line shack, Father was telling us about the piece of land on Cherry Creek. It was about 10 acres with 400 feet of frontage on the South Platte and 1,075 feet on Cherry Creek. Father said the area was large enough for our home, a blacksmith shop and livery if we had that much capital. Only Mother knew what our finances were for sure. Jay and I knew that if we ended up with a livery stable we would be the ones to run and maintain it. Charles had been father's right hand man and had become a fine blacksmith in the previous three years. A lot of possibilities were going through father's mind as he became quiet when we passed the confluence of Cherry Creek. I anticipated an entertaining evening, listening to father talk mother into going along with his dream that he has come up with.

CHAPTER 21

"Richard, you must be out of your mind. How much money do you think we have, anyway?"

"If we are to do everything you are talking about we will have to borrow at least 25% from some bank."

"Elizabeth, things are cheaper up here than in Kansas City. What I am saying is that we find a saw mill to get the lumber directly for half what it costs in Missouri. There is enough lodge pole pine on the 10 acres for Jay and Jack to build their corrals. Ben says we can stay here till we have a home finished."

"Tell you what. You and your buddy, Ben, find a bank that will loan you enough money to build a small boarding house for me to have a way to contribute to this plan of yours and we might have something to talk about. You and your boys have this all figured out, but Mary Alice and I have to be involved or this move to the Wild West won't work."

Needless to say all that mother asked for, she got, so we started on a two month project through June and July, to put everything together in an organized way. I was torn due to my duty to help Diego with his shop and store, so I worked early each day for him and with Jay in the afternoon and evening. We finished Diego's store by mid June. He was taking in enough work to keep him busy all day and he was also selling a new Colt Navy Revolver quite regularly. We had the livery stable and corrals in order by the end of June. We built the stable as far from the creek and river as the lots would allow and the corrals were facing the creek and river with a wide road between the water and the corrals. Father's shop was 100 feet farther up Cherry Creek and as far from the water as possible. We were not sure what water levels are like in the spring yet. Mother had a local builder that is putting her dream home and boarding house together. It was set at the farthest southeast corner of the 10 acres.

By the end of July, our area was known in town as the Knight compound. The builder said we could move in by the 15th of August. Mother had four bedrooms on the family side of the house. She had nine nice sized rooms: one large dining room for the serving of breakfast and supper and eight for guest rooms. She had one guest already as Diego had asked if he can have the downstairs front guest room. Mother had agreed. The August 3rd *Daily Rocky Mountain News* front page had nothing but war news on it. In July, the battle of Gettysburg was won by the Union but a correspondent from somewhere up north said that because Union General Meade failed to follow Confederate General Lee as he fled with his men back to Virginia, the war would continue for another year at least.

Harvey was doing well. He, along with Carl and Art, had put together a freight company and named it H C and A Freighters The company had got a contract to keep some of the Overland Stations supplied, also they hauled lumber from the mill we saw on the east side during our exploring trip. Father sold him one of our wagons and he had the two he and Hershel brought to Denver City.

Hershel and his family had moved into town. When we arrived in Denver City, Hershel was devastated to find Clark, Gruber & Company had sold their mint. But then, when he went to the building at 16th and Market, he found that the United States Government had purchased the Company and turned it into an assay office and they needed someone with his background. He was now a supervisor for the assay office and doing well.

Jay and I had the eight horses we brought from Kansas City. We rented out Father's wagon and the six remaining oxen. We had 20 inside stalls for rent and we now had three buggies to rent also. Charles and Father were busy with work from all the new construction in town and there were still five large mining companies southwest of town that are always bringing equipment in to be reworked.

By December 24, 1863, my 15th birthday, Denver City had three daily newspapers, four churches, two banks, two theaters, five brick stores and many gambling houses that lined up behind Blake Street, the main street downtown. Mother felt I had completed the schooling I need for reading, writing and arithmetic but she had found a book on American history and demanded that I study it just like I was in school and in three months she would give me a test. The family had been so busy with all of our projects and accomplishments we have more or less forgotten about the war back east. I found a paper that had President Lincoln's memorable "Gettysburg Address," and a story about General Sherman's push toward Atlanta after the Union soundly defeated the Confederates at Chattanooga.

There was a lot of talk about some of the Denver City citizens forming a unit to serve in a Colorado militia to help maintain peace with the Cheyenne, Arapaho, and Ute Indians. Charles was the right age for the Conscription Act but I think father would have had to volunteer in order to get into uniform. Chief Black Kettle and his tribe had been quiet and living with the treaty they signed with Indian agent William Bent in February, 1861, at Fort Wise. They had a large reservation a 160 or so miles southeast of Denver City called the Big Sandy, but whites kept infringing on their territory and this could be trouble, in time.

Father had friendly encounters with Chief Black Kettle as he has loaned his big bull, Bolivar, to some of the Cheyenne and Arapaho tribes to keep their cows giving milk for the small children. Chief Walking Bear of the Ute tribe was the first to use Bolivar's services shortly after we arrived in Denver City. Father never said what he gets for Bolivar's time but he seemed to be happy with whatever it is. Bolivar was possibly the busiest and happiest bull in the Colorado Territory!

CHAPTER 22

Colorado Governor John Evans seemed to be spoiling for a fight with the Indians. He was pushing for statehood and wanted to be one of Colorado's first senators. I think he felt that if the Indians went away more whites will come in and cause this to become a state. Then he could make his dream of becoming a senator a reality. Troops from the 1st Colorado Veterans Volunteers with Colonel Samuel Tappan in charge attacked a party of Cheyenne at Fremont's Orchard in April 1864 and were the catalyst for continued trouble with the Indians.

Warm spring rains and melting snow brought a destructive flood down Cherry Creek on May 19, 1864. Water got to the foundation of our home; water was inside father's shop and the livery stable and all our corrals washed down the South Platte like toothpicks. Most of the southern part of town from 15th Street to 20th Street including Market Street was wiped out. We were lucky. Father had us move our livestock down to Harvey's pastures when the rain got heavy, but we did lose our buggies and a lot of tack and gear. The south side of the creek bank rose rapidly so the run off was into town and down the South Platte River. Jay and I lost a lot of hay we had overhead in the livery, but saved our oats and barley that were in sacks by running it over to the rear of father's shop. We had 16 of our inside stalls rented out but got all of the horses out before the stables washed down the river. The fire had done a lot of damage but I thought the flood will make some people have second thoughts about rebuilding again.

Several families had left and were going farther west, but I saw clean up and buildings being rebuilt just three weeks after the flood. Carl, Harvey's son, lost a wagon, six mules and almost his life when a bunch of Indians that he called "Dog Soldiers" attacked him on his way to Latham, Colorado to restock Frank Root's Overland Stage station. Dog Soldiers are Cheyenne that would not sign the treaty along with Chief Black Kettle and had continued to cause trouble in northern Colorado since the treaty was signed. Carl was shot in the shoulder and bled so much they thought he was dead, but they were in such a hurry to get away with the wagon and its goods they didn't stop to scalp him.

Walking Bear and his Ute braves found Carl and took him to their village and got the bullet out of his shoulder and two days later delivered him by travois to the line shack on the South Platte that was Harvey's office. It was late summer now. We had rebuilt the livery, stables and corrals. Business was slow. Denver City was almost cut off from the outside world. Nothing was getting through from the east. The Cheyenne and Arapaho tribes had made it impossible for wagon trains or freighters to travel the eastern trails. The Indians were cutting the telegraph lines both east and west, and outside communication was almost non-existent.

Harvey was only working locally and most of his work was with the saw mill, moving lumber to town for what little building was continuing. Prices on food or any item you wanted to buy was out of sight and everyone was looking to Governor Evans for relief. The Overland Stage Line was at a standstill due to raids by the Indians on the trail all the way to Fort Kearney. Governor Evans was wishy-washy. First he wanted whites to go after the Indians; then he thought better of that and wanted to form a Cavalry of what became the group called "100 dazers." These were volunteers from Denver City that enlisted for a period of 100 days to quell the Indian uprising.

On September 28th Cheyenne and Arapaho tribes, with Chiefs Black Kettle, White Antelope and Neva, along with three other Arapahos, came into Denver City for the Camp Weld Meeting. Governor Evans was not happy about the meeting but could hardly turn down an offer to talk peace. John Evans turned the meeting over to Colonel John Chivington, telling the Indians it was out of his hands and they would have to work out something with Major Edward Wynkoop and Colonel Chivington.

Colonel Chivington made the final statement of the conference. "My rule of fighting either white men or Indians is to fight them until they lay down their arms and submit to military authority. You are nearer Major Wynkoop than any one else, and you can go to him when you get ready to do that."

The local papers had pictures of everybody hugging and leaving in good spirits, but father said, "This is not over. Wait till winter sets in. Our Governor has confused everyone, Indians and whites. Nothing has been settled at that conference and things will get worse before this peace we are looking for comes."

Father and Charles enlisted with the 100 days home militia, or the 3rd Colorado Cavalry, but all he and Charles had accomplished is to put new shoes on the horses and mules of the 2nd Colorado Cavalry and the 3rd Colorado Cavalry. Winter had set in with severe blizzard conditions in October and November. In late November, Father and Charles, with their two companies of the 3rd Cavalry, were sent down the South Platte to try to keep the telegraph line in operation. Father was very concerned. When he and Charles leave he told us all to be watchful for trouble as the Cheyenne were getting short on supplies and hungry down on the Big Sandy. I made a trip to Father's cattle that we left south of Harvey's home and office and found three less cows than last week. Following the tracks, I felt some hungry Cheyenne had taken them south as the horse tracks suggested that the horse had not been shod.

CHAPTER 23

Late in November 1864, Governor John Evans was pushing Colonel John Chivington to take the "Bloodless Third" and control the Indian population before their 100 day enlistment is up.

Colonel Chivington took the 10 remaining companies of the 3rd, and a detachment of the 1st Colorado Cavalry, to Fort Lyon on the Arkansas River. He picked up 125 more men for artillery from the 1st Calvary and, with an overnight march through bitter cold, found the only Indians in the area. Early on Tuesday, November 29, Colonel Chivington led a charge on Chief Black Kettle's camp on Sand Creek. They killed about 150 Indian men, women, and children, losing 10 of their own soldiers.

Now called the "Bloody Third," they and Father's company returned to Denver and were mustered out on December 31, 1864. The Sand Creek Massacre intensified the trouble between whites and Indians and Denver City was more isolated than ever. Now that I was 16, Diego had confidence in my abilities and said he now needed to pay me for my work. His business had grown and he had a woman who did leatherwork. She produced holsters, belts, and now was making fancy bridles for horses. Her tooling was more delicate than some of Diego's work. Diego now sold the .44 caliber Henry repeating rifle. It went for $ 42.00 but Diego could get $ 50.00 each for the ones he had left because no freighters are getting through from the east.

During January 1865, the Cheyenne and Arapahos killed at least 30 ranchers, soldiers, and travelers between Denver City and Plumb Creek down on the Platte River. They had stolen 1,500 cattle and burned all the buildings at Julesburg, Colorado. Frank Root survived but Ben Holladay was trying to get Congress to pay him $120,000 for his loss of station, supplies, livestock, and coaches. In early March, Chief Black Kettle, who survived the Sand Creek Massacre, came to see father one night. He told him that "Dog Soldiers" were going to raid the Cherry Creek area and that he and the family should leave for three days. Father told Black Kettle that all the Indians knew that he and his family were helpful and wanted peace with them, so no harm would come to us. The Chief was upset that father will not listen to his plea and left with a stern warning that we were not safe.

The next night, when we were all asleep, Chief Walking Bear with 10 braves came to our home and kidnapped all of us, including mother and Mary Alice, taking us to their village for two days. When the Utes brought us home, Diego, who had watched the raiding party from upstairs after hearing the noise last night in our corrals as they turned the stock out, said, "They came in the house downstairs and were unhappy you were all gone but never came upstairs to look."

They burned two buildings across the creek. They burned four of the homes farther up Cherry Creek and killed two of the families that had no children. Mother's only guest at the time was Diego, so we lost no one in the Indian raid. Walking Bear told Father that even though he and Black Kettle were enemies they needed one another to help their mutual friend, Richard Knight, and Black Kettle had no braves at the time to help him. When the Ute braves came for us, Thor was in the livery, I guess. He must have stayed out of sight when the "Dog Soldiers" came because they would have taken him back to their camp and made supper out of him.

Winter was almost over. We were getting daily news again as the telegraph lines were remaining up and working. Abraham Lincoln was reelected and on March 5th the Daily News had his second Inaugural Address. One of our papers was giving General Sherman good reports about his march to the sea from Atlanta and his path of destruction. The other paper was questioning whether he had crossed the line since the Union was winning and his destruction was not necessary for total victory.

It was April and Denver City was growing with the warmer weather. Mother had all of her rooms full. Father had to hire a shoer to help him and Charles in the shop. I was working four hours, six days a week for Diego. Jay and I had hired Lewis, Hershel's son, to work after school in the livery and stables. One afternoon Thor came looking for me and barking for me to follow him to the front of the livery.

As I walk out the front door, I was greeted by Artimas York, the sergeant from Fort Kearney, Nebraska. "Hi, Jack, how are you, anyway? You have put on some weight and grew a couple of inches. I see Thor is no worse for the wear. I hear they need hard rock miners up Georgia Gulch. Suppose your dad could tell me who I need to talk to up there?"

"Artimas, Father knows all the owners up that way and he would be glad to point you to the best of the lot. Some of them you would not want to work for."

"Come on over to the shop and meet father. We are full at the house but we have a comfortable couch in the office in the livery. After supper you can bed down in the office."

"Lewis, take this man's horse, put him in a stall, feed him some oats and give him a good rub down."

We walked over to father's shop. "Father, meet Artimas York. He is the sergeant I told you about who wanted to buy Thor from me at Fort Kearney."

"Artimas, I'm Richard Knight. Jack has told me about you."

"Well, Richard, the story about wanting to buy the dog sounds good but the truth is if I thought I could have stolen the dog I would have. That is until I saw how Jack uses that whip he carries. I thought this boy would be an easy mark but he changed my mind real quick."

"I am glad you two worked it out. I believe Jack would kill for his dog and I sure would not want that to happen."

"Father, I have asked Artimas to stay for supper and offered him the office to sleep in tonight. He has heard the mining companies are looking for help. Would you recommend one of them for him to apply for a job?"

"Sure, we can talk about that after supper. Jack, take Artimas up to the house and let mother know we have a guest to grace our table tonight."

Mother was pleased to have company and made Artimas sit for coffee and a sweet roll she was baking at the time.

The next day, April 10, the *Denver Daily News* had the story about the terms of surrender between General Lee and General Grant at Appomattox Courthouse. This was great news since we all had been waiting for this day since the war started in April, 1861.

Then on the 15th of April, 1865 we got the horrible news about the assassination of President Lincoln at Ford's Theater in Washington, D.C., by some actor by the name of John Wilkes Booth. Mother said, "I remember. I believe it was on New Years Day 1835. President Andrew Jackson was at a funeral for a Congressman named Warren Davis when a fellow named Lawrence tried to shoot him with two different derringers and both misfired. I was only 11 or 12, but we talked about it in school and I guess you retain some things you learn, especially when you are young."

CHAPTER 24

As spring left and summer came, periodic Indian raids extended all the way to Fort Kearney in the east. Prices for goods and services kept rising due to the lack of consistent flow of provisions and items from the Overland Trail. Mother had enough chickens to keep eggs a plenty for the family and her guests. Father had a good supply of beef that he kept with Harvey's herd south of town.

But in Denver City, eggs were $1.50 a dozen. Beef costs $.45 cents a pound. Flour was $20.00 per 100 pound bag. Potatoes, when available, were $15.00 a bushel. Lumber from the local mill was $200.00 per thousand board feet. Hay, when we can get it from the south, was $100.00 per ton.

We got $25.00 per day for a wagon and team and $17.50 for a horse and buggy for the day. Sam Getts, one of Ben Holladay's stage drivers between Denver and Julesburg, Colorado, came in to Father's shop for new shoes for his horse and told us Billy Cody is driving the stage between Fort Kearny and Plumb Creek over on the Platte River.

Sam said, "That boy out ran a band of several hundred Sioux Indians with Lieutenant Flowers, a division agent, riding shotgun and six heavily armed passengers. He kept whipping the horses and the rest were firing rifles and pistols as the Sioux rode next to the stagecoach. Billy had a long whip and used it on the Indians that got too close and over the heads of his horses until they reached Three Crossings, where the Indians broke off the charge. Flowers was wounded, and two of the passengers were killed, but Cody got the stagecoach to safety."

Father told Sam, "Bill should be around 20 by now. He always was full of spunk so the story doesn't surprise me."

Carl, from H C and A Freighters, came by the livery with a wagon to be repaired at father's shop. Carl told Jay and me, "The Cavalry is going to start patrolling with our wagon trains to help get provisions into Denver City. We will be relaying with wagons out of Fort Kearny, at Julesburg, Colorado. This should help Denver City and most of the residents get back to normal. We have six wagons and outfits now and are still looking for drivers to keep them all on the trails hauling freight.

"We had two riders in here yesterday looking for jobs." I told Carl, "I know one of them. Thor knocked him off his horse a couple of years ago when he and his partner, Larry Logan, tried to snake the herd we brought from Missouri away from us and I thought they were jayhawkers. When they rode up the drive to the stables yesterday, Thor met them before they got off their horses in front of the livery. Josh Bean remembered him and would not get off his horse until I came out of the office and called Thor off. Josh had no idea he was riding up to my door until Thor, ready to jump him, let him know he was in bad territory and Josh said he and his brother Able, the fellow with him, joined the Army the week after our little meeting and he had not seen Larry Logan since he enlisted in the Kansas Cavalry. Further more he said he and Able drove wagons and artillery pieces off and on for the last two years in the Army. I think Larry was trying to lead Josh astray back then, Carl, but Josh has grown up in the Army since we first met and I think his brother is older by a year or two. They told me that they were going to try and get a room at the Colorado Hotel, for a night. Mother's boarding house was full so we had no place to put them."

"Loan Powder to me," Carl said, "and I can ride over to the hotel and check them out. I will probably go by and see Diego, also, if you can spare Powder that long. By the way, did he and Thor get along when he left?"

"Yep, no problem." I replied.

"That is good enough for me. Can you get that wagon over to your father's shop? He knows what it needs to fix the problem."

As I tried to get up on the wagon to take it over to father's shop, Thor walked in front of me and wouldn't let me mount the wagon. "Thor, get out of the way." He pushed me side ways and barked. Again I tried for the wagon step and he bit my boot and I went to the ground.

As I got up, I heard why Thor had been trying to keep me out of the wagon. Just behind the seat on the wagon was a Prairie Rattlesnake all coiled up and ready to strike. They were not big snakes but their fangs carry a lot of poison and can sure make a man awful sick for a while. Father came over from the shop when he heard Thor barking and for some reason he had a rifle with him. He got a long stick and tossed the snake on to the ground. Shooting his .44 caliber from the hip, the bullet split the head of the snake between the eyes.

I said, "That is a great shot. I have seen you do that before when killing a snake but to split his head by a shot from the hip must be a trick."

"No trick, Jack, you just have to get the snake watching the end of the gun barrel and squeeze the trigger. Don't pull on it or the end of the barrel will jerk and break his eye contact."

When Carl returned from town he said, "I hired both of those Bean boys. I think they will make a good team for our southern route down into Santa Fe; they were raised in that area as kids."

CHAPTER 25

Late in July, with the warm weather causing us all to sweat profusely, Jay and mother noticed that the hair on my face was showing red in the sunlight. Diego said, "Must be time for me to make this boy a strop. We just got some leather from Salt Lake City that should make a fine strop."

Mother said, "Richard, when we were in the Mercantile last week, you were looking at some straight razors. What kind should Jack have?"

"Well, the best ones come from Solingen, Germany, I believe. The Wilkerson razor I have came from there. We should find another one like mine." Then father said, "It might be easier to have Chief Walking Bear show him how to push the hair inside and bite it off with his teeth."

Mother replied, "Sometimes, Richard, you are impossible to have a serious discussion with."

"Okay, Diego, you make Jack a strop. Mother and I will get him a cup and the straight razor. Now all we have to do is figure out who will teach him how not to cut his jugular vein."

After a few more wise remarks around the table, Charles said, "Jack, come to my room in the morning and we will start you out right. I don't wear a mustache like all these other critters around the table so I can show you how to shave and save your top lip at the same time."

So on Monday, July 31, 1865, in a formal ceremony at our dining table, I was presented with a beautiful new strop, cup, and razor, and a bronze plaque stating that James Alburn Knight shall no longer be called a boy as of this date.

I had been so busy working for Diego six days a week and spending the rest of everyday with Jay, the livery, and stable that my hobby with my bullwhip had suffered. I needed to practice an hour or so a day to stay proficient. Thor must have wondered why we no longer hunted for game like we used to. When we were taken to the Ute Indian camp in January, they fed us quail. I had no idea where they got quail that time of year, but if they could get them then they must know where Thor and I needed to go hunting since fall was just around the corner.

It's Sunday, so I saddled Powder and rode off with Thor north, toward Chief Walking Bear's village. After a two hour ride, Thor took off running straight for Walking Bear's large tee-pee and ran right in through the door flap. When he came out, he had Walking Bear's beautiful, white husky bitch with him and Walking Bear was right behind them. Walking Bear greeted me with hand sign and I reciprocated just like he taught me to do. Walking Bear says, "Jack, you need to see what Thor left with us on your last trip to see me. Come in tee-pee and have a look see."

On a buffalo robe in the back of the tee-pee were six of the most perfect puppies you would ever want to see. Walking Bear said, "Those will be fine dogs when they grow up. Look at the size of the paws on the four man dogs."

Looking Walking Bear in his eyes, I asked him, "I thought Ute's have dogs for food in winter months. You won't use these for food will you?"

"No, these will be hunting dogs for all my sub-chiefs. Thor and momma dog do too good of job to make these big animals."

Two were black; two were white, and the other two were black and white. I agreed with the chief they must be from Thor. The big white dog let Thor lie with the pups and he licked all of them one at a time like he was making sure they are all in good shape. Then he came over to me and pulled on my leg to get me closer to the puppies.

I told Walking Bear that I came to ask about hunting in the area where the quail are like they served us in January. Walking Bear looked at me sort of puzzled, "I see no shotgun. How you going to hunt birds with no shotgun?"

"Thor and I have a game we play. He flushes the bird and I pop it with my bullwhip, and he retrieves it for me."

"Ho, ho, me have to see this with my own eyes. Never see any white man hunt that way. I get pony and take you to where birds are at."

He brought Chief White Feather with him and I knew this is for his protection. If some whites saw us, they might try to harm the Indians if they saw me riding with them. We rode north for about two miles and came upon a very large berry patch. Thor was looking for birds already and spotted an area and made his sniffing warning for me to follow him. He rushed two birds, but I only got close enough for one of them. Crack and it went down. Thor ran and picked the bird up and brought it right to me.

We circled the berry patch and got three more birds before riding over to see the chiefs sitting on their ponies, shaking their heads and laughing. "We not believe this if not see it with our eyes. You use bullwhip better than stage drivers we see on trails."

Thor and I got five more quail and that was enough for mother to fix supper for all of us at the compound. I thanked the chiefs with hand sign, turned Powder around and headed for home. That night, Mother steamed corn on the cob from her garden and we had stuffed quail, with buttermilk biscuits and homemade butter. Thor got a baked quail all his own for the help he gave for such a great meal.

CHAPTER 26

"Jay, why is Betsy, Harvey's wife, spending so much time with Mother, lately? She has been to see mother everyday this week. I was up at the house early in the week and she had that Morgan girl with her. You remember the Morgan brothers down on the South Platte with the big ranch in the valley that we both liked?"

Jay said, "That girl, Ida, is the daughter of one of those Morgan brothers and Mother and Betsy have eyes on Charles for Ida to marry"

Boy, I missed a lot around here being with Diego so much of my time. Speaking of marriage, "Did you know Diego has been spending a lot of time with Margo, the Mexican lady he hired to do the leather work for him?"

"I wondered where he was at night," Jay replied. "Sometimes he never shows for supper and a couple of nights I did not hear him come in, must be something serious going on someplace."

"Well, Jay, what does Charles have to say about this thing with Ida Morgan? Is he ready? She is very nice looking and much prettier than the gal he chases down at Booker's Hotel."

We got a customer for the wagon and team so our conversation was put on hold. It took both of us to set up the rig for a six mule team to get the man and his son on the trail. While Jay completed the transaction, I walked over to father's shop and looked for Charles, who was mounting a new wheel on an Overland Stage. I said, "Charles you have a new love in your life and you didn't tell me about her. What am I supposed to tell Nancy over at Booker's when I have lunch there and she asks, where is Charles? He has not been around lately."

"Well," he said, blushing bright red, "I really do like Ida and she is more my age. Nancy, you know, is 29 and mother says 6 years difference is too many years to make a good marriage for me."

"So you want me to tell Nancy you won't be in to see her anymore?"

"No, no, that I have to do that for myself if I want to continue going to town and seeing Nancy on the streets" Charles continued, "Nancy and I never discussed marriage, or anything like that. But we have been seeing one another for almost two years, so I owe her my own explanation for breaking our relationship."

"Well I'm glad that's not me that has to explain something like that. I need to remember not to let myself get that close to a girl and have to cut ties with her."

As I headed back to the stable, Betsy and Ida Morgan drove past me on the way to see mother again. I wondered how long this courtship could last before Charles was on his way to married bliss. I sit down in the stable office with the *Daily Rocky Mountain News*. The Civil War was over, but the first week of October 1865, the big news out of the east was about the superintendent of the Andersonville, Georgia Confederate prison being tried by a military commission run by General Lew Wallace. The main body of the commission wanted to hang Confederate Captain Henry Wirz. They sure did drag some of these things out. The war was over in April and this is just now being tried.

Father walked into the office and pulls up a chair. "Boys, we need to talk. Mother has worked hard for over two years, with Mary Alice's help, of course, and I am sure you don't know it, but she has paid this compound off at the bank and we own it lock, stock and every barrel on the property. Jay, you are 21 this year and Jack you will turn 17 in December. It sounds like Charles is about to be married to Ida Morgan. Mother and I are tired and both you boys have the education and drive to make it without us any longer. We will, of course, give you each a good grubstake, say $2,500.00 apiece. Your work has been instrumental in this success."

Jay said, "But Father what about all your work to build this business and develop this property?"

Father stood up and said, "I have been approached by the fellow who owns the 20 acres behind us. He wants to develop the whole 30 acres into a section for town of all brick stores and buildings. He wants to keep the boarding house open and will build Charles a new shop for him to lease at a very reasonable rate. His offer is eight times what your mother and I have invested now. The gentleman does not want possession until June of next year," Father continued, "So we have eight more months to stay and reap the rewards of our work."

"As for mother and me, my older brother, John, your uncle who lives in Ottowa County, Kansas, has asked us to join them on their 160 acre farm and help raise horses. Mary Alice will love working with the show horses."

Jay said, "You mean the uncle who is six-foot-eight inches tall, and likes to fight anybody who will challenge him."

"Yep, that uncle."

I said, "Father, that is a generous grubstake and I will handle it carefully, but I don't think I will stay in Denver City. We have a few months to get used to this turn of events so we will see what comes up."

As father headed for the house, Jay said, "Well, Jack, are we going to part company or you want to have a partnership with an out of work livery boy?"

"We have a long time to think about the future so we don't need to commit to anything today, brother."

As I headed for the house, Charles was getting his horse and saddle from the stable. I sure was glad I didn't have any problems like he had that night.

CHAPTER 27

When Charles came down to breakfast the next morning, I was taken back by his attitude and how happy he was. I said, "Well, you must have had a great evening in town. What was going on that would give you so much glee?"

Charles got his coffee and said, "While I am trying to explain to Nancy that we should probably see other people and not just one another, she tells me that she has been trying to let me know she is leaving for San Francisco in two weeks for a hostess job offered to her by a restaurant owner that was in Denver City last week. He bought her ticket and gave her travel money. He says Nancy will fit right in with his restaurant that he has built in the new hotel district."

By the time Charles told his story, the rest of the family is at the table and mother said, "Now we can set a date for your marriage to Ida."

"Wait a minute," Charles said, "We need some time to get to know each other a little bit. I don't even know if we like the same things. She might want me to become a rancher like her father and uncle. I'm a blacksmith and I want to stay one."

Mother said, "You're right, Charles I'm possibly putting the cart before the horse. I can tell you one thing for sure she wants to live in the city. She likes horses, but I think her only wish for cattle is a good steak."

Father said, "Charles, I heard of a couple of lots available on the river between here and Harvey's place. You might want to check them out for a great place to build a home. Sounds like you need to start thinking about someplace to hang a hat and a yard for my grand-children."

Charles got up from the table. "I am going to work now. If all you guys have to do is draft my future you don't need my input for your fairy tales."

Father said, "He is getting touchy. We must be getting close to his real thought process."

When Diego, went back to his shop he left yesterday's paper. As I thumbed through the inside, I found that Buddin Jeanette was going to be appearing at Apollo Hall on Larimer Street this weekend. I had not seen Buddin since he went away to Military school in 1861. I had to get Jay to go with me. He knew Buddin and they got along well. Unless Buddin's mother had told him, he had no idea Jay and I were in Denver City and we would surprise him. From several articles I had read, Saki had become an accomplished actor and had been in plays in New York, Chicago and New Orleans, just to name a few of the cities he had worked in.

As Jay and I walked through the lobby at the Apollo, there were large prints about the play. In one, Saki was wielding a sword over an English Officer as if he was about to strike him with it. We found our seats and the curtain was raised. The play was very well put together. The story was about an Irish farm boy conscripted into the English army who became a proficient swordsman and, as fate would have it, the Irishman ended up running his sword through his English Commander and had to flee England. He returned to Ireland, changed his name and talked his three brothers into doing the same and they all escaped to America. Hard to believe a Frenchman could play the part of an Irishman that well but Saki pulled it off.

After the fourth curtain call, we found our way back stage and found Buddin in a dressing room cleaning his make-up off his face. He glanced in the mirror and saw me. "Jack what a great surprise and Jay great to see you both. Remember Blue Feather, our Arapaho friend? He told me he thought you had come out to this part of the country." I said, "Saki get that stuff off your face and let's go over to Booker's and have a sarsaparilla."

"Okay, but Jay, is he still only drinking that medicine? I figure you would have him on the good stuff by now."

"Buddin, he is just like paw; he has never had a drink or a smoke except from a Ute peace pipe and he won't even have a chew."

I said,"Saki, where did the playwright come up with the story for the play you folks did tonight?"

"Well, Jack, I wrote the play. I think I had heard a story about like that when I was living in Kansas City. Why?"

"Oh, no reason, I just think you have put together a very nice piece of work and will entertain people from coast to coast."

Buddin said, "I sure hope so. We are opening with the same play in Omaha, Nebraska in two weeks and then on to St. Louis and Chicago. If we get curtain calls in those towns like we did here, maybe we can take it to New York City next year."

As we walked to Booker's hotel, several people asked Buddin to sign their programs and he seemed in his own world and Jay and I were not even there. I felt actors lived in a world that only they understood. We entered and found a table. As we sat, Buddin returned to our world and we spent the next hour hearing about military school and his leaving that and going on to an actors' guild that he became involved with. Surprised that he was interested, Jay and I spent the next hour telling about our adventures and accomplishments over the past four years.

Buddin was staying at the Booker Hotel. We left sometime after midnight and rode home having enjoyed the whole evening. Jay said as we were pulling the saddles off our horses, "Buddin is not as self-centered as he used to be. But he sure lives in a different world than you and me."

All I could say to that was, "Yep."

CHAPTER 28

As cool November weather was upon us, we had to winterize everything at the compound. All of our grains had to be set up on pallets so the ground moisture or a rise in the creek did not get them wet and freeze them to the ground. We had as much of the hay as the top story of the livery would hold and we even filled the stable attic this year. We had insulated mother's chicken house so the chickens didn't freeze and stop laying eggs. The two wells we had on the property were walled-in during winter. The one for the boarding house was always covered on three sides but in winter a door was installed at the front. We had cut and stacked 30 cord of wood for the compound since Jay and I liked to have a stove in the livery office for us and the comfort of our customers. Father's shop was always warm since he keeps his forge alive all day.

Sunday, November 12, 1865, *Daily News* had a story about the hanging on Friday of Captain Henry Wirz at the Old Capitol Prison. He must have been a real hater of the Union considering the way he treated the men at

Andersonville Prison. As I put another piece of wood in our potbelly stove, Carl and Art came in the office and found a chair.

"Well, how goes the battle with H C and A Freighters?"

Art said, "This is the first day in three months we have been in at the same time. Pa keeps those wagons rolling. Hey, those two brothers you recommended are a fine team. They cut two days off our time to Salt Lake City and back."

"Hold it," I said, "I never recommended them for that job. I never have and never will recommend anybody to you for a job. I just pass information on and you make up your own mind about the person. Father has shown me enough cases where people recommend someone and they fail to live up to the recommendation given and then you blame the one who did the recommending. No, no, not me."

"Okay." Carl said, "We get your message but just wanted you to know they are working out just fine."

Art walked to the window looked over at the shop and said, "When is Charles going to marry the Morgan girl? She stays at our house waiting for him to ask, because she doesn't want to go back to her father's ranch. Mother is delighted to have her as she is good company for her while all of us are gone."

Carl added, "It is nice to have a sister around, but she would be happier with Charles. Did you know she went to college for two years in New York? She is a qualified teacher and writes poems. Some I like, when she writes about nature. You can almost feel the trees and streams she writes about."

Changing the subject, I commented, "Have one of you been to California, yet? I found a book on California the other day at the Mercantile. It says there is unlimited possibility for growth in any business you want to be involved with in that state."

Carl said, "We thought we were going to go there when we went south of Las Vegas, Nevada to pick up four wagon loads of borax for a mine over in Breckinridge. But when we got to the ferry on the Colorado River, they had already gotten our load across so we had no reason to go over into California."

Art said, "You boys want to go into town with us for the afternoon and have a beer or try your luck over on Larimer Street?"

"I think I will pass Jay and I stayed down there past midnight a couple of weeks ago and I am not sure I have caught up on my sleep, yet."

"All right," Carl said, walking out the door. "We will see you both next time we make it home. Pa is sending us on the new southern by-pass trail that Holladay has cut to avoid both Julesburg and the Sioux that have moved south."

As Jay was finishing the bookwork for October, Father and Charles rode into the stable. They had left early to go up river to look at the lots Father had heard about. Father passed the office and headed for home, but Charles walked in to the office and right to the pot-belly stove.

Charles said, "I need to buy both of those lots. They both face the river and about in the middle of the two lots there is a set of rifles that has to be a great spot to catch supper now and then. Both lots are over an acre each with a total of 300 feet of river frontage. The property rises over 100 feet to the rear of the lots so if the South Platte decided to run over her banks, the home and barn, if situated on the rise, would be safe."

I said, "That place is about three miles out. Do you think that is close enough to town for Ida to be happy?"

"You know what? I like it and I am going to make an offer on it tomorrow. If Ida wants to marry me she will have to like it too, or go back to her father's ranch," Charles said as he went out the door.

Jay lamented, "Whoa, I have never seen Charles so one way about anything. He must really like that piece of property. I know right where those lots are and he is right, the spot is great and in a couple of years it will be part of the town, anyway."

As daylight faded I told Jay, "I think I will go to the house. Say, by the way, is Lewis still going to work after school this month?"

"No, it gets dark too soon and his mother would prefer he not be riding home in the moonlight. Can't say I blame her."

I said, "That's right. They live clear on the north end of Blake Street. That must be three or four miles from here. You sure we pay the boy enough to make that trip."

"Don't worry about it, Jack. He is well paid."

CHAPTER 29

In mid-December, Mother found out she was losing her longest renting boarder. Diego and Margo were getting married. Margo had a small house in town that she rented. Diego had made arrangements to buy the property and Margo was happy with that; neither she nor her family had ever owned property since leaving Mexico. Diego acted like a kid; he whistled and hummed all day. Sometimes I missed his history and geography lessons that I was used to getting wrapped up in. That's all right he was starting to repeat some of the stories about Spain and Europe. Margo was Catholic and I think Diego was raised in that faith although he had never talked about religion with me. The small mission on the east side of town was filled and people were standing outside to congratulate both Diego and Margo after the ceremony. I had no idea that so many people knew Diego well enough to come see him get married. He had been an important part of downtown Denver City for over two years. Booker's Hotel is having a Sunday afternoon brunch in his honor. Food and beverages were there for those invited.

Tyler Booker and Mother, with Mary Alice right in the middle, put this party together, so the Knight family had to attend. Mother even made Jay and me wear ties or else work the kitchen detail.

Mother said they invited 350 people to attend and at least that many were there, with a few more that breached the back door. Harvey and his wife Betsy were there with Ida Morgan. Hershel and his family were there, of course. Carl and Art must have been on the trail or they would have been there also. I saw the owner of the *Daily Rocky Mountain News* and his wife. Ben Holladay was there and gave a nice toast to both the bride and groom.

The week after the big wedding and the Sunday before Christmas was my 17th birthday. Margo and Diego came to dinner at our home. After we finished eating, Diego went out to their buggy and brought a load of wrapped presents in the house.

Father said, "Diego, just take those into the tree in the living room."

Diego stopped and said, "These are not Christmas presents, they are birthday presents for Jack and kindness presents from Margo for all you did for her wedding."

Margo stood, picked up a package and said, "Jack, Diego say you use pistol with cross draw. I design this belt and holster for you. Also, Diego and me sew this vest from the antelope hide you get many years ago." Margo continued, "Hide not big enough to make two coats, but big enough for coat for Elizabeth and vest for you." Margo took a pure white, soft leather coat from a package that looked like it came off a princess you see in paintings. It had pure silver buttons, with silver shields on the sleeves and pockets. Mother was almost crying as Margo helped her into the coat.

"Oh dear, this is the most beautiful thing I have ever seen. Your work is beyond belief. Are you sure you want to give this away?"

"Elizabeth, there is no one else in this world who deserves this coat more than you." Diego said.

Mother thanked them again and kissed them both on the cheek. I had never seen mother kiss anyone but a family member before. Margo saved enough leather from the antelope hide to make a very ornate purse for Mary Alice. She loved it and kept it with her all day. Diego tossed a present to Father and when he opened the package, his eyes were beaming. He pulled a heavily tooled leather belt with an oversized silver buckle from the wrapping.

"Margo this is just what I need to go with that suit mother made me buy for your wedding."

Charles received a new strop with a silver handle. When Charles was teaching me to use a straight razor, I noticed his strop was not in great shape as he had inherited an old one from Father. I had forgotten I had told Diego about his strop. There was one sack left on the table.

Diego stood up and says, "Over the years I have known the Knight family, the one boy I have had little to do with is Jay, probably because we have very little in common. I spent time with Edwin, talking about ancient history, one of his favorite subjects. Charles learned about metallurgy and geography. Jack maybe learned too much of what a younger person is not ready for. But Jay and I have never sat and just talked about anything that I can remember." Diego continued, "Maybe we need to go set on a bank and fish for a day. But, in the meantime, to show my love, and it is love for all the Knights, I want you to have this new six shot Navy revolver and the belt and holster Margo produced for you."

Jay, the one person always ready with a quick come back, was silent and trying to gain his composure. "Diego, you are without a doubt one of the most intelligent people I know, except for my adopted mother, sitting over there. You are right we have, up to now, had little in common. But if you like to fish, I bet we will become two of a kind on the banks of the South Platte, if Margo will let you have time to fish. I always felt you had my back when needed and I assure you I had yours. I think the brave who shot my ear had a bead on my head when you shot him and spoiled his aim."

Diego laughed and said, "I had forgotten that incident. Yes, he was one of the Indians the Cavalry had tied onto a pony and sent back to his tribe, as I remember now."

Father stood and said, "We will miss you and Margo. Elizabeth and I are selling out in May, next year, and moving to Kansas. My older brother wants us to help him and his family raise horses back there. This is not for public notice but we know you will not spread it around. Charles is staying with a new blacksmith shop. The other boys have not made any plans that I know of."

Diego stood and said, "Margo and I have wondered how much longer you two were going to keep your noses to the grindstone. You both will be missed in our fine city."

CHAPTER 30

In January, Charles had his offer accepted on the two plus acres south of town and he and Ida had set a date.

Every Saturday and Sunday in January, Jay and I took turns and help Charles thin the timber and stack it for split rail fencing on his property. After it dried out for three months it could be split into rails easily. Charles had cleared and leveled the area for us to build his barn when the weather warmed up.

Charles and his neighbor to the south had a very large project they are working to put together. Their plan was to have a two lane road between the two properties and a bridge high enough to let spring run off pass under it as the South Platte swelled during snow melt. First thing they had to do is get permission to build up a grade to raise the bridge on the west side of the river to meet the trail that runs on that side of the river. We had four 110 foot trees behind father's shop to span the river if we could figure how to get them to the site. Father would figure that out when the time comes. Charles and his neighbor, William Hardesty, had purchased 10,000 2nd quality bricks to build the retaining walls on both sides of the river for their bridge and had permission to join the trail west of the South Platte.

Diego showed up in late January to supervise the footings and taught Jay and me bricklaying and how to back fill the retaining walls so the river would not wash away our work and the bridge.

We were fortunate, as January and February were mild. We had a lot of good days to work on Charles' project.

By the end of February, we were ready for the large logs to span the river. Father built an "A" frame wagon to haul the 110-foot logs to the site, one at a time. Then we had to get the special wagon across the river to use as a lift and pull machine to set the long logs on our retaining walls and span the water. Father used six oxen to lift and pull each log in place.

At the end of the second day, with the four logs notched and in place late Sunday, father said, "Charles you and Hardesty are on your own now. I think the boys and I have contributed to your success long enough."

"Father I am happy with the help and the logs you provided. The brothers have gone beyond what was expected. I know I can never afford to pay for what all of you and Diego have given me. But please know it is appreciated by both Ida and me."

It is dark when we got the oxen back to the corral and fed. I looked around and I didn't see Charles. I asked Jay and Father, "what happened to Charles?"

Father said, "The last time I looked back he was running back and forth on his new logs crossing the river. I hope he stopped before dark. It is 14 feet down to the water. I would hate it if he fell off and drowned in two feet of water."

When we got to the house, mother was frying buffalo steaks for everyone at the boarding house table. Harvey had killed a young buffalo coming back to Denver City by the Smoky Hill Trail and dropped half the critter off on his way home.

I said, "We didn't see him go by out at Charles place. How did we miss him?"

Mother, getting ready to cook our steaks, said, "He said he was headed to Hershel's. Betsy and Ida went to stay with them for his short trip to Plumb Creek."

By the time mother had finished cooking supper, Charles walked in the door. "Father, Bill Hardesty came by after you guys left. He said they told him at the saw mill that the 8 x 12 timbers for the deck on the bridge will be ready to pick up Tuesday. I need to use the big wagon and at least six oxen Tuesday afternoon. It will probably take three trips."

Father said, "I sure hope you don't have to pay for those timbers. Archie over at the Mercantile told me they were getting $200.00 a thousand board feet for lumber still this year."

Charles said, "The mill had to get money up front to run that timber and William Hardesty paid $160.00 a thousand when he paid in advance."

"That sounds fair. Then that is what I consider charging you for the four logs you got off the compound for your base," father laughed.

"How did you fellows come out on the bricks for the retaining walls?" Father asked as he gets another cup of coffee.

"We did well. The bricks were 75 percent of wholesale and they gave us all the sand for the footings and mortar."

Father said, "You have a bridge that would be there even if we got the water we had two years ago. Just be sure you tar the logs and the backside and ends of all that timber good so bugs don't start living in your bridge."

Charles washed up and found his chair to bring to the table. He seemed nervous and unsure what he wanted to say to Father.

He started and said, "Father, I want to build a brick home in the area I laid out on the rise on the south end of the property."

"Son, Mother and I said we would help you, but if you want to build a home like that you need to see a banker. You own the property and if you had a nice barn and your roads in place I don't see why it would not be enough percentage of the value to get a loan to do what you want. Just remember, what you borrow has to be paid back and when you say you will pay, that is when it is due."

"Mother, will you take Charles to see Mr. Jessup, next week and see if what we talked about is possible?"

"Sure, I have to go to town Tuesday anyway so Charles, let's do it before you go to work Tuesday morning."

Charles was taking on more than I would want. He was getting tied to an area and couldn't just pickup and do something else. That was good for Charles, he probably would never leave Denver City but I had to be free to see more country.

CHAPTER 31

As winter left the high plains and we were less than three months from the breaking up of a family that has been together for the 17 years of my life, I was looking for spring with a heavy heart.

This family had grown and prospered since Father and Mother left Sandusky, Ohio in 1852. Father had always worked for someone until he came to Kansas City. Mother had told me the story of how hard it was for Father to leave his two older brothers, John and James, in Ohio, but he had a bad marriage and knew he had to leave that part of the country for him and Elizabeth, my mother, to make a go of his second marriage.

Mother taught school and father started his blacksmith shop at a house they rented for two years until his business had grown and he was able to move into downtown Kansas City, Missouri.

I had to figure out what I wanted to do and where I wanted to end up. I would have more than myself to worry about and take care of. Powder had to have feed and a place to stay. And Thor was mine also. These animals had to be part of my thought process. I had a trade; Diego said I can repair any firearm that has been made. But I really didn't like to be confined in a shop all day. I wanted to see California, but what part? Sacramento was growing. It was becoming an agricultural area and that area was growing because of the railroads. That was a temptation for me to follow. Some day we would be able to travel all over the west on rails.

To solve my problem, to start with, as soon as father said we could let people know that he was selling out and moving to Kansas, I was thinking I would ask Harvey if I could drive wagons for H C and A Freighters.

Might just hook up with a train going to California. I could leave Powder at Harvey's spread and Thor could ride with me on a wagon. Ben Holladay knew about the deal father had with our neighbor because he had introduced father to Terrance Grant, the developer. Jay had a stage driving position with the Overland Stage Company whenever he was free of the livery and stable.

Bill Cody was at father's shop when I walked in to talk to Charles. Bill said, "Jack, you sure have filled out since I last saw you. What do you weigh now?"

"Last time on the livery scales I hit 205 and father measured me at six foot two inches and growing." I continued, "What brings you to Denver, you know they dropped the City part this year?"

Bill pointed to a satchel on his horse and said, "I am delivering a couple of dispatches to your Governor, if I can wake him up later in the day. Went by his home on my way through town and no one answered the door so I came to see your Pa and Charles. I am still attached to the army."

Thor had to get his licks in. Bill was the only person outside our family that Thor paid any real attention to. He had to get a kiss on the ear and Bill talked really low to him. I'm not sure it was even in English.

"Are you going to stick around for the big wedding this weekend? Charles and Ida Morgan are going to tie the knot."

Bill said, "Wish I could but I have to get a report from the Governor back to Fort Ellsworth as soon as possible after he responds to the dispatches that I have for him." I knew Bill came to see father and Charles so I used sign language and left so he could spend time with them.

Walking back to the livery, I looked toward the house and saw three Indian ponies, one with a travois still attached, at the hitching post in front of the boarding house. I turned around and went to the house.

As I entered the big dinning room, spread across the table and the chairs was this huge pure white buffalo hide. Walking Bear said, "This a cuddling robe for Charles and his new wife. I kill this animal white man call albino. Cheyenne say killing white buffalo bad medicine, but Ute use them to give great hunters as wedding gift. Last winter Charles bring two large brown bear to my camp for winter meat. Tribe very fond of Charles."

I felt the robe and it was soft like a blanket. The hide and fur were snow white and it was as pretty a piece of leather as my antelope vest.

"Mother, how did you get Walking Bear and White Feather to come in the house?"

"When he brought the robe to the door I said you bring it in, I go in your house, you can sure come in mine," Mother said. "Now go get your brother Charles so Walking Bear can present this magnificent gift to him."

I went to the shop and told father and Charles they needed to come to the house as mother had guests who would like to see them. Bill Cody was still there so I invited him too.

As we walked from the shop, Bill said, "Those are Ute horses. They braid the mane out of the animal's eyes." I had been around the Utes a lot and never had noticed that until Bill pointed it out.

We all walked in. Bill and Father started talking in sign and smiling at the two chiefs. Bill walked around the table and hugged both Indians like they were brothers. Walking Bear said, "William Cody, my friend for many moons. Know him when he just a boy riding on Platte River. Deliver white man's messages."

"Charles, this robe for your marriage gift from all tribe. Many work to make for you," Walking Bear said, as he put his hand on Charles' shoulder.

Bill said, "People, I have to go. I have to see the Governor and he should be about by now. Good to see you, Elisabeth Knight. It has been too long."

Bill talked sign to the two chiefs and left the room with Charles who walked him to his horse.

The party was over as Charles returned and the two chiefs walked to their horses. Chief White Feather said, "You Knights come to our village after Charles marries. Bring his wife and we eat all day."

That was the first time I had ever heard Chief White Feather say anything in English. Charles returned to the dining room and folded up his treasure. He said, "I know where this will hang for the rest of my life. When Ida sees this, she will want it to hang well above our fireplace in her living room."

"Son," Father said, "If you could only know how many hours of work went into that robe you might put it in a trunk for safe keeping."

"I don't think that would be what the tribe would want done with it," Mother said.

Charles said, "After the honeymoon and we cuddle in it for a few days we will put it away until our home is finished."

CHAPTER 32

The morning of Saturday, March 17, 1866, started very early for everyone in our house. Today was a big day. The second oldest son of Richard Knight was getting married. And it was Saint Patrick's Day also.

Even Edwin Richard, the oldest son, had made the seven day trip from Kansas City, Kansas, by stagecoach, to be the best man for his brother Charles Godfrey. Mother was proud as a peacock of these boys as she raised them into manhood and saw to the education of both men.

Mary Alice was happy to be the ring bearer and has put her first store bought dress on first thing this morning. Mother made her take it off as the wedding was in the afternoon and said she has lots to do before time to dress.

Jay and I had to take care of the livestock at the stable, but Father made signs to post for his shop and the livery office that said we were closed for a family wedding. Mother and Mary Alice had to feed the guests' breakfast for the boarding house and they put a platter of bacon and a big plate of hotcakes with a jar of huckleberry jam at our table for all of us to dig into.

Edwin said, "I have waited over three years for these hotcakes, so pass the butter and some of mother's huckleberry jam to cover them with."

It is hard to believe it has been three years since all four of us brothers have been together. Mary Alice came to the table and even though she is going on 12, she had to sit in Edwin's lap to eat her breakfast.

The First Presbyterian Church was full. The north side had Ida Morgan's family, including her uncle and his wife. Ida had two brothers sitting with her mother and father. Harvey and Betsy sit with Carl and Art on the bride's side of the church. After the Knights took up the first row on the south side, Diego and Margo sit with Charles' neighbors, William Hardesty and his family. I saw a few people I don't know but most are customers of the blacksmith shop or the livery.

Strange, every man in the church seemed to have a beard or mustache except Charles and me. I needed to work on that.

The ceremony was much longer than Diego and Margo's. Ida wanted the vows read from some writings she found when she was very young and had held on to them just for her wedding.

Mary Alice had a tear in both eyes but was beautiful in the dress mother sent to St. Louis for. She used a small pillow to carry the ring on. Margo had made it from the white leather left over from mother's white coat.

All the invitations were for both the wedding and a gathering at Booker's Hotel for sarsaparilla or for whatever punch Booker made up for such occasions. This was early in the day and not nearly as many people were here as when Diego got married. Father gave a toast to the bride and groom. As he finished, Diego got on a chair and gave a little speech and a toast in his best form. When he finished, Arnold Jessup was helped up on a chair and said, "I know this is not a business occasion, but as Charles' banker, I wish him and Ida many years of health and happiness in their marriage and in the home they are building down on the South Platte River."

Charles met Mr. Jessup when he and mother went to talk to him about a loan. But until the toast, he had no idea he would receive the loan from his bank. Charles and Ida thanked everyone. Both had changed into riding clothes and made their way to the front door.

I am the only person there who knew where the couple was going on their honeymoon. Chief Walking Bear had a tee-pee prepared for them on a creek bank 200 yards from his village. For three days, the squaws of the village would bring food and water three times a day and would light a fire by the creek for two nights.

No one would bother them and unless they wanted to ride for a while, their horses will be taken care of also.

This was traditional for sons and daughters of Chiefs in the Ute nation. For two years, Charles had helped this small band of Ute Indians with health and education for the young children and food in the winter.

He had even seen to it that over 20 young braves had been baptized. He walked in the village as one of them. Charles and Chief White Feather are blood brothers. Chief Walking Bear tried to keep his tribe together but some young bucks wanted to live with bands of Ute that moved around and married into those roving tribes, giving them an excuse to leave this small peaceful band living in the Denver area.

CHAPTER 33

By the middle of May, Father started settling all accounts and had let the word out that he and Mother
were planning on leaving Denver and moving to Ottawa
County on the Solomon River in Kansas. He had very
little to sell off as everything in the compound except our
personal horses and tack went with the deal.

Mother had agreed to let all the silver, dishes and
linen, except her best set of each, go with the boarding
house. She had a large trunk for everything she was keeping. She even gave her sewing machine to Margo DeLacruse so Margo would have a machine at home. We finished the barn on Charles and Ida's land. We added a tack
room on the north side that was large enough for them to
live in while their home was being built by a local contrac-
tor. Ida had turned out to be the rugged type woman who
Charles needed to survive his steps into the future.

Mother and Mary Alice were busy training the
new managers for the boarding house. When we left,
they could expand the house and have four more rooms

to rent. The managers could live in Mother and Father's bedroom.

Mary Alice was looking forward to having nothing to do but go to school and help with the horses. She might find serving breakfast easier than using a curry comb on horses everyday. And cleaning the stables was not the same as mopping the floor in the kitchen and dining room every day. She said, "Jack, you are outside most of the time. Remember, my work has been inside, always. I can't wait to be outside and smell the fresh air."

Mr. Terrance Grant, the gentleman father was selling to, spent the day laying out roads and has chosen the far south east corner of his property on which to build the new blacksmith shop. He had a survey team laying out roads, and lots, staking each one with a number that corresponded with a number on a plot plan. We had short red stakes all over the front of the livery and blacksmith shop.

When I looked at his plot plan, I understood just how large his project was and understood why father's property was worth what he was paying. Mr. Grant said, "Jack, this will be called lower Denver and we will develop the other side of the river with another 40 acre site in two years."

"What are your plans, Jack? Mr. Speer, my partner, and I are always looking for young talent to work for us."

"Mr. Grant, I would be a very young what ever. I am only 17-years-old and I really don't know anything about your type of business."

"Jack, I am surprised. You act and carry yourself like most 21-year-olds and have the greatest personality for a teenager I have had the privilege to meet."

"I take all you say as a compliment and thank you for the kind words. Most of my life has been around people older than me so I guess I try to be like them."

"Well, good luck, Jack, and come by and see me whenever you're in Denver.

Harvey must know by now that Father has sold out so I need to go talk to him about a driving job with his outfit."

As I saddled Powder, Thor ran into the stable with his tail wagging and sniffing as if to say come outside. I walked Powder outside to find my friend, Jim Bridger, still on his horse and leading two pack mules.

"James, is that you? Remember me from Kansas City? I just left Diego DeLacruse in town and he says you are here where the creek runs into the river." Jim continued, "Where is your pa and Charles, the older boy? I sure would like to see them."

"Jim Bridger, sure I remember you. You used to come down the Missouri river to have father do iron work for you. You used to tell me about the Great Salt Lake and Yellowstone. I have not got to either one yet. Father and Charles are in that shop right over there. Come on, they will both be glad to see you. Give me your horse and mules to put in the corral, right here."

As we walked to the shop, Jim told me he had been with General Grenville Dodge, helping to survey the routes for the railroad to pass through the mountains when they are ready to complete the coast to coast rails.

Charles and Father both stopped what they are doing and invited Jim to sit with them at a table by the front door.

Father said, "Jack, run to the house and bring us all something cold to drink. I am sure Mother has something made up." Mother sent a large pitcher of cool apple juice from last year's juice canning. Father had made an apple press last year and it worked so well that Jay and I pressed over six gallons of juice for canning.

As I returned to the table, Father said, "Jim, you look tired and worn out. Are you well enough to be traveling by yourself?"

"Richard, I am only 62, but time is not on my side. My eyes are starting to fail and I know this is my last trip to the mountains. I am headed for Fort Bridger and this will be my last trip through Denver as I am going to my farm outside Kansas City, Missouri, That's where I am going to stay put."

Father talked Jim into staying with us for the night. I took care of his horse and stripped the mules for the night. I slept in the livery office and let Jim have my room so he could sleep well his last night in Denver.

I promised to come to Fort Bridger before Jim headed to Missouri. I was thinking that Harvey had a run to the Dakota Territory and felt he would hire me to drive for him.

Jim left early next morning and headed for Latham and then was on to the Dakota Territory and west to Fort Bridger.

CHAPTER 34

As I rode south along the South Platte River, passing the place Charles and Ida were building their new home, I saw the bridge that I helped build. I thought back to the first day I drove the small herd of cattle and horses past this very spot on the way to Ben Holladay's line shack. I remembered the feeling of accomplishment of completing the 700 mile trip from Missouri to Denver.

It seemed like a long time ago but it had only been three years since we made that trip. Wow, I was only 14 that year but I really felt more like a man than just a teenager. I wondered if I missed anything not being like other boys who chased hoops with a stick. Saki and I never shot marbles with the boys at school. We didn't have time for that kind of play. Father played marbles with Charles and Jay, in the back yard, but I would walk away and play with my bullwhip.

As Thor and I were crossing the river to head for Harvey's barn and office, Betsy, in her buggy, pulled up and motioned me to stop. Betsy said, "Jack I am going to see your mother. She has been such a good friend I will miss her so. Harvey and the boys will all be home this weekend. I want to have a party at the house. Diego and Margo are coming and I have to see that Hershel and his tribe come, also. Harvey is in his office if that is who you wanted to see."

Harvey was standing, looking at a map of the area west of the Mississippi river. "Jack, come in." Harvey continued, "H C and A Freighters just acquired four new wagons and 24 mules to pull them. Well, they are not new but in good shape."

"The man who had them was killed up in Dakota Territory, along with two other drivers, by raiding Lakota Sioux. The army showed up too late to save the three drivers but saved the fourth man and the wagons. The owner's wife lives in Latham, Colorado and Frank Root told her I might be interested in the rigs. All four are Studebakers and Frank says they are in good shape and the mules are not that old. Carl and Art will be home Saturday, so next week we can go to Latham and pick them up. The fourth man would like to stay since he trained all the mules and has been with the group for 18 months."

"Harvey, that is great! What I came out here to talk to you about is to see if I could hire on as a driver when my family moves to Kansas?"

Harvey said, "Jack, are you sure this is what you want to do? Diego tells me you can repair any firearm out there and that you are a fine mechanic. Why would you want to drive a lumbering freight wagon?"

I really had to think about what Harvey had said because I didn't need to sound stupid when I give my answer. "Harvey, I don't think I want to drive wagons all my life, but right now a work bench and a forge are not what I am ready for. The outdoors and the adventure that is left in the West is what I grew up with and I guess I have to follow that trail for now."

"Well, Jack," Harvey went on, "if adventure and outdoors is what you need you have come to the right place. H C and A just happens to need a driver that can handle an 18 foot bullwhip and loves the outdoors. I can hook you up with Carl for a couple of trips to get you adjusted to living in the wild. You have been a city boy for too long and you need some fine points worked on. Welcome aboard, Jack."

Riding home, Thor must have thought I was crazy. I used my whip to pop acorns off the oak trees as I rode by. My whole body was excited. I had a job with nothing but adventure and hard work ahead. Carl had to teach me now. That was great! I used to be his teacher.

After I rubbed Powder down and fed him some oats, Jay came in the stable to tell me about the party at Harvey's this weekend.

I said, "Jay, I met Betsy on the trail and she told me. Guess what? Harvey hired me to drive for him. He just bought out another outfit from Latham and needs several drivers to add to his stable of Wagoner's."

I did not tell Jay how and why Harvey was able to buy the outfit because I didn't need him repeating the story so that mother would hear what happened. Mother was superstitious sometimes about happenings and worried about her family when it involves someone else's tragedy.

I walked to the shop and see if father has kept his 18 foot bullwhip. I need to practice with one that long since mine is only 12 feet.

I asked Father, "Can I borrow your 18 foot bullwhip to practice with for a few days? I am going to drive for H C and A Freighters and Harvey tells me I need to use a longer whip than I am used to."

Father said, "Sure, but if you wait a little while I can probably save you a pain or two with a trick I learned a long time ago with long bullwhips."

Having been around Father as long as I have, I have learned he is just a little smarter than me. So I said, "Whenever you have time I'm ready."

That evening we had a lesson about long whips. Father said, "Jack, the handle is about six inches longer than your 12 footer. The thong is where you pick up five or so feet. The fall is about the same, so your focus has to be on the thong. It will come and get you unless you change your timing with the wrist action. Now watch the timing with my wrist."

Father popped a couple of rocks he set on the corral posts and I watch his rhythm and think I can match his movements.

"Okay, you try after I replace the rocks," Father said. I missed all three rocks and Father walked to the house saying, "Keep at it, you will find the target soon."

An hour later, and with a welt on my neck I think I have it. Thor lay a safe distance and just watched.

CHAPTER 35

Well, the big day had arrived. We had cleared the compound and mother and Mary Alice were staying at Booker's Hotel. Jay had all his gear on a second horse and was ready to leave for Latham, Colorado since that would be his new home base with the Overland Stage Company.

Charles and Ida had moved to their new barn and were told they could move into the new home in October of this year. Charles would be working out of the old shop for about three months while his new brick blacksmith shop was being built.

I had all of my belongings, two saddles and tack, my Henry .44 rifle, three bullwhips, my hand gun and belt, Powder, one pony, Thor and two carpetbags of clothing. I headed for Harvey's place, my new home for who knows how long. Betsy had asked me to stay with them and sleep in Art's bed. Art would not be back before Carl and I left to take four wagons to Santa Fe, New Mexico on July 5th. The freight was a load of lumber from the Denver sawmill.

Father had gone to see Chief Walking Bear. He has cattle business to finish with the tribe. He told mother he would return tomorrow because he wanted to spend a little more time with Chief Walking Bear, as this could be the last time they would see each other in this life. Margo and Diego were serving supper for mother, Mary Alice, Betsy, Carl and me. Harvey and Art were out of town.

Father returned early to catch the Overland Stage. They loaded mother's trunk and the rest of the baggage. Father took the saddle off his big Bay horse and tossed it up on the stage. He walked the horse over to Diego and said, "You always liked this big horse so now he is all yours, Diego."

Diego stood speechless as the stage pulled out at 9 a.m. right on time. Everybody waved both ways as the stage headed for the Smokey Hill Trail and east to Kansas.

As I was riding south and passing the compound, the crew Terrance Grant has hired was pulling the corral posts out of the ground to make room for the frontage road on Cherry Creek, according to his plot plan.

By the time I left town next week, the barn and stables would be gone without a trace of the work Jay and I did, left to see. This is what father called progress.

Thor crossed the South Platte like he was going home and I had to call him to follow me. He shook his head and crossed back to the trail to Harvey's with his head down.

Crossing the river onto the H C and A Freighters place, I saw Carl changing some wheels on the wagons we were driving to Santa Fe. I was an employee, so I was expected to get in the saddle and help.

Carl said, "Go ahead and put your horse away. We have four wheels you need to take in to your brother for new bands. Get one of the older buggies and we can load them all and you and Thor can deliver them to the blacksmith."

"Tell Charles these are spares, so just work them into his schedule in the next two weeks."

"Carl, how far is Santa Fe, and who else is driving since we have four wagon loads to take there?"

"Well, it is about 400 miles each way so you can tell your sweetie you won't be back for at least a month. Probably one of the Bean brothers and another new hand will go with us." Carl said.

As I loaded the wheels, I told Carl, "I never have had a steady girl so that is not a problem for this guy. You are going to have two greenhorns on this trip?"

Carl helped load the last wheel and said, "No you're the only greenhorn. Harvey hired Burt Culy the driver that survived the trip with the wagons he bought up in Latham. I have not met him yet, but Pa sure likes him."

I said, "Carl, we never talked about if it was okay for Thor to travel with me. What would other experienced drivers have to say about that?"

"After they see how he is around the stock we use, and watch him help keep them in line he will be one of the boys. Jack, I know what help he can be. Don't worry about Thor." Thor and I took off with the load of wheels for the blacksmith shop. I had Thor jump up on the seat to see if he could stand to ride and not walk or run for a little while.

I said, "Now Thor, don't get used to this riding thing, you have work to do also when we travel, but sometimes you can sit with me."

Charles heard us pull up and looked out and opened the big door so we could get the wheels inside and said, "Ida has quail for supper and said if I saw you to invite you to sit with us tonight."

"Thank you, I believe I can do that. Carl and I have more wheels to grease yet today. What time are you going home for supper?"

Charles continued, "I plan on leaving about 6 o'clock and Ida said supper would be ready about 7:00. She is still trying to figure out the new kitchen stove so I hope everything works in her favor today."

"I have had Ida's cooking before. You should not worry about her. She has been around a ranch house a lot in her life and her momma taught her well."

As I walked to the buggy, Thor jumped on the seat beside me. Maybe I had started something I might have a hard time changing.

"You have to remember Thor you are a work dog and I depend on you to help me just like a brother. So don't get used to the seat beside me. Lazy dogs are like lazy people they have no place in the West."

CHAPTER 36

We were loaded and ready. All the lumber was 16 feet long so the wagons were full and stacked a foot above our seats. This was all finished lumber for siding and for door and window sash.

Santa Fe must not have had the trees for this kind of wood or they would not want to pay the freight rate, otherwise. 1866 rates out of Denver were about one dollar per 100 miles per 100 pounds of freight.

Able Bean, Burt Culy, Carl, and I made 100 miles in four days. We passed only one outfit hauling railroad ties headed for someplace in Kansas. The head driver told Carl that there was a company out of Atchison, Kansas running rails all the way to Santa Fe, New Mexico. The next leg of our trip was more stressful as we were skirting the San Isabel Mountain range and it rained every day. It took us seven days to make the next 125 miles to Raton, New Mexico.

As we camped the night just out of Raton, Carl said, "Jack, get your bullwhip ready we now have to run this bunch around the Sangre De Cristo's and through

Apache Canyon. It is only about 100 miles as the crow flies to Santa Fe, but we will be five days getting there as we have to go south before we go west to get there."

Carl was right. It took us five days before we saw Santa Fe, and the Dahl Brothers Warehouse where we were to deliver the lumber.

It was late in the day and Carl said, "Jack, get the wagons inside that fence and help Able with the stock. Get the animals in the corral across the street and feed them all the oats left in my wagon." Carl continued, "Burt and I are going to the National Hotel, three streets up the hill, after I let the dispatcher know we are here. You and Able come on up when you are through feeding those animals. We all need a good bed for tonight."

My first thought was what to do with Thor? Well, he would have to guard the wagons so he had a job and he would do it. I would go into Dahl Brothers and get him something he liked to eat and get him settled in a bed under my wagon seat.

Later, after a bath, I had a shave at a barber shop next to the hotel, my first in a public bath, by the way. We were finishing our supper as the local Marshal walked in and wants to know if the boys who parked their wagons in Dahl Brothers lot were in the room.

Carl stood up and motioned the Marshal to our table and said, "Yes, we drove them in earlier today. Why?"

"Well, one of you needs to follow me down there as a big black dog has two fellows pinned down. I think they were going to help themselves to whatever you have loaded in those wagons. I was making my rounds and heard the dog barking and went to investigate what all the noise was about."

"By the way, I'm Marshal Tiggs. The two guys say the dog just attacked them but they have a wagon parked behind Dahl's fence and for the life of me I don't think that dog went outside the fence and made them come to where he has them pinned down." Tiggs continued, "The dog won't let me get to the fellows and they are really afraid he is going to get them. If one of you will come and call the dog off I will arrest the guys and let them stay in jail until you leave town."

We were finished with our supper, anyway, so all of us went with Tiggs to help rescue the villains from their fate.

Thor had them cornered in a doorway and the Marshal was right. There was no escape. I walked up to Thor and his tail wagged on my leg as if to say, look what I have done. He backed away and Tiggs made his arrest. Thor was excited so we had to sit and talk about his good deed and get him relaxed to go back to his bed.

Marshal Tiggs asked Carl if he wants to press any charges and Carl said, "Not any reason for me to, but the Dahl Brothers probably will have a complaint." Burt Culy helped Marshal Tiggs walk the two prisoners back to his jail and met us in the hotel bar when he returns.

Carl said as Burt returns, "See, Jack, I told you Thor would end up just one of the boys. Well, I'm tired.

One more drink and off to sleep for me. Jack, you want another sarsaparilla?"

"No, this is two for me tonight. I had one with supper. Mother says this stuff has something in it that makes your pants shrink so I watch how much I drink."

Burt said, "After we unload that lumber you must have a load ready for us to pickup and head back for Denver."

"Yep, Pa has us set up to haul flour from the Aztec Mill. Twelve ton, I believe, that should be about 60, 100 pound sacks for each wagon. The most important job, besides delivering the flour, is keeping it dry."

Carl said, "The mill is supposed to have wax coated canvas to wrap the cargo in and place over the top of the load. In good weather, we let the cargo breath and in bad weather we keep it covered."

It took all day to unload the lumber at Dahl's and to drive to the Aztec Mill and load the 240 sacks of flour with the care needed to protect the flour. Carl had made arrangements to leave the wagons inside the fence at Dahl Brothers for the night, so we stayed at the National Hotel one more night.

That night we were having supper and Marshal Tiggs came to our table to let us know the two gentlemen that Thor cornered the night before, swore to kill the big black dog before he left town.

I was finished eating so I bid everyone goodnight and headed for the warehouse. As I turned inside the yard toward the wagon I left Thor in, he was at my side.

We headed for the door way and I heard footsteps behind the next wagon. As we walked in front of the wagon both men hade their guns in hand. I yelled, "Thor." Thor straddled one with teeth bared and I had the other with three loops of the bullwhip around him. Tiggs, who followed us, picked up the two guns and took the two gentlemen to jail again.

CHAPTER 37

It was time to head for Denver. We started hitching up before daylight.

Carl said, "The loads are lighter than the lumber. I think we can make it to the Raton toll road in four days if we have good luck and no rain. July can have summer storms come up clear out of Mexico. They call it the monsoon season but with luck we can out run it."

The first night out of Santa Fe, we camped where the Santa Fe Trail came out of the north end of Apache canyon. Burt asked Carl, "That toll road we came over must be new. Was it here last year when you and your brother came this way?"

Able said, "No, we came over Raton Pass on the old route. It took almost 3 days to go 30 miles on the old trail. But, it was raining also, and the rain would wash part of the trail out and we had to make new trail for the wagons."

I said, "My father knew Dick Wootton before he started that toll road. By the time he was half way through the project, Father was amazed with his tenacity and with his engineering ability to cut and fill and build all those bridges. You know he had to figure the drainage on the sides of the mountains to keep his road from washing out and ending up like the old trail."

Carl added, "We pay him six dollars to use that road and it saves us about two days because of his 27 mile dream."

Able added, "They call him Uncle Dick Wootton in these parts. You know he lets the Indians use the trail for free. Any white man pays .25 cents to ride his horse on the road."

Carl was right; we skirted the east side of the Sangre De Cristo range in good time and were on the north side of Raton, New Mexico, on the fourth day out of Santa Fe. Warm winds were blowing from the south and that meant monsoon conditions for the weather. Usually, late in the afternoon the rains, along with thunder and lightning, came to drench the land.

As we made camp for the night, we could hear thunder in the south and the wind was starting to blow. We had to tie our tarps down to protect the flour as the rain sometimes was blown sideways by the wind.

We set the wagons so the wind attacked the rear and kept the rain from the flour. We picketed the 32 mules so they would not stampede and scatter from the effects of the thunder and lightning. Parking the wagon on the highest ground, we wrapped a tarp around the rear and wheels on both sides and settled in to wait the storm out, under the wagon.

The wind was strong so we had no fire for coffee or supper. We dined on hardtack and pemmican and drank water. Thor had never liked pemmican but he must have been aware that if he did not eat what I gave him, he would go without.

We had rain, but not a lot. Able told us he had seen monsoon rains wash trails away in just hours. And never set your camp close to a dry creek bed as water can get three or four feet high washing down in some rains during the monsoon.

The next morning Carl said, "We were lucky last night, no damage to any equipment or livestock. Today I hope we can make Uncle Dick Wootton's ranch by dark as there is always good food and shelter at his stage stop and there is a corral for our mules to feed in."

As we were making good time, we were stopped and had to cut and remove a tree that was hit by lightning and fell on the road. It was still burning so the area close to the tree was about to start a fire. The rain had helped control the burn until we arrived. By the time we cleared the road and made sure the fire was out we had lost an hour on our time to make the ranch by dark.

There were wagons going south but that did not hold us up. The area we passed was wide enough for wagons to pass without one group stopping to let the other by. That group of 20 wagons had started at Topeka, Kansas and had followed the Santa Fe Trail across Kansas bringing commodities to the Santa Fe, New Mexico area and farther south.

It was dark as we pulled into the toll gate area and, we were waved on to the stage stop. Inside, we all had a cup of coffee and asked for an area to park and camp for the night to rest the mules and to get them feed from Dick Wootton's livery that was designed to accommodate freighters passing both ways.

As a rancher, Dick raised feed on his ranch and sold to customers that stopped at his place and he was also in the freighting business himself and delivered grain and hay to the areas within 100 miles of his ranch.

Father was right about Dick. He was a very ambitious, hard working Scotch-Irishman, living hard, working hard and loving everyday of his life. Uncle Dick Wootton and Carl's father were very good friends so we got the royal treatment as far as supper and breakfast. H C and A Freighters were good customers and also hauled freight for the Wootton ranch to and from Denver. It rained on us four of the next 10 days on the trip returning to Denver. Carl had us stay at stage stops on the rainy nights and tips the stage agent to let us sleep in the barn overnight. It was raining the afternoon we arrived at Harvey's place and Carl said, "We don't need to rush to the Mercantile in town. They won't want to unload in the rain so we can stop here."

While we were gone, Harvey and a couple of drivers, waiting for a trip, constructed a bunkhouse for the single drivers to use when in town. It was nice, and large enough for eight men to sleep at a time. A very small kitchen area had room enough to make bacon and eggs.

It had a pot belly stove for the cold winters and enough windows for good air in the summer.

Harvey said, "Next week the cabinets for each driver will be delivered and each driver will have a safe place to keep belongings while on a trip." Over the next year I logged over 6,000 miles with H C and A freighters. I had seen the Great Salt Lake, been to St. Louis, and seen Texas twice. I was 18 now and still not tired of the roaming life of a freighter.

We just returned from a trip to Texas, and fought the monsoon all the way through New Mexico, and southern Colorado. I would rather fight Indians.

CHAPTER 38

Thor had caught a cold in his lungs and was having a hard time with breathing. With all the rain we encountered last week, I thought maybe the dampness caught up with him. I believed this is his first illness since he was born.

I let him ride in the seat next to me a lot and that was probably a mistake to let him lay down when he was wet. Charles said, "Go see Chief Walking Bear and ask his squaw wife Elk Woman to make you a poultice to wrap Thor's chest and back with and I bet you in three or four days his fever and congestion will be gone."

Wow, I didn't know what Elk Woman put together but I had to wrap Thor and leave him in the barn as no one could stand the smell close to the bunk house.

Thor never tried to chew the poultice off and after two days he started eating and his fever was gone. I took the wrap off after three full days and nights. He was still weak but ready to stand and walk the barn back and forth.

I kept him in the barn for two more days and rubbed him down twice a day, keeping him warm and dry. I had to bury the wrap deep as it never stopped reeking from the odor released the first day. Harvey had a trip going north into Dakota Territory scheduled for next week. It was heavy because he was using the Conestoga wagons and 16 oxen getting ready for this trip along with four other wagons and 32 mules.

He picked the Bean brothers, Burt and Art, along with me to go with him deep into Lakota Sioux territory. We had six wagons full of lumber to forward to Fort Fetterman, a new fort being constructed on the Bozeman Trail.

Fort Fetterman was named for Captain William J. Fetterman, the captain in charge of 80 soldiers killed during an ambush by Lakota Sioux, Northern Cheyenne and Arapaho warriors December 21, 1866.

Captain Fetterman and his men were ordered to rescue a besieged wagon train three miles from Fort Phil Kearny. He and his 80 men were led over Lodge Trail Ridge into a trap by a small band of Lakota Sioux headed by a young Lakota warrior, Crazy Horse, along with 1,000 warriors. The entire troop was wiped out and mutilated in the same manner as the Cheyenne were at the Sand Creek massacre. This was the worst defeat suffered by the United States Army at the hands of the Indian nations in Army history.

Fort Fetterman was around 220 miles from Denver and was within the southern area of the Lakota Sioux and Cheyenne fall hunt for buffalo.

On our fourth day out of Denver, we ran into a survey crew on the 4th of July 1867. Harvey said, "We should stop here and rest the animals. We have good water and plenty of feed for the mules and oxen." We camped away from the survey crew but my curiosity got the best of me and Thor and I wandered over to where the crew was laying markers like the men did at our compound in Denver. I asked for the man in charge and am introduced to General Grenville M. Dodge. I introduced myself and he told me he knew of my family if they were living in Kansas City, Missouri in 1860. What a small world. My father did some alterations on a wagon for him seven years ago.

General Dodge told me they are laying out plots for a town to be named Cheyenne. He says, "This will be a stop for the railroad when it is run into the Dakota Territory and Cheyenne will grow rapidly when this happens."

"When do you expect all of this to happen," I asked.

"Jack, I expect the rail will be here before the end of this year and this town will have probably a 1,000 citizens living here by then. The railroad is going to change the way all the freighters operate, but you will still be needed for the short runs where the rails don't go. When the railroad is coast to coast you will see great herds of cattle move out of Texas, north to the railroad, for delivery both east and west to feed folks on both sides of this great country."

"Well, General, I have to get back to the wagons. We are headed to Fort Fetterman with lumber to build the interior of the fort."

"Jack, I knew Captain Fetterman. It was a travesty for that to happen to him and his troop. We all look for peace, but situations like that strengthen our resolve to put the Indian on reservations and away from white civilization."

As I headed back to the wagons, my head was swimming with General Dodge's portrait of things to come. The building of a town where I stood, a railroad with steam engines crawling across the prairie was amazing to envision. Large movement of cattle across vast waste lands, and worst of all, the thought of friends like Chief Walking Bear and Chief White Feather having to live on reservations set up by white men, complicated the future. I gathered sticks and wood for the fire on the way back to the wagons. Harvey and the boys had a fire going and Burt was cooking some of his great cornbread in his Dutch oven for our supper. I told Harvey and the boys about the town and that General Dodge felt the railroad will be here by the end of this year.

Harvey said, "I don't think the railroad will hurt our business, just shorten our trips and that is a good thing. The more rails bring more people and more work for us and our wagons."

That night I dreamed of the cattle drives and wondered if I was tough enough to stand the hardship of a trip out of Texas all the way to northern Kansas on the back of a horse. Why not? I made 600 miles on a horse from Kansas City, Missouri to Denver, Colorado and I was only 14 then.

The next morning we harnessed the mules and oxen early and were on our way before the sun was over the horizon. We still had over 125 miles to go before we unloaded and Harvey says the Lakota liked to hunt this area at this time of the year so we had the never ending thoughts in our heads about Indians.

CHAPTER 39

O n the second day out of Cheyenne, we watched Indians watching us as we travel north, crossing several small streams. Every time we crossed water they seem to get closer. On this day, we saw a large herd of buffalo about four miles east of our position. Watching the band of Indians following us, we saw them all turn and go after the buffalo. We heard around 30 rifle shots and the herd headed straight south, with the Indians gathering where they made their kill.

Looking through his glass, Harvey said he saw a lot of squaws riding to the kill area and begin the skinning of the buffalo. If the women are that close that meant their summer camp must be in the area to the east of our trail as we had not seen any tee-pees during our travel and we see nothing ahead.

We spotted the Indians about a half-mile from our trail but they just followed us and never got any closer. That night, Burt Culy told us we are in the area that his wagons were attacked 18 months ago and said the Indians watched them for two days before they attacked their wagon train.

From our camp, we could see two different fires burning. Harvey said, "They know what we have in the wagons. As I watched one warrior who had a glass, he saw me as I was looking through mine. We smiled at each other. He was looking at our train from front to back so all he saw was lumber in every wagon."

Art said, "If they attack us and burn the wagons and lumber I guess they would feel they have stopped a build-up of the white man's advance into Indian country."

Harvey continued, "This area has been the hunting ground for the Indian for many years. Those cliffs we passed yesterday have quite a story to tell. This creek we are following is named Chugwater Creek. It seems, many moons ago, a Mandan Chief was hurt and unable to continue his leadership of the hunt. His son, "The Dreamer," had to take charge of the hunt. His plan was to drive the herd of buffalo over the cliffs. As the buffalo hit, they made a chug-like sound probably from the bursting of their stomachs. So the Indian called the place, "water at the place where the buffalo chug." Hence we have Chugwater Creek. This is big hunting grounds and, I am sure, even with Fort Laramie just to our east and now Fort Fetterman to the north all tribes feel we are gaining ground that belongs to them."

As we harnessed up the next morning, the fires from the Indian camp were out and they are not to be seen.

Burt Culy said, "We must be alert as there are several places ahead for ambush by the warriors."

Burt was right. Not two hours from last night's camp, we saw them crossing the creek and headed straight at us and we had no place but open prairie on all sides. We had nothing to do but circle the six wagons as tight as possible to try and repel their oncoming attack. As they began circling us, I saw that they all had repeating rifles. I could see the brass receivers of the 1866 Henry rim fire rifles. They all started circling clockwise and fired only as they saw one of us in an exposed position. We all had only one place to get directly out of their line of sight and that was under our seats in the wagons. I had my Henry rifle and my Colt .36 caliber pistol. I could shoot outside our circle with my rifle and when a brave jumped inside the wagons, I used my pistol to shoot at close range. After 15 minutes with three dead or injured braves inside our circle, they broke off and rode out of rifle shot and stood still on their horses. Harvey jumped out of his wagon and made sure the three were dead who had fallen inside our circle. Harvey called to everyone and got an answer from all of us. Able said he was bleeding from one leg but had it under control. Art was hit on his left hand but said he had it wrapped with his bandana. Harvey made sure we all had enough ammunition for another charge and just made it back to his wagon when the Indians started their whooping and riding at us again. We all waited till they were almost to the wagons before we opened fire and quickly we had knocked eight braves off of their horses.

The remaining braves ran next to three running Indians and hauled them onto their horses, doubling up, and galloped back to where they stood before the attack.

Again Harvey checked on everyone and we were still in the same shape as before the last attack. The five Indians on the ground never moved and as we counted with the three inside and two more dead from the first charge, we had 10 bodies on the ground. We had been at this now for almost an hour when they decided to make another run at us. They had built a small fire and we saw a couple of them with a bow sitting on their horse with no rifle. Art yelled, "They have arrows with wraps on the ends. I think they are going to try and burn us out."

Sure enough, at the next charge six braves each had a bow and arrow with a fire on the head of the arrow. They started shooting from way back trying to distract us from the fire arrows. Two of the arrows hit different wagons and the canvas covers caught fire but burned slowly. One arrow stuck in my wagon and was burning near my rear wheel. Two arrows ended up harmlessly inside our circle. I never saw the last one. As they circled, this time our aim was not as good and some of the braves actually would ride on the far side of their horses and shoot from under the horse's neck. We only shot one horse and rider and he got up on another horse and got away as they headed back to the small fire.

I jumped out and put the fire out on my wagon, but had to hurry back as the braves started another charge with fire arrows.

When all the shooting started again, we heard the most beautiful sound in the world. A bugle trumpeted from the north and the Indians heard it about the same time and rode east across the creek and kept going.

It was a troop of the 4th Infantry from Fort Fetterman. Major William Dye, the construction supervisor at the fort, said he knew we would be in the area and brought a troop to escort us through because he knew the Lakota were here hunting for buffalo and wanted to make sure our cargo was going to make it to the fort with no trouble. I never was clear about whether he worried about us or the lumber. After we had time to check all our wounds and get bandaged up, we had all been hit by rifle fire or from splinters from the wagon used for our cover.

Able Bean was hit the worst. He had a .44 bullet in the muscle of his right calf and had to have surgery to remove it. Art took a bullet just behind his little finger on his left hand but the projectile was gone. Harvey was grazed on a shoulder and a bullet went through his hat and grazed his head and his head was bleeding when he took his hat off. Josh Bean had wood splinters deep in his left arm and a corpsman had some surgery to do on him. Burt had a bad cut on his forehead over his left eye and my right foot was hit on the fleshy part in front of the ankle. I ruined a good pair of boots but I guess I would have to wear them home.

As the troopers laid the dead Indians by the trail, I counted the bodies and there were only nine. One of those braves crawled off in the confusion and we never found him. The next two days to the fort were slow and uneventful. We were shot up and sore but we had survived a Lakota Sioux raid and not everyone can say that.

CHAPTER 40

Thor was sniffing the tightly wrapped and tied bundles of salt and hide. We were loading and freighting 600 65 to 75 pound green buffalo salted hides to Latham, Colorado to be picked up and carried on to a tannery in Kansas City, Kansas.

The six of us were well and ready to go after a week of rest and medical attention. Able Bean was still limping on his right leg but could handle as much loading as the rest of us and we had the wagons loaded in two days.

Bill Cody arrived at Fort Fetterman while we were recuperating from our encounter with the Sioux. He had been buffalo hunting for the Kansas Pacific Railroad crews, giving them meat to feed the army of workers building the rails west from Kansas. Leaving the mercantile with a load of supplies for our trip to Latham, I saw Bill walking in on the boardwalk to the store. "Hey, Jack, great to see someone I know in a lonesome place like this. What are you doing in this part of the world?"

I explain our reason for being at Fort Fetterman and continued with, "Bill you should have been with us 10 or so days ago. We had the Lakota Sioux attack us 40 miles from here. We had to circle the wagons in open territory and stand and fight. We got nine or 10 of them, but they got some licks in. Nothing was too serious to any of us. I believe it was on the fifth charge Major Dye, with the 4th Infantry, rode in and saved us, sending those Sioux scrambling east as fast as their horses could take them back to where they came from."

"You were lucky, Jack, they would never have let you get away if the infantry had not come to your rescue. The Lakota Sioux have a pact with the Cheyenne to kill every white man on their land. And you were right in the middle of their hunting grounds," Bill said, "When are you headed back to Colorado?"

"Tomorrow, Bill. We have six wagons loaded with green buffalo hides on the way to Kansas City, Kansas for tanning. We have contracted to haul them to Latham, Colorado and someone else will carry them to Kansas."

Bill said, "I am headed for someplace south of here called Cheyenne so if your wagon master will let my companion, William Comstock, and me ride along we would be grateful for the company part of the way at least."

"Bill, you know Harvey already. He will welcome you to ride with us however far you would like."

"Jack, some of those hides you have, I am sure I killed. But it makes no difference who killed them, the Sioux know what you are carrying and that makes you a target as long as you are in the same area as they are. You need an infantry contingent, of some sort, for protection, part of the way out of this country."

I said, "Bill, I don't think the army is going to help a civilian wagon train through Indian Territory just to save some buffalo hides and six Wagoner's."

Bill said, "Let's go see Harvey before I make an appeal for help for your wagons and cargo."

We carried the supplies back to the wagons and Harvey saw my helper as we rounded the corral, heading for our camp. Harvey greeted Bill, "William, it's been too long, how are you doing? I heard you were at the fort but I have been too busy to look you up. It is great to see you. We hear a lot of stories about you and hope they're not all true. You would have to be 10 years older to have done what we hear."

"Harvey, I may be only 22 years old but I've been rode hard and put up wet several times. But wouldn't trade it for anything I know of. When you hear of me just remember I'm only human, just trying to get through this life with my skin in one piece. Let's get serious. You have a real problem facing you and your crew. The Sioux are just waiting for you to leave this compound and I assure you they have not forgotten their loss from your last meeting. My friend, William Comstock, and I would like to travel with you since we have to go south to Cheyenne, but that is only two more guns. Would you consider going to the Commander of the fort and asking for some army help at least to Chugwater?"

Harvey said, "Bill, I'm aware of the danger and thought about what to do about it. Do you think the army would help us? I've never had any escort offered before cept when Denver was having trouble getting supplies when the Cheyenne were on the war path and have been in troubled spots several times."

Bill said, "Won't hurt to try. The worst that can happen is they tell us no and we are no worse off than we are now. Let's go see Major Dye."

I had no idea why Bill and Harvey asked me to go with them to see Major Dye at headquarters. The three of us walked into Major Dye's office like we owned it. Come to think of it, we did.

Looking up the Major said, "Mister Cody, gentlemen what can I do for you? You all have such serious faces. I can't imagine what is so concerting for three men of your stature."

Bill said, "Sir, we are concerned about the safety of the six wagons and the men operating them as they pass through the same territory you found them in two weeks ago."

"Gentlemen, I have had the same thoughts as time for you to leave has gotten closer. I feel that under the circumstances I should, in order to give comfort to the train, send a detachment of 20 men with a sergeant to accompany you well past the Lakota hunting grounds."

Harvey said, "Major, sir, you have given much comfort to my men and myself. William Cody and his friend

William Comstock are traveling with us and I am sure it will give a lift to them, also."

The Major asked, "Harvey when are you planning on leaving the fort?"

"First light in the morning, sir."

"The troop will be ready and waiting as you pass through the gate. We here at Fort Fetterman were happy to get the lumber you hauled up here. It will make us all more comfortable and that is always a good thing when you are so far from home." Good luck and God speed."

CHAPTER 41

As Harvey rode herd on the front wagon, I could see the 21 troopers getting ready to saddle up. My wagon was last in line so Bill Cody and Bill Comstock were waiting to saddle up next to my rig. Bill was busy talking into Thor's ear and with his big front paws on Bill's exposed chest, Thor had his tail wagging side to side like he knew just what the man is telling him.

As I cracked the bullwhip well above the heads of the six mules of my team, both Bills saddled up.

Within 20 minutes we were all moving south toward the place where we ford the Platte River, about 10 miles from Fort Fetterman. All was very quiet and as the sun started over the horizon to the east, Sergeant Fitzpatrick sent three troopers ahead to scout for us. I'm sure the sergeant didn't want to see us ambushed while crossing the Platte.

Our progress was good. We were making 22 miles a day. Late July was usually dry in this part of country and animals had plenty of feed and water to keep them going. The two Bills kept us all set with meat. After the first day out, they killed a buffalo so the army and the wagon train had steak for supper. Sergeant Fitzpatrick, a big 6 foot 4. Irishman, even larger than my father, was not much on army protocol, so we all camped together at night and around the fire we heard stories from Bill Comstock about Indian fights and buffalo hunting that let your imagination about the two Bills run wild.

On the third night out the sergeant said, "Gentlemen, tomorrow night we will be passed the Chugwater Cliffs and my detachment will be leaving you before daylight the next morning. We have only seen some wandering Arapahos hunting for winter meat. Hopefully, after we part company your party will have continued good fortune."

Burt Culy was setting next to me and said, "Jack, the hair on the back of my neck stood up a couple of times today and I searched the whole country trying to calm it down but nothing helped. I just have that feeling we are right around the corner from something unpleasant."

As we all headed for our bedrolls, everyone was quiet, not like our other nights in camp. Even Thor seemed uneasy and paced between Bill Cody's bedroll and mine a couple of times before he lay down to sleep.

On the fourth morning out of Fort Fetterman, we had coffee and hardtack to eat to get an early start on the day. Sergeant Fitzpatrick sent a group of five troopers to scout ahead of the train.

Bill Cody climbed on the seat next to me and wanted to know how Father, Mother, and Mary Alice were doing in Kansas.

Bill said, "William and I will be taking off this morning as we have to ride over east into Nebraska and hunt meat for the boys working on the Kansas Pacific Railroad headed for Cheyenne."

The sun was coming over the horizon and I handed the reins to Bill so I could take my coat off. Just as Bill got comfortable the five troopers came riding back and passed us as fast as their horses would carry them. Harvey had stopped the head wagon so we were all stopped. Sergeant Fitzpatrick rode passed us and on to Harvey's wagon. A trooper rode to us and said, "We need to get over near those ledges and bunch up. There are about 50 Sioux waiting in ambush for us a couple of miles ahead. Grady and the troopers spotted them when a few of their horses were moving around."

All the wagons headed east for the protection of some rock outcroppings and shale ledges. We got set with our backs more or less covered and hoped this forced the Indians to ride north and south in front of us and not be able to get behind us.

Art, Harvey's son, said, "Sergeant, what makes you think they will come to us when they had a plan to ambush the train as it passed them."

Sergeant Fitzpatrick said, "Grady saw them start for the horses when they knew they were spotted. They are spending time looking us over right now." It was very early and the sun was still rising from the east so we wouldn't have the sun in our eyes unless they waited till later in the day to charge.

All of our horses were behind us and the mules were more or less protected by the wagon behind them. Looking straight west and out of rifle range, we saw them assemble in a line. Grady had said there were 50 braves. Bill had a glass and says there are close to 90 of the critters by his count.

William Comstock commented, "That is about three apiece."

Harvey made sure all six of us with a wagon had plenty of ammunition and gave both Bills repeating rifles to replace or back up the slow buffalo killing rifles in their saddle scabbards. We were as ready as we can get.

The Sioux rode straight at us and we waited till they had to split and some went south while the rest headed north. I think we all shot at once and 10 braves hit the dirt as they rode away. They all gathered in two bunches and came back from both directions with some firing under their horse's necks. This time past us, they hit a couple of troopers and several mules. We only hit four more, as they rode by.

Harvey had time to check on everyone and ran by each wagon to make sure we all survived.

The Indians were building a fire so we knew what is coming on the next charge: fire arrows. This charge was by the whole bunch from the south and we could see a dozen braves with bows and flaming arrows headed our way.

They came in two columns, front line, rifles and right behind them the flaming arrows. The front line was firing fast and furious, trying to keep us down so the bow-man could hit the targets.

This was the heaviest exchange yet. We had nine more braves on the ground as they passed us. Two went down firing arrows that never left the bow.

Two more troopers took lead and another mule was down. The fire arrows all hit inside our wagons or on the ground. As Harvey checked the wagons, he found Able Bean took a bullet in the forehead. He never felt a thing, as Harvey put it.

Bill Cody took his buffalo gun from his saddle scabbard, loaded the chamber and laid it on my wagon rail.

Bill said, "Watch that Chief when they start this way again. He leads the charge and drops back about the time they get in our rifle range. I think I can pick him off before the braves pass him with 'big momma' here."

The Indians started a charge like before with two columns with the fire arrows behind the braves with rifles. Bill was right, the Chief was leading the rifle column and I watched Bill level his sights on the front Indian.

You could see the Chief start his move to the side. There was a big boom and at the same time the Chief was knocked off his horse as if he ran into a rope across his path. The two columns collapsed into a circle around him. We couldn't see what was happening but shortly we could see they had tied the Chief across his horse and they all started riding north.

Sergeant Fitzpatrick, with a couple of troopers, walked out to check the 20 some braves lying on the killing field in front of us. Only one was still alive. The sergeant caught an Indian pony and helped the brave onto the horse and smacked the pony toward the war party riding north. He picked up the rifles by the dead and brought them back to return them to the fort.

Harvey was cutting a hide bundle open. Josh, along with Art, was carrying Able to lay him on the hide in preparation to bury him.

Josh said, "Able said everyday the Lord gives him is a bonus as he really expected to die in the war."

CHAPTER 42

By the time we laid Able to rest and had cut the dead mules from their traces, it was late afternoon.

We lost five mules, so that left us with an extra wagon and no animals to pull it and we were also short one driver. We loaded the hides by dividing them between the remaining wagons and we drove five miles to leave the bodies of the braves so their people could recover their dead.

That night, Sergeant Fitzpatrick said, "Harvey, I have five troopers that need continued medical treatment besides what we were able to give on site. I know Mr. Cody and Mr. Comstock need to head east to meet their party. I feel the Sioux will be of no further danger to your wagons and your party. Saying that, I will head my detachment of men back to Fort Fetterman early in the morning. God speed to all of you gentlemen."

That night the troopers camped away from the train and the five of us, with both Bills sitting around the fire telling stories of experiences, we enjoyed with Able through the years. Thor had an instinct about people when they were hurting. I watched him and he was not leaving Josh Bean's side. Thor laid his big head on Josh's feet as Josh sat on a log close to the fire.

I told the story about the first day I met Able. Josh and Able rode up to the livery and Thor wasn't going to let Josh dismount. Josh got a smile on his face when I told everyone why Thor acted the way he did because of me telling Thor never to forget this man at our first encounter back in Kansas on my trip to Colorado.

Art said, "Able and I made a trip to Salt Lake City last year. We had a two day layover waiting for some grain to be sacked for our load back to Denver. He met a lady when we went to a picnic in the town square on Sunday since there was no where else to go. She took right to him as we walked to the serving table. She said, 'Well, tall man, what can I do for you.' 'I--I would like one of those corn cobs and some butter.' She was hooked. I walked away and never saw him until much later that night at the hotel. With a big smile all he would say about the girl was. Nice lady."

Josh told us, "Able and I had very little in common. He was two years older than I, and didn't approve of my friends. He got me to join the army with him. We became close after that and because of him I gave up the wild and risky side of life."

Harvey said, "Able was a quiet man but everyone he met was struck with his down home charm and ability to mix in any situation. Able was a real man." With that, it was time for the bed roll.

Before daylight, Harvey had bacon and coffee ready for an early start. Bill Cody and William Comstock had their bacon and coffee, and swung into the saddle and rode east. It was getting light by the time we got the wagons and mules together and we headed south. I looked back and the troopers had left ahead of us. We passed Chugwater cliffs by high sun and the rest of the day dragged on. We made 23 miles today.

The next day and half of travel we found ourselves back in Cheyenne. General Dodge was right. There were about 15 tents set up and there was a crew scraping a road bed for the railroad. It had only been three weeks since we left this area and civilization had moved in. Well, two more days and we expected to arrive in Latham, Colorado to unload our cargo of hides. Harvey decided to stop and camp for the night just as we got into Colorado territory. We got the mules all rounded up in an old corral left by the army with the wagons in a circle and a good fire for making supper. Harvey asked us to sit and listen to him for a minute.

Harvey said, "Boys I have run this company for four years now and nothing that has happened up to now has affected me like the loss of Able. I feel I need to do something else but have no idea what that would be."

Josh stood up shaking his head, "Harvey, all of our hearts are heavy at the loss of my brother, but he was doing what he loved and would not want you to change the life you also love because he died. He was proud of the life you gave him and enjoyed your guidance. He loved you like a father. For his sake, Harvey, let him go and please continue with the life you enjoy."

Art said, "Carl and I would expect you to go on if something happened to one of us. I knew you were tender hearted but Josh is right, this loss has to pass for your own good and health."

Harvey said, "I have to sleep on this. We can talk later. Goodnight."

CHAPTER 43

The mules ate every stalk of grass that was in the old corral so I expected they would be ready to go after we watered them from the barrels we carry for that purpose.

Harvey said, "Jack, take the head wagon and let's hear your bullwhip start us on the way to the rest of our lives."

I didn't see the usual sparkle in Harvey's eyes, but it was great to hear his husky voice give a positive command.

Over the next two days, we all healed to a degree and all we were looking for was the outskirts of Latham to show up.

As we were passing the Overland office on the way to the warehouse to deliver our load, I noticed a stage behind the building.

After we unloaded the first two wagons, I asked Harvey if I could ride the extra mule we have with us back to the Overland office to see if my brother, Jay, had been in town lately. It only took five minutes to get back to the Overland office and I could see the stage was still where it was. I hitched the mule and told Thor to wait at the side of the office out of any traffic that would come by. I walked into the office. Frank Root was behind his desk as I entered. "Jack Knight how is the bullwhip kid? Heard you had a run in with some Lakota Sioux a few weeks ago up in the Dakota Territory. Had a fellow in here yesterday that was at Fort Fetterman several weeks ago and said you guys got shot up in the scuffle."

"Yep, we took some lead and an arrow, but survived when the army came riding in to save us. Have you seen my brother lately?"

"Yes, Jack, he is upstairs asleep right now. He's been up there for about six hours so just go up those steps and he is in the first room on the left. Wake him up. He has a trip in about three hours so he needs to get up anyway."

I knocked on the door and walked in. Jay was dressed and sitting on the bed with a navy six shot revolver pointed at my belt buckle.

Jay said, "Jack, I'm sorry. I thought you might be a fellow I met the other day who thinks I want his girl. Not so, but he can't get it through his head that we were just two people that knew one another in Denver."

"Sounds like you have a real problem, Brother. It's good to see you. We just got in from the Dakota Territory and I thought I would check with Frank to find out where you were."

Jay stood and said, "I have a stage to drive in a couple of hours. Let's go downstairs and have something to eat while we talk." We found chairs in the stage house restaurant and sat down.

Jay said, "I saw Father and Elizabeth about two months ago in Kansas. They are fine and doing well. The horse farm is very profitable and growing every month. Mary Alice is almost 14 now and she is beautiful. Handles horses like both of us."

"Jay, you don't call my mother, Mother anymore?"

"I'm sorry, Jack, that was a slip of the tongue. I always call her Mother or Mom when I'm around her. Uncle John and Aunt Ann are fine and happy with their success with the horse farm."

Jay continued, "Jack, I heard you had some Indian trouble a few weeks ago up in the Dakota Territory. Everybody come out alright?"

"We all survived that time, but this week we were attacked again just north of Chugwater cliffs and Able Bean didn't make it. He took a Sioux bullet in his forehead and Josh his younger brother was with us when it happened."

Jay said, "I remember Able. He was the older brother of the fellow we took the boots from back in Kansas when they tried to take our herd from us. Yep, I liked Able he was a real man's man. Sorry, Jack."

"Well it was sure hard on Harvey. He said he was ready to give up the wagon business but Josh helped turn him around. Never thought I would see Harvey in a condition like that. He took Able's loss like he was his own son. Jay, I need to get back to the warehouse and help unload those hides. I'm glad you are in Latham and I got to see you. We need to find some time to go fishing again when we can spend a couple of days together."

"Jack, that would be great, let's do it this fall before the snow starts and the lakes freeze over. See you later little brother." We shook hands and hugged. A burly fellow walked to the table and put his hand out to Jay and apologized for his conduct yesterday. I guess that was the guy Jay was talking about when I walked in to his room. Don't think I would have wanted to mess with him in a dark alley either.

Thor was waiting with the mule and ready to head back to the warehouse.

CHAPTER 44

The trip back to Denver was a good one for Harvey. Beachham's warehouse had a hundred sacks of grain going to Denver so we returned home loaded instead of five empty wagons running with no revenue.

Harvey said, "Nothing can replace Able. But Josh is right you just keep going and take what life hands you."

Not a word about the loss of the wagon and the five mules we left up in the Dakota Territory from the Indian attack.

It was August now and we were having the warmest time of the year up here in the high country. The water from the South Platte kept our mules with fresh water and in good shape. We made Fort Lupton the first day so we were making very good time on our leg home to Denver.

After we got the mules in a corral and fed with some oats that Harvey bought from the Overland station, I wandered with Thor into the fort. A big man I recognized, but couldn't put a name to, walked up and began a conversation about father, and when was the last time I saw father.

He said, "Knight, you don't recognize me but I remember you. We met at your father's blacksmith shop back in '64. I'm Jim Baker, one of Jim Bridger's close friends. Just left him 2 weeks ago. He and his father-in-law, the Shoshone Chief Washakie, are trying to put together a treaty with a land deal in the Wind River country for the Shoshone tribe."

Jim said, "Bridger is losing his eye sight and said after he helps the Chief with his plan he is heading back to his farm in Missouri. Chief Washakie signed a treaty in '63 at Fort Bridger but he wants a better defined boundary for his band of about 900 or so Eastern Shoshone."

Jim found a box to sit on and said, "Bridger knows I live in Denver and asked if I had seen the Knight boy with the bullwhip, lately, and if I saw you before winter to let you know he was leaving for his farm."

I said, "Jim, when I get home, I'll send Old Gabe a telegram and tell him we talked. I need to offer him my help if he wants it. I probably would not be doing what I love if not for his stories I used to hear him tell on the banks of the Missouri River. Thanks for the time you took to talk with me today. By the way, the entire family is doing fine." As Thor and I walked back to our camp I recalled of the many times spent with the man many people call the Blanket Chief.

Harvey was helping Art with the supper. Tonight we had lots of bacon and some of Harvey's sugar baked beans with real buttermilk biscuits and fresh milk.

"Harvey, what have you got going that I need to be involved with for the next three months?"

Harvey said, "Jack, you have been going at it steady for two years now. If you need some time off you have earned it, can I ask why you need three months to do what you want?"

"My friend, Jim Bridger, is moving from Fort Bridger up in the Dakotas to his farm outside of Kansas City, Missouri. I think I can help him if you don't need my services for that long."

"If Jim needs more help, Jack, you let me know. I probably owe him for a couple of favors he has done for me over the years. Sure, you go if he will accept the help. Have you talked to him about this? He is touchy about what people do for him. He says never let yourself be obligated to any man."

"No, Harvey, I'll send him a telegram when we get home and offer my help." The next day we arrived early at Harvey's headquarters and I brushed Powder down good and saddled him for town. Thor was ready to go as he watched me change from the 18 foot bullwhip to my 12 footer. He probably thought we were going hunting.

As I rode into town and got on Market Street where the Western Union office was located, I looked at street signs and the name of the street had changed to Holladay

Street. It must have been because of Ben Holladay's big new brick building for his office.

When I dismounted in front of the telegraph office, there was a boy selling the Rocky Mountain Newspaper. I saw it had a picture of my friend Bill Cody on the front page. I bought a copy and read the story about Bill and William Comstock having a contest for the right to be called Buffalo Bill. The story continued and says William Frederick Cody won the contest with the higher buffalo kill numbers in eight hours and from now on can use the handle of "Buffalo Bill Cody." That would give him something to tell his grandchildren when he is old and gray.

I had almost forgot what I'd come to town for and started to get back on Powder when I saw the telegraph office and remembered why I was there.

My telegram was short. Jim, Stop Am offering my help to you for coming trip. Stop If interested send reply. Stop Jack Knight, Denver.

The next day Thor and I took a buckboard to town with a list of supplies to buy for Betsy as she had a bunkhouse full of drivers to feed for a couple of days. After the trip to the Mercantile, I went by the telegraph office to see if Jim had sent a return.

Sure enough it was there. To; J. Knight Stop Bring bullwhip Stop We go Stop J. Bridger

Well, that plotted my life for a couple of months anyway. Thor was waiting in the buckboard guarding our supplies. Everyone going by the rig walked to the other side of the street as Thor was standing over our packages just daring them to try and take them from him.

I drove to the blacksmith shop on the way back to Harvey's. Charles was sheathing some stage wheels with iron rings as I arrived. Charles said, "Jack, good of you to come by. Heard you had a go with some Lakota Sioux up north. Also heard about Able, sorry."

"Yep, not our best trip. Charles, I stopped to tell you I'm going to help Old Gabe get back to his farm outside Kansas City. Probably be gone two or three months. I will try to go by and see the family in Kansas on the way back."

Charles said, "Tell Jim 'hello' for me and do go by and see Father and Mother. Ida and I are fine. Tell them no grandchildren yet but maybe next year."

With a big hug I said, "Charles, always good to see you. Tell Ida 'hello.'"

CHAPTER 45

Powder was saddled. I had another horse with a very light pack saddle and a few clothes and some trail food for both Thor and me. Most of our stops would be in small towns and stage stops so we could travel with the minimum baggage.

The route I had decided on was about 385 miles to Fort Bridger. Changing horses a couple times a day, I expected to make it to Jim's in about nine days.

I had to stop at the Ute village and see Chief Walking Bear and Chief White Feather as it had been almost a year since I have been to their camp. I knew Charles has kept them informed about me but I missed them like family and wanted to see that they are surviving in good shape. Both Chiefs were getting old and needed help for their tribe.

Thor knew where we were headed and takes off to announce our arrival in the village. Sure enough when I rode up, Chief Walking Bear was standing outside his tee-pee with his white dog and Thor was standing on his hind legs with his big paws on the Chief's chest. Walking

Bear said, "Jack Knight, you been gone long time. Come tell me about big fight with Lakota. You kill big Chief. I hear Chief Blue Knife take one bullet in right eye and go to happy hunting ground right away."

"Chief, I had no idea which Chief was killed but that was Bill Cody's bullet, not mine that did him in. Yep, he was dead when he hit the ground. Just one shot from Bill's single shot buffalo rifle."

Walking Bear said, "Lakota big enemy of Ute tribe. Always try to steal our horses and take young boys and girls for slaves. Stole my first wife many years ago. She took two moons to get away and come back to me. That why I have two wives."

"Walking Bear, I'm going to Fort Bridger to help Old Gabe get him and his family to Westport, Missouri. His eyesight is failing and he needs to retire to his farm he bought several years ago. I probably won't be back this year before the snow falls. I know Brother Charles helps you in the winter, but since I am leaving I want you to take these five, 20 dollar gold pieces to help you and your small tribe 'til I get back. No hand signs, Walking Bear. This you do for me."

He said, as he hugged me, "Jack, how your brother say? Gods speed. Tell our friend Bill Cody thanks for Blue Knife. Sorry White Feather gone elk hunting. He will be sad he miss you." Thor ran ahead of me as I mounted up. Even with the side trip to the Ute village, we could still make Latham before dark if we hurried.

We made Latham after the sun has set. Frank Root had me feed the horses and put them in the Overland barn for the night. He let me take Thor to the same room I met Jay in last week.

As Thor and I awoke, it was still dark outside. I dressed and washed my face in the bowl on the dresser. Blowing out the candle as I walked out the door, I heard someone talking loudly at the stage ticket window. I walked on my toes and made Thor stay behind me. Looking down the stairs I could see someone had a pistol pointed at the window and had his other hand out reaching for something. Before the man behind the window got the money to the outreached hand, my bullwhip had taken the gun from his left hand and the second whip motion had him by the throat.

Before I could stop him, Thor was on top of the would-be hold-up man and had his big paws pinning the man's shoulders to the floor.

I picked up the gun and asked Jeff, the man behind the window if he needed help getting the critter over to the jail.

Jeff Holzgang said, "Whew that was so quick I didn't see anything 'til the dog was on top of him. No, Jack I can get him over to Walter Johnson's with no problem."

I crossed the street to have coffee and some eggs. Frank Root joined me. Frank said, "Thanks, Jack. Jeff said you saved the receipts for the last two days. I should never leave that much in the drawer. Learned my lesson on that."

"No problem, Frank, glad I was there. I sure didn't want anything to happen to Jeff. He must be getting close to retirement. Don't need him hurt now. Well, Thor and I must get on the road."

As I left, Frank remarked, "Don't go by to pay Jeff for the room or the stable bill. It's all on Ben and me. Tell Jim Bridger I said 'hello.'"

"We might be by here on the way to Missouri. Have to see what Old Gabe has on his mind for the route to his farm."

The stable boy had brushed both Powder and the other horse down good last night. He was sleeping on a couch in a room at the front of the barn. I had one silver dollar in my pocket so I slipped it in his shirt pocket. When he saw we have gone, he will know where it came from.

CHAPTER 46

T he trip to the Colorado line was uneventful. Powder was back in the swing of traveling. He carried the pack when I traded rides and showed no hesitation anymore.

Thor chased a grouse now and then. He looked my way as if to say, "Why don't you pick this one off for supper?"

I decided to follow the route General Dodge surveyed across the mountains for the Union Pacific railroad. Amazing the speed with which civilization takes over an area when the railroad was planning to build their line. Following the survey stakes and the men working the roadbed, it looked like a railroad needed a stop for water or something about every 20 miles as the stops were laid out for that.

Telegraph poles and the line were already up along the right-of-way. Looks as if every 40 to 60 miles a town had been laid out.

On the 7th day out of Cheyenne, I rode into a town they called Green River. The livery boy says it was about 50 more miles to Fort Bridger. Butch, the livery boy, told me about the hot springs south of town. That sounded good as I needed a bath and shave before riding to Jim's house.

This town would grow when the railroad gets here. There must have been 600 people living here right now. I saw 12 new buildings and 50 some tents lining the streets.

I spotted a hotel sign. A bed sounded good for tonight. Next to the hotel was a bar that advertised buffalo steak dinners for 45 cents. I could handle that now that I was clean and had a bed for the night. They even had sarsaparilla to drink. I had two. I got a late start the next day and after about 35 miles, Powder was giving out so I stopped at a fresh water creek and made a camp. I started a fire and put a pot of coffee on and it was done when I heard something from behind me.

"In camp, I come in?" I was surprised. Thor had given no warning that someone was coming up on my camp. I turned around and across the little stream was an Indian, fully dressed in moccasins, buckskin pants and vest, carrying a Henry .44 by the barrel and handing it to me to show he was not going to use it.

He said, "I hunt elk. Horse step in hole break leg. Have to shoot. Me belong Shoshone people. Near Fort over there." I took his rifle at the barrel end and handed it back to him. He smiled and showed me the whitest set of teeth I ever saw on an Indian.

I said, "I'm Jack. What do they call you?"

"My name Stands Tall, but am just 'Taw' to all at fort. Work for Jim at fort. Hunt for meat and teach his little ones to ride horse."

"You like coffee, Taw? I have an extra cup if you do."

Taw said, "I like coffee. No sugar, Blanket Chief say not good for teeth. He show me how brush teeth with soda when just boy."

Taw was about 5 foot 10 but he did seem taller as he stood straight with his shoulders back and really looked big.

"Well, Taw, have some cold bacon and a biscuit with your coffee and tomorrow we can ride together to the fort."

"Taw walk or run. Only 12 miles or so. Good for body to run. You carry rifle, Taw run."

Taw said, "You go to fort see Jim? He say he leaving to go grow food a long way from here. He call it farm."

"You speak good English. Did you learn from Jim? Do many in your tribe speak English as good as you?"

"When Taw young, old Shoshone woman come to our village from far away. Teach some of the people white man words. Jim teach me to talk with him."

We both fell asleep as the fire went away. Thor woke me at daylight and Taw had built a fire and was heating last night's coffee. He moved so quietly it was scary.

I saddled Powder and loaded the pack horse tying Taw's rifle to the pack saddle. Taw said, "Go straight, no road, too slow. You follow, we get there quickly." He took off walking fast and the horses picked a trot to keep up. As Taw hit open range, he sped up and ran like that for about three miles. I pushed Powder to catch him and asked him to stop. When we were stopped, Taw was not even breathing hard. What a body this man had.

We did another five miles and I had to give the horses a rest. Thor was having a great time running with Taw but he panted while Taw just was breathing normally.

Looking and pointing west, Taw said, "Jack, after that hill you see fort. I run like wind, you not try to keep up. See you at fort, later."

As I hit the hilltop, I had to call Thor, who was chasing Taw and falling back.

CHAPTER 47

Walking the horses toward the entrance to the fort, I saw a line of Indians standing and sitting, waiting for Jim Bridger to scratch their arms and pat them on the behind as they leave the line up.

Jim hailed me and said, "Jack, have a seat on the buckboard and rest. I'll be done in an hour or so. Have to stop the pox from spreading around here."

I said, "Jim, let me take my horses to the livery and get the saddles off them. We have been chasing Taw and they worked up a sweat."

"Ho, ho, that was not a good match. I believe Taw can out do most any horse we have here at this fort. Just go straight and you will see the horse barn on your left, about center of the compound."

I walked the horses to the livery and a young Indian boy grabbed the reigns from me and said, "Taw want you over there."

The boy pointed to the building across from us. Taw walked out with a cup of coffee and handed it to me before I could untie his rifle from the pack frame. He recovered his weapon and motioned me to a bench in front of the livery.

Taw said, "Blanket Chief do his best to save all Indians, Shoshone, Bannocks and Arapahoe. He love little papooses. He give medicine and no charge to the people. We miss when gone. Government send man to be in charge, but we not think he have our people on his mind. Most white man work for self."

I said, "Taw, what will you do when Jim leaves? Will you work for another white man here at the fort?"

Taw said, "I take my family and go to Wind River reservation. Jim Bridger help our chief, his father-in-law, Chief Washakie; get government to give Shoshone and Bannocks a reservation, back in '63. Jim trying to get Washington to write down good boundaries for our people so Chief and people know where we can go to hunt. Jim say next year the white man's chief will take care of this."

We talked about reservation life for the Indian. I told him of my friends at the Ute village in Colorado and the way Chief Walking Bear had been a great friend of my family since we arrived in Denver. He laughed when I told him the story of the kidnapping and why it happened. He was aware of the sand creek affair but said the Cheyenne are bitter enemy of the Shoshone tribe.

Taw said, "I have one wife, two sons and a little girl. I am good hunter, have 10 horses and am strong. We will live well with Chief Washakie protecting us."

I looked toward the front gate and saw Jim walking with his buckboard headed for the livery. He saw Taw and me when he gets close to the barn. A big grin appeared on his face as the stable boy came out and took hold of the bridle on the horse next to Jim. Jim said, "Jack, you are a sight. I expected you some time this week. Sorry I was busy when you hit the gate but that was important. Tomorrow I hope to get about 40 old men and young braves to show up and that is all the vaccine I have. I really need some help getting to the farm. I hoped you had time for an old man in need. Your family has helped me several times. This should be the last."

"I don't see any wagons or a corral full of mules. How are we going to move you without wagons? The railroad has no rails up to the fort yet."

Jim walked into the livery and called, "Jack, come and see what I have back here in the back of the barn. Look at that, Jack. It's a stage I bought just for this trip. There is just my wife, Mary, and two little ones. I sent everything else we will need on a wagon train last month. This is to be a fun trip, just Mary, the two kids, you and me driving this stage. All the older kids are at Westport in school. We follow the stage routes, stay in the stage stops and enjoy. I might even tell you a story you have not heard me tell."

This was not the Jim Bridger I had known for almost 10 years. He had never talked about enjoying anything but a sunrise and sunset. Watching him squint when looking around, I knew who will drive that stage most of the time. That's ok, now I know why he was so happy I came.

I said, "Jim, we have a lot of Indian hunting ground to pass. Have you thought about the danger to Mary and the young ones? A lot of the lower Dakota Territory is Sioux and Cheyenne buffalo hunting country."

"Jack, you have little faith in your old friend. I have hired 30 Arapaho braves to follow us past the Colorado line. We will probably never see them, but they will be there just in case some Sioux or any other tribe want to challenge us."

"Sounds like you have it all figured out. When would you like to start this adventure? I would like to meet this Chief Washakie before we leave."

Jim said, "It's Thursday today. The Chief usually comes to the fort on Saturday. Let's leave early Monday morning, rain or shine."

Friday, Thor and I walked the streets of the fort. We checked the settlement store but I didn't see anything I couldn't do without. As I walked toward the livery, in the walkway between the livery and a hay barn I saw a rattlesnake coiled, almost at the wood sidewalk. Thor saw him too and stiffened at my side. I was about 12 feet from him so he was an easy target. I planned on taking his head off, but he struck at something and was hurled on to the street with the return of my whip. I had to act fast since the snake starts at me. He was too close to use the whip so I had to kill him with my pistol. Wow! What a lucky shot. I had not pulled my gun for quite a while.

The livery boy came out of the barn. "Mister, can I have him to make a belt with?"

I said, "Sure, after I cut his head off and his fangs are gone, he's all yours."

Taw walked out to where I was and says, "I think that same snake I see a couple of times this week. Bad to get bite from that kind of snake. Most pass on."

Thor and I walked back to the main house and Mary had some squash soup and fresh biscuits for me and some raw meat for my dog.

Saturday morning, Jim had me walk with him to the settlement store. We sat on a bench in front of the store and discussed our upcoming trip. Before noon, four Indians rode to the hitching post in front of us. Jim stood up and started with the sign talk. Three younger boys went into the store and the older one walked over to Jim.

Jim said, "Jack, meet Chief Washakie of the Agaiduka Shoshone tribe. Chief, this is my very fine friend, Jack Knight. Jack, when Washakie was about 60 his tribe wanted a younger Chief. Washakie left the tribe for a couple of days and brought back six enemy scalps. From that time on, no brave has challenged his place. As we are leaving the store Taw walks toward us. I remember I have an extra horse now and have no need for it. "Taw you say you have 10 horses. I know you lost one last week. I would like to give you that sorrel I used for a pack horse to get here with."

Taw had a wide grin, "Jack, that one fine horse. She will make fine colts. My family thanks you."

CHAPTER 48

Early Monday we were on the trail with Jim driving and me riding shotgun. I really didn't have a shotgun, but that's what they called the second man up front on a stage. Mary had her hands full with an eight-year-old boy and a four-year-old girl. Both were great kids and traveled well. Mary liked to have Thor inside because the kids left her alone when he was in the coach. I let him ride five or so miles at a time, as he needed to keep his legs limber and I'm sure he got tired of the kids pulling on his ears.

Traveling was much better now than when the family came out from Missouri over five years ago. There were well built stage stops and most had horses to trade if you have some extra cash to put with the trade. All had feed to sell for your stock and most had a room or two to rent for a night. At some you could even get good home cooking to keep you from having to camp and cook in the wild.

The first day we traveled the 50 or so miles to Green River and stayed overnight. The next day, Jim let me drive. We made the 60 miles to Table Rock station.

Wednesday, Jim had me push it over 70 miles to Fort Steele. Fort Fred Steele was still in a building stage. We had to camp out and sleep under the stage for the night.

The next morning, Jim and I went to see the man in charge. We found there was a Major who is the driving force. He apologized for the conditions, but told us the fort would be the main protection for the railroad workers and the trains against the Indians in the lower Dakotas when it was finished. I never got the Major's name.

Jim said, "Jack, let's get to a station between here and Laramie. We can't make Laramie by tonight, it's over 90 miles. As long as the weather holds out here on the prairie, we might as well take advantage of it."

I looked to the south and saw a cloud of dust headed our way. I have Jim use his glass to see what it is. As I was slowing the stage, an Indian rides up and yelled "buffalo" and points toward the dust cloud.

Jim said, "Jack, head for that rock outcropping over on you left. Get your braves up here with the stage."

The rocks Jim pointed at were 500 yards off the trail but I snapped the bullwhip over the horses' heads and they took off across country. I saw the braves catching us and we made it behind the rocks and gathered as close as possible next to the rocks. I had Mary let Thor inside the coach.

For the next hour, we watched a herd of 10,000 or more buffalo trot past our position behind those rocks. The 30 braves made a rope corral between the stage and the rock pile for their horses and then sat on top of the rocks to watch.

Jim said, "Jack, you may never see that many buffalo in one herd ever again. That is the most I have ever seen at one time in the last five years."

As the last animals were passing, one of the braves shot a young bull. They would have a good meal tonight from that kill.

As we were driving away, I had forgotten about Powder who was tied to the rear of the stage. I looked and he was not there. I stopped and stood on top to see if I can see him. The braves were working on their kill. Inside the rope corral was Powder with the Indian horses trying to get out, without success.

I climbed down and let Thor out of the coach. We ran over to rescue Powder from his rope prison. I was so excited getting the stage behind those rocks I forgot about my horse. I'm glad one of the braves had Powder's welfare in mind.

We drove another 15 miles and saw one of the Butterfield's stage stops. Jim said, "We can stop there but I don't know anybody. Hard to say what kind of a reception we will get."

The place was quiet. No livestock was in the corral, no smoke from the chimney. We pulled in front and the door to the shack was open. Jim got down in one jump and was in the door. He came back out fast.

"Jack, get my medical kit from Mary. We have a man with a bullet in his shoulder. Get a fire going for me and have Mary get us some water."

I helped Jim get the man on the only table in the one room station. He was a big man, 250 pounds or more. He had lost some blood but his coat and shirt covered the wound when he went down. It probably stopped the bleeding or he would have been dead.

The fire started easily as there were still hot coals in the stove. This must have happened in the last two or three hours when the man had a good fire going. Mary found a small kettle and a large pot to warm water in. Mary helped Jim cut the man's coat off so Jim could get to the wound.

Jim said, "Look for some whiskey. This fellow is coming around and I need him quiet when I go after that slug. Look in that cupboard, Mary. Good, that will work fine. Jack, try raising his head up and put as much of that stuff, as you can, down his throat." Jim took the small kettle of warm water over to the table. He grabbed what was left of the whiskey and poured some into the warm water. He had cut the shirt away from the entry wound and now he cleaned the area with the whiskey.

"Jack, hold his upper body if you can. Mary, hold his legs down." With steady hands, Jim had a probing instrument and went steadily after the bullet. Within a few seconds, Jim came back out with a piece of lead. He cleaned the area again and placed some white patches from his kit over the wound and added a towel to hold them in place. The man woke up about 20 minutes later.

"Remember man wanted to buy a-a-a horse. Only have two sets of six for coach. Need to keep. He says if you not sell, I take one anyway and he pulled his gun. All I remember 'til you wake me up."

I said, "Friend you have been shot. There are no horses in your corral so he must have taken them all. I'm Jack, and the man that saved your life is Jim Bridger and his wife Mary. What is your name, sir?"

"Raymond Vance. Most people just call me 'Ray.' Only been here for about a month. We usually only have a stage come by every other day, for now. I sure am obliged to you. You the real Jim Bridger from that fort farther west of here?"

"Yep, that's me. Just happen to come this far on a hunch you had hot food and a bed. Got two little ones out in the stage. Ray, can you sit up so I can wrap your wound. Jack, why don't you ride Powder back to the Arapaho camp and talk them out of some of that buffalo they killed today? They will be camped within a half mile of us and close to the trail. You can't miss them."

CHAPTER 49

Ray was sitting up in his big rocking chair by noon the next day. His stage had been there before 10:00 a.m. and had to continue without a team change. He sent a message with the driver to send by telegraph whenever he got to a place with a telegraph. Jim said, "Ray, I'm sure your company will have someone to help you and some more horses here by tomorrow. Mary has left a stew and a dozen biscuits for you. Jack has brought enough wood inside to keep the fire going for two days. We need to try and make Laramie by tonight. You going to be alright if we leave?"

Raymond answered, "I'll be ok. I can't thank you all rightly for what you done for me. Sorry 'bout the accommodations, but we are gonna make it better. I can feed the stove, eat an' sleep right in this big chair. Yep, I'll be fine."

We loaded up and headed for Laramie. About two miles down the trail we saw a horse with his hind leg held off the ground. Jim said, "Stop."

We got off the coach and checked the leg. The tendon is pulled and broken on the left rear leg.

Jim said, "Jack, this must be why the guy wanted to buy a horse from Ray at the stage stop. This thing is in misery. Why would the fella shoot a man and not a horse with a leg like this? Don't make sense to me."

With that statement, Jim walked to the front of the horse and shot him behind the ear. The horse was dead before it hit the dirt.

When we got back to the stage, Mary was trying to explain why their father shot the horse and that it was better this way.

We made the Overland Stage Depot in Laramie before dark. Parking well behind the depot, we picketed the horses in a good level area to feed and water them.

Jim found that the depot had a large tent to accommodate families that were traveling and wanted to rest for awhile. Also, a cook in the stage depot building would put together a meal for weary travelers. We were not the only travelers who wanted to eat. Another couple traveling west was staying over and eating also.

Jim and Mary sat with the children at one table. J.C. and Diane Williams, the travelers from the east, invited me to eat with them. The cook served beef stew.

J.C. said, "We came over the Smokey Hill Trail into Denver. From what we heard the old trail along the South Platte is not safe from Indian attack. We are traveling to San Francisco from Leavenworth, Kansas. My firm, Woodruff and Kelly are transferring me to open an office in the Bay City."

I said, "That sound like attorneys to me. My brother, Edwin, is an attorney in Kansas City, Kansas. I don't remember the firm he works with. He went across the river as an intern in 1861."

J.C. said, "I know a lawyer from Kansas City. His name is Edwin R. Knight. He is a partner with Abbott and Bunch. Big firm for a small town."

"That's my brother. I had no idea he was a partner. A couple of years ago he said he wanted to end up in San Francisco working with banks."

As J.C. attacked his pie he said, "Edwin can write any ticket he wants. He has put together some big companies in the railroad, and cattle industries. Because of some of his deal making you will see Kansas City, Kansas become one of the largest cattle and meat processing cities in the country. I'm not sure what Cecil Abbott saw in Edwin, but he gave him his head and Edwin is a driven man. Nice guy, also."

"J.C., I'm his little brother, Jack. I am just a freighter. Thanks for the update on Edwin. The family over there is Jim Bridger, his wife, Mary, and two of their children. We have a coach like you are riding in and I'm helping Jim get to Westport, Missouri where he has a farm to retire to."

J.C. said, "Bridger, like Fort Bridger in the Dakota Territory. He is a legend. How did you get to know him?"

"Well, I remember him as a family friend from when I was say seven or eight years old. He used to come down the river and have father make things for him. He used to tell me about the Great Salt Lake and Yellowstone with its geysers and big bears. He was my hero when I was young and now I can help him with his dream."

Getting up from his chair, J.C. put his hand out and shook mine. He said, "Diane and I are going to rest in the tent before our stage leaves. Jack, it has been a joy to talk with you. You and your party have a safe trip. Go through Denver and take the southern route."

I walked over to Jim's table and said, "Jim, the couple I had dinner with tell me the trail along the South Platte is not being used by the Overland Company. They came over the Smokey Hill to Denver. Suppose we should go that way, also."

"Jack, I left two shot guns with Diego to repair and was going to have him ship them to me. We can go through Denver and pick them up. Probably be better for Mary and the children anyway. I really like that South Platte country and was looking forward to seeing it one last time. Yep, let's go to Denver. They have nice hotels there. I might take Mary to a theater. She has never been to one."

I said, "We can make Denver in two days if we keep a steady pace. I know we can buy a new team from Frank Root in Latham, Colorado. Are you going to send the Arapaho guard home today or after we make Cheyenne?"

Jim looked serious and said, "Jack, let's keep them 'til we get to Cheyenne. There is a lot of open hunting area between here and there. They are well paid and have no problem for another day."

We made Cheyenne early in the afternoon and Jim climbed on Powder bareback and rode to tell his honor guard goodbye. When we got to the Overland station between Cheyenne and Latham, it was getting dark.

The following day we traded horses in Latham, had a meal with Frank Root and made Denver before dark. We dropped Mary and the children at Booker's Hotel and drove to a livery three doors from Diego's shop. Diego was still working at his forge and got a big grin on his face when we walked into the shop area.

"Jim, Jack, what a surprise! Please, have seat while I finish this hammer for a customer. Business good. Have another smith working. Not good as Jack, but ok."

Jim said, "Diego, remember the two shotguns I left. Jack and I were in the neighborhood and thought we would stop and pick them up."

"Sure," Diego said, "Both guns ready and wrapped ready to ship. You pay too much to fix and now no ship. Diego have no change to give you."

Jim said, "Diego, just seeing you is enough change for me. How is Margo? We are staying over tonight so I can take Mary to a play if there is one at one of your theaters.

Diego holds his hand up and said. "Jack, bring those two kids to the house tomorrow evening and Margo and I will enjoy serving you supper and let Jim and Mary have the evening together with no little ones."

CHAPTER 50

The next morning at breakfast Mary asked me how far it is to Westport. From former trips to St. Louis, I knew we still have about 650 miles to Missouri.

I said, "Mary, I know you and the children have to be road weary by now. We still have around 650 miles to travel. If it's any comfort once we get off this high plain, the trail is much better riding and should make the travel more enjoyable in the coach. When we get into Kansas I would like to take the boy up with me and let Jim ride with you inside. He can rest better there and give you some company also."

Mary said, "Jack, you know Jim was going to try this trip without you. I don't think he would have made it. Please don't tell him I said that, but it's true. He was as happy as I have ever seen him when he told me you were going to help us."

"Mary, this is a trip of love for me. Jim was the first man that gave me his time and told me the stories of the west and of adventure beyond a small boy's dream.

He was and is my hero and always will be. I will miss him and his stories."

Jim walked to the table and said, "All right cross draw, we rest today and hit the trail early in the morning. Mary and the little ones need to rest for a day. Tomorrow we ride. Jack my bones hurt from the stage. You think Powder would let me ride him for a few hours tomorrow?"

"I think Powder would like that. He has to be tired of following that coach on a rope. You might even scout ahead for us. Never know what's out there. Jim, by the way, when we level out down in Kansas can the boy come ride shotgun for me and you ride the coach with Mary?"

Jim said, "Jack that would be good for Taw. He will like that. How about that Taw? You want to ride shotgun for Jack?"

First, I had heard the boy's name. I thought there must be a connection with Stands Tall, back at Fort Bridger. Had to remember the boy is half Shoshone.

Taw said, "Jack, can I handle the reins? I can drive a buckboard just as good as father. Well, almost as good. When can I go up on top, Father?"

This boy had been quiet and reserved this entire trip and now he was as excited as I was when my father gave me my first bullwhip and showed me how to use it. He and his mother spoke English better than Jim. Must have been a good teacher at the fort.

Jim, true to his word, took Mary to the Apollo Theater to see a musical. Thor and I took both children by to see Charles and Ida before going to have dinner with Margo and Diego DeLacruse in a rented buckboard, giving Jim and Mary some time alone.

Early the next morning, Jim mounted Powder and we took off on the Smokey Hill Trail headed for the Kansas line about 175 miles away and around 2,000 feet lower in altitude. For two days, Jim rode Powder for about four hours a day. The third day Jim brought Taw on the top seat to get him used to the different sway and jerk from the height at the top of the stage. Taw got the feel immediately and his body took to the stagecoach movement easily.

The fourth day out of Denver, Taw rode all day with me and loved every minute of it. He watched my use of the bullwhip and I saw him draw his arm back like I do as if he was the one prodding the horses on with a whip.

After the fourth day, we were less than 200 miles from Salina, Kansas the largest town in central Kansas on the Smokey Hill Trail. I was sure when we get to Salina that Jim will want to stop for a day of rest. I knew I would be ready.

Seven days and four teams later out of Denver, we arrived in Salina, Kansas. Jim said, "Jack, we have less than 175 miles to Westport. I will be happy to get there but I sure will miss your company when this trip is over. Sometimes you seem like a son to me. There are few men I have traveled so many miles with. A lot of my travel over the years has been by myself."

After a day of rest and three days of travel, we arrived at the Bridger farm in Westport. What a gorgeous home. I heard he moved it piece by piece, board by board from Pennsylvania, several years ago.

Mary had no idea what was in store for her. She seemed more than content with what she saw. I heard there were six more children in school who lived here with a surrogate mother waiting for the family to relocate.

Jim asked, "Jack, what do you think? With my family helping me on these 160 acres, you feel we can make a living?"

"Now that you are all together," I replied, "you will be fine. Whatever you plant on this land will grow. The two Kansas Cities, right here, will use what ever you raise. They are going to continue to expand. Yep, Jim, you will do great things."

I continued, "Jim, I would like to stay tonight and saddle Powder up tomorrow and ride over to Kansas City, Kansas and find my brother, Edwin. It has been my pleasure to help you and your family. I can never thank you for the time you have spent with me. You have helped mold me and I appreciate it."

CHAPTER 51

Thor seemed delighted as I saddled Powder and started our ride to Kansas City. I'm sure he was tired of being mauled by Jim's children when riding the coach. As we crossed over into Kansas, I had no idea where the office for Abbott and Bunch would be so I had to find the telegraph office. Following the poles into downtown, sure enough, I found the office. The operator directed me to a building on Riverview Road. After I got on that road and close to the address he gave me, I saw a livery and rode Powder through the open door. Getting Powder taken care of and in a stall, I told Thor to stay with him. I asked the livery boy if he has a place I could leave my gun and bullwhip. He showed me his closet for wet weather clothes and said they will be safe in there.

Walking the two blocks to the office of Abbott and Bunch, I felt naked without my gun and whip. I always wore them in Denver, but this is a big city and I should have no use for them here.

As I stepped inside the building and search for the lawyers' office, I was surrounded with men in suits and ties. Everybody was dressed, fit to kill, except me. I found the office I'm looking for and walk in. A well dressed lady behind a desk said "How may I help you, sir?"

"I-I'm looking for Edwin Knight."

She said, "Sir, Do you have an appointment with Mister Knight?" That's the second time she had called me "sir." Now if I were dressed like everybody else around here I guess "sir" would fit.

I said, "Miss, I'm Jack Knight. Edwin's my brother. I just rode in from Denver to see him. Is he here?"

"Yes, of course, sir, one moment please."

She stepped from behind the desk and walks down a hall into another office. As she reentered the hall she motioned me to come to where she is. She said, "Mr. Knight will see you now." I walked into an office large enough for four lawyers. Standing behind a desk as huge as I have ever seen was Edwin. He had grown banker's sideburns and his mustache had filled out. He was wearing a three piece suit, vest and all.

He came from behind the desk with his hand out and said, "Jack, what a great surprise. You have grown even more since the wedding. What are you doing in town? Please sit over here and have some coffee."

At a round table with chairs around it, there was a silver service with china cups and saucers. The silver coffee pot had a candle keeping the coffee warm.

"Edwin, this is sure fancy. I met one of your lawyer friends on his way to San Francisco the other day. J.C. Williams from Leavenworth, I think he said. He told me you were a partner with this firm now. You have done well."

"This is all for show, Jack. Some of my clients expect this kind of treatment so we have to oblige them. Say, have you seen your buddy, Cody, lately? I hear they call him Buffalo Bill Cody now."

"Yep, we had to fight some Sioux together a few months ago, up in the Dakota Territory. That was before he killed all those buffalo. Edwin, I thought you wanted to go to California. You still going to do that?"

Edwin said, "Jack, as soon as they get a railroad over to San Francisco, we are going to put an office there. I will be the managing partner. I seem to have a knack for putting people together in ventures and that is an advantage for our firm. California is ripe for that kind of work and I can't wait. But we need the country to be easy to traverse for some of my ideas. Jack, in a year or two Kansas City will be the beef capital of the country. The railroads running out of here will carry cattle to both coasts. Get in the cattle business or get connected with a railroad. That is the future. Are you going to travel to the horse farm and see Father and Mother?"

"Yep, I'll take the Smokey Hill Trail back to Denver. I believe the farm is just north of Salina, Kansas. Edwin, I have Powder and Thor in a livery a couple of blocks from here. Is there a hotel close, I can stay in and have dinner with you?"

"No need for that. I have a suite across from that livery. You can stay with me. I have two bedrooms. Thor is welcome to stay in the room also. Let's walk you over there. You don't want to hang around here all day."

As we walked, Edwin suggested we get Thor on the way. When we were crossing the street to the hotel where he had his suite, it started to rain. We all made it inside without getting wet and went to the second floor. His suite faced the street and you could see the river to the right. "Well, this is it. You guys make yourselves comfortable and I will return around six tonight. We have a great restaurant on the street behind us. If you are hungry now, my kitchen has some food in it. See you at six."

It was still early. As I was looking out the front window, I saw a mercantile a block from the livery across the street. I needed some new clothes for dinner. No need to look trail worn with Edwin dressed and me, not. I gave Thor a biscuit and water and told him to "stay," after finding him a blanket to lie on.

What a great store. They even carried boots. I needed new boots, but thought I would get some in Denver. With new pants, a heavy wool shirt and new belt, the old boots looked bad, so I pick out boots and some new socks also. The prices were better than Denver so I got a deal. I went by and picked up my gun and whip on the way back to Edwin's place and felt whole again.

When I returned to the hotel, I asked where the closest barber was located. The doorman tells me that there is a bath and barber behind the hotel and three doors down from the restaurant on that street. Just what I need. Salina was my last bath.

After a haircut, shave and a bath, I dressed in my new clothes and boots. The doorman said, "Mr. Knight, you look very nice. Good thing you favor your brother I probably would have turned you away otherwise."

I spent the rest of the afternoon with the boots off and lounged on Edwin's leather couch. He had given me several things to think about: the railroads, the cattle business, and what should I be doing to prepare for the time the wagons and freighters will disappear like the buffalo? I fell asleep until Edwin came home.

"You clean up good, Jack. I was planning to put on some old clothes for dinner so as not to embarrass you. Let me shed this vest and we can go eat."

CHAPTER 52

The restaurant called The Butcher's Block was way ahead of what we had in Denver. They even had big chandeliers with clusters of oil lamps on them and of course, white tablecloths and starched, white, cotton napkins.

Our waiter knew Edwin very well, and asked if he would have his usual. Turning to ask what I would have, he almost dropped his pad when I said, "I'll have sarsaparilla before dinner and milk with my meal, please."

Edwin smiled as Franklin, the waiter walked away. "Jack, you have to excuse Franklin. Most men that have dinner with me order Scotch or Brandy. He was just taken aback for a second."

"That's ok. I'm totally out of my element in here. But I think I could get to enjoy this type of living. What is the best steak served here?"

Franklin arrived with our drinks and Edwin said, "Franklin, we will both have the Kansas City cut medium rare with baked potato and some of that apple pie, later."

I said, "I fell asleep thinking about what you said about my needing to settle into something beside wagons and mules. I'll be 19 this December. All I know about the cattle business is from Father. You have a bull and a cow and they make a calf. Now, I know you need to know more than that to be in cattle ranching. What and where would the railroad need a young buck, like me? Maybe I should find out more about cattle. That is outside work for sure. If I wanted to be inside, I am a very good gunsmith and always have that to fall back on."

"Jack, I put a company together for a fellow in Abilene, Kansas. He has opened a stockyard in Abilene to gather and ship cattle to the eastern markets by railroad. Joseph McCoy encourages Texas cattlemen to drive their cattle across the Chisholm Trail to his stockyards. He will purchase the cattle, feed them and sell them to the markets in the east by shipping them on the railroad. I will write you a letter of introduction to Joseph McCoy. You and he might find a use for your talents. You will like Joe. He is even-tempered, like father and enjoys all people like you and father. He will have cattle in Abilene before the year is over."

Our steaks arrived and Franklin served them on an iron platter still sizzling from the heat. The meat was just right, blood dripping from the middle and brown on both surfaces. Franklin almost forgot my milk and was very apologetic when he does serve it. Both Edwin and I just ate and have no conversation while we attacked the food. I had heard the best steaks were from Kansas City.

Now I could agree. Also the coffee and apple pie was not something you wanted to pass up.

"Edwin, Jim and I came through Abilene last week. It is a growing area. I saw some stockyards on the south side of town, but I wasn't paying much attention to anything in particular. I think I will go see the family before I go to meet your friend in Abilene. It can't be over 40 miles back to Abilene from Uncle John's horse farm on the Solomon River. Have you been to see the folks since they moved to Ottawa County?"

"Oh, yes, when I saw Joseph McCoy in Abilene last month, I rode up to the farm. I will draw you a map and save you some time finding the place. They are all prospering from the farm. Father and Mother look younger and are really enjoying life. Father works hard but nothing like he used to when he had the blacksmith shop. Uncle John and Aunt Ann are fine. Their two kids, Mary Lou and John Jr., are doing well. Mary Lou is 15 now and John Jr. is 3 years old. Our sister, Mary Alice, is growing like a weed and you won't recognize her. She looks older than Mary Louise and is too pretty considering the rest of us." Edwin continued, "If it was me, I would stop in Abilene before going to the farm. You might hook on to something with Joe and have more time to spend with the family. If you like what you hear you might end up in Texas before the end of the year. Can't tell. You might like the cattle business and stay with it. You could become a buyer and get involved with processing of beef. Who knows? The field is wide open right now and you could get in on the ground floor."

"Edwin, I promise I will stop and talk to Joe Mc-Coy. I really like what I do now but realize it won't be the same a couple of years from now. I have wanted to go to California and check that out but have not had the time. I'm still young and have a few years before I have to think about settling down. Maybe a cattle drive would be a good trip for Thor and me."

"Well, you do what you want. McCoy would be a good start if you really want to go on a cattle drive. He has partners in Texas that bring large herds into Kansas and he can send you to a rancher that knows what he's doing."

I said, "Thanks for all of the advice and the straight talk. I put faith in your wisdom not just as an older brother, but as a wise man with common sense. You have an eye on the future of this great country."

As we were walking back to the hotel, it stopped raining. Hopefully, the sun would shine and a breeze would dry the trail toward Abilene.

That night with Edwin, just listening to his conversation about what would happen to our country over the next 10 years with the expansion of the railroad and the prosperity of people moving west, made me, more than ever, yearn to be part of that western movement.

The weather was cold, but the sun was out, as I saddled Powder for our 120 mile trip to Abilene, Kansas. Thor and Powder could leisurely make 30 miles a day if

I walked part of those 30 miles. Tonight we would stay in Lawrence Kansas, and visit Richard Knight, a cousin, and oldest son of Uncle John and Aunt Ann. He was a couple of years older than my brother, Edwin, but fun to spend time with. Being a dentist, he had great stories to tell about some of his patients. He cut hair when the dental business was slow, but said that was boring. The next few days were slow moving because with just one horse you are limited on the miles he could handle with your weight.

When we made Abilene in the afternoon, I rode to the south side of town and found Joseph G. McCoy's office at the stockyards.

As I stepped into his office, I pulled Edwin's letter from my shirt pocket and start to introduce myself. The man behind the desk got up and said, "I'll bet you're Jack Knight got a telegram from Edwin over in Kansas City. I'm Joe McCoy. So you want to be a cowboy? Yep, Edwin is right; you will probably be a good one."

CHAPTER 53

Joe came from behind the desk and shook my hand like I was a long lost relative or a buddy he hadn't seen since the war.

Walking out the door, Joe said, "What you see here, owes a lot of thanks to your brother. He helped with the land deal and also got the Kansas Pacific railway to put that spur into our yard. Found lumber in Hannibal, Missouri for the three story hotel across the street and got partners together to make this happen, all since July 1st. Now, in just over two months, we have a herd of 2,400 Texas cattle arriving here tomorrow. This fellow, Colonel O. W. Wheeler, and his partners were going to drive their herd to California but decided when he heard our price, to sell them here in Abilene. We will sell and ship some to Chicago, some to St. Louis and Kansas City. I bet we have 20,000 more head here before the end of the year when the price we pay gets back to Texas."

I asked, "From what part of Texas do the drives start? This fellow Wheeler, you know him well enough to introduce me to him? I figure a cowboy is no account to him but he can tell me where to start, anyway."

Joe told me, "Jack, I think this bunch started out of San Antonio. This fellow, Jesse Chisholm, started a wagon trail out of there and it comes up through Wichita, Kansas. He has a couple of stops built along the trail for people to buy necessities and the cattlemen are following his trail because of the feed and water for the animals. I guess it can get hairy in Oklahoma Territory, because the Osage and other tribes think the area is theirs. We will know more when Colonel Wheeler gets here."

I was the first paying customer at the new hotel. Powder got a rub down and a stall for the night and Thor had a bed in the same stall. I walked a block toward town and found a restaurant in a big tent. Everyone was talking about the herd coming to town and what the cowboys would be like in a town with only one saloon. Abilene had a lot of growing to do to become a big cattle town.

I was in San Antonio last year. Wow, that must have been 700 miles straight south of here. I bet Oklahoma was a tough place to pass through. We went through New Mexico Territory on the trip to Texas last year.

The next afternoon, longhorn cattle started filling Joseph McCoy's stockyards. It took three hours to get the 2,300 or so longhorns into the feeding pens.

The last three cowboys bringing up the tail end of the drive were the partners who owned the herd. I picked Colonel O. W. Wheeler out of the three easily. You could always tell an ex-officer because he is the one in charge.

I walked to the stockyard office and was inside when Wheeler came in to see McCoy. Joe knew I was anxious to meet Wheeler so he motioned me to his desk and introduced me to the drover right then.

"Colonel Wheeler, this is Jack Knight, he would like to have a word with you while I get this tally from the counters straight. I believe he wants to become a cattle puncher."

Wheeler said, "Well, that can be arranged. You look like you can handle yourself. Ever use that bullwhip you got there?"

"Yes sir, I can pick a fly off the wall with any whip, up to 18 feet and leave no blood. I have been a freighter for the last two years and have been from the Dakotas to Texas in that time. Mr. McCoy says you know the cattle business and I am willing to learn whatever it is I need to know to thrive and survive."

The Colonel said, "Well, you need to drive a herd from Texas all the way to Abilene and you will have a good start. In four days we are headed back to Austin, Texas and you are welcome to travel with us. We will bring another herd north, shortly, or you can hook up with another drover down in Texas. We only pay a dollar a day and grub so you won't get rich, but you will learn about cattle."

"Mr. Wheeler, I have family up in the next county on a horse farm. I need to see them before I leave. I want to go up there and see them and I can be ready to ride with you in four days. By the way, I have a big dog that can handle a steer or two. Can he ride with me?"

"As long as he is under control and doesn't bother the other cowboys," the Colonel replied, "Just remember he is your responsibility. This is Tuesday. We plan to leave early Saturday morning. I hope to see you Saturday morning in front of the hotel over there. Ride careful, Jack."

It was only about 20 miles up the Solomon River to the farm so Thor, Powder and I took off that afternoon to find it. Less than three miles out of Abilene, we found the Solomon River and followed it north on the east side of the water. The land was flat and there was a lot of good grazing along the river. As it got dark, I saw a couple of farm houses a few hundred yards from the river with dim lights in their windows. The trail I'm following was supposed to terminate at the front gate of Uncle John's farm.

It was late September so we had a large full moon lighting our way. Edwin had said there were two homes on the farm. Mother and Father had built a small home just past the gate and off to the right of the wagon trail. As I passed the gate, I saw the lights from a house a 100 yards from the trail.

As I rode up to the light I said, "Hello in the house, anybody home?" The front door opened and Mary Alice was around my neck as soon as I was able to dismount Powder. She turned loose of me and had Thor around his neck.

Mother met me at the porch with a kiss and said, "James, we thought you would be here yesterday from your brother's telegram."

"Mother, I got tied up in Abilene and stayed a night there to meet someone." Father was getting up from the kitchen table as I walked into their home.

I said, "Mother, who is this man with all the gray hair at your kitchen table?

Father blurted out, "Don't get smart Jack. I can still whip you if you forget your bullwhip and maybe even then if I get inside your range. Good to see you son."

The next two days flew by as I spent time with Uncle John and Aunt Ann. The whole family was busy. They had over a 100 horses to care for and had buyers at the farm from daylight to dark, it seemed. Father stayed busy with the shoeing and has a small blacksmith shop close to the main barn. Mary Alice, true to her word, had learned to handle horses as well as she did a mop at the boarding house. Mother was happy and as relaxed as I had ever seen her. She tended her garden and home and says that was enough after the years in Denver.

CHAPTER 54

Thursday night at dinner I gave the family the news that I was going to become a cowboy for a couple of drives out of Texas to learn the cattle business.

Father questioned the decision, but backed off when mother interrupted and let him know they gave up the right to question their boy's life decisions back in Denver when they left us to make our own way.

Father said, "Your mother is right. It is none of our business. I just hope you know what you are letting yourself in for: cold and wet nights, hot and wet nights, cattle stampedes, unreliable companions, deep rivers and bad food. And those are probably the better things about a cattle drive."

I said, "Well, father, I will be 19 years old this winter. If I spend the next year or so learning something about cattle, by the time I'm 21 I should know what I want to do with my life. Maybe a buyer or I might want a stockyard on a rail head some place. Who knows? I have to check it out."

Friday morning, Mother put a spread on for our breakfast, thick cut bacon, farm-raised eggs and biscuits with her apple butter. Mother said, "James, you might not get another breakfast like this for a long time so I hope you enjoy this one. I expect you to come see us every time you come to Abilene. You don't need to stay in that hotel when you're this close."

Mary Alice said, "Why don't you leave Thor here with me? He will be fine and he must be tired running all over the country with you."

I said, "Thor will be fine. He can be a lot of help on a drive. Let's see how he does on my first drive and we can look at your suggestion later."

I headed for Abilene by noon and had a leisurely ride to the livery in town. Passing the telegraph office, I remembered I needed to send a note to Harvey explaining my reasons for not returning to Denver and my apology for any inconvenience to him. Leaving the office, I saw several fellows that looked like cowboys from Colonel Wheeler's outfit and asked if they came in with the herd last Tuesday.

One of the guys put his hand out and introduced himself. "Hi there, I'm Nolan Heardman from Austin, Texas. Yep, we're from the drive that came in this week. The Colonel said you might be heading back with us. I guess you're the one he was talking about, tall fellow with a bullwhip and cross draw with a big black dog. This is Curtis Ellis from down San Antonio way."

I said, "Nice to meet you both. My name is Jack Knight. How long you boys been running cattle for Colonel Wheeler?"

Curtis said, "My first drive, but I been around cattle since I was a young boy working with my father on the Rio Ranch, out of San Antonio. Nolan, here, is an old hand at ranching. How long you been working cows, Nolan?"

Nolan said, "Well, let's see. I'm 32 and was 12 when my pa died and I had to go to work. Been 20 years since I roped my first steer I guess."

"Well, I run nine cows and a bull with 10 horses from Kansas City to Denver back a couple of years ago so I have a lot to learn about herds the size you guys are used to handling. We had five wagons with us so I guess the miles we traveled were faster than if you want beef to remain on your cattle."

Curtis said, "Jack, you got half of the game already in your head. Weight is the name of the game in the cattle business. We only travel about 10 miles a day."

Nolan said, "Your dog know what to do around cows? I knew a dog once that could handle cows better than a man on a cutting horse. He has the same look and I saw him walking close to your horse when you rode in. Not afraid of hoofs."

I looked down and Thor was one pace behind me on my left just as always. He learned early to stay clear of my right side as the whip comes out from there.

"Thor can hold his own with cattle, mules and horses. Yep, he is a help to me with animals and seems to enjoy it."

Curtis and Nolan walked toward the big tent that had the restaurant in it. Nolan said, "How 'bout some supper, Jack. I'm going to eat and get some shut eye in a bed before we head out early in the morning. The Colonel is an early riser and is usually up before daylight. He sold the wagons we brought with us to carry the grub so all we got going back are 24 horses and the ones we ride tomorrow. Should be a fast trip back to Austin."

Before daylight, there were eight riders waiting at the livery. Shortly, two riders with 24 horses, four with packs on their backs, moved to where we were waiting.

Colonel Wheeler said, "Boys, I guess you all have met Jack. Jack this is Grady, he is my foreman. Well, we have over 600 miles to cover. Let's see if we can do it in 12 days."

By the end of the fourth day, we camped on the north side of the Canadian River about 225 miles out of Abilene. The Colonel was pleased with our progress and said the stock had done well.

Thor had become the wrangler for the relief and pack horses so the cowboys welcomed his participation and all tried to over feed him at night. The Colonel waited for daylight to cross the Canadian River. We rode up stream to a place that only reached the flanks on our horses so we didn't have to swim.

We spent two more days riding the dusty trail the cattle had just come over on our trip to the Red River and over into Texas. We camped at Red River Station, Texas for the night.

After supper, the Colonel said, "Boys, it's only 160 miles to Waco. If we make that by Saturday night, I will put us all up at Brown's Hotel for the night. We can eat in a restaurant and have a drink in a nice bar. I'll even buy the first drink."

Everybody was up early and ready to go the next morning. We were going to have to average 80 miles a day to make Waco by Saturday night. I remembered Bill Cody telling about his 90 and 100 mile a day rides, but he changed horses every 15 or so miles. The Colonel seemed to know what he was doing but the horses would be worn out when we got there. We changed horses every 20 miles and let the others rest with no one on their backs. Powder was keeping up better than Thor. The big dog laid down and rested every so often but never let us out of his sight. About dark the Colonel called a halt and said, "Over there on your left is Fort Worth. I think we are half way to Waco, so let's give it a rest."

Nobody wanted to argue, so we made camp. Nolan got the coffee out and Curtis and I had a fire going before Nolan had water from the stream. All we wanted for supper was biscuits and cheese with the coffee and as many hours of sleep as possible before daylight. We made Waco and forded the Brazos River in early evening. The Colonel rode to a livery and had the stable boy feed all the horses oats for their dinner and paid for rub downs for every animal. True to his word, Colonel Wheeler put us all up in separate rooms at Brown's Hotel, less than a block from the livery. We were having supper and the Colonel told the waiter that all the meals and drinks were on him.

When we had all finished our steaks, the Colonel stood and addressed all nine of us. "Boys we have come a long way together. I hope you will all be at the ranch when I get there. I have to take off to Lampasas Springs, west of here. I want some cattle from over there on our next drive so Grady and I will be a week or so before we get to the ranch. Nolan, you take the other boys to Austin and out to the ranch. Start rounding up the strays south of the bunk house. Jack, all these boys that came back with me are on the payroll so we need to get you on the ranch rolls starting today if that is alright with you? Nolan, you're in charge 'til Grady is back at the ranch. Good luck and have a good trip home."

Over the next two years, I worked with the rocking W Ranch on five cattle drives to Abilene and one to Cheyenne, north of Denver. Nolan, Curtis and I fought Osage Indians, floods, stampedes, rains that turned the prairie into mud flats, and wild fires. By October 1869, and our fifth trip to Abilene, I decided that was enough driving cattle and ranching for me.

It was time to pick up Thor from Mary Alice at Uncle John's farm and head toward Denver. Thor had been with her since my first drive to Abilene.

CHAPTER 55

Thor saw me from the main turn off of the road into the farm. He ran down the short drive to meet me. I knew I had to get off the horse before he got to me as he would jump up and knock me from my mount. He was as glad to see me as I was to see him. I felt bad about leaving him, but the first drive we made from Texas, to Abilene was just too much for him. I was sure he would work his body to the death as he was always rounding up stragglers and strays. He thought that was his job on a drive.

By the time he was done licking me, I grabbed his ears and saw a few gray hairs coming in around his mouth and above his eyes. I had forgotten that he was over nine years old now and not many dogs had the mileage he had on him.

I led my sorrel up to Mother's hitching post in front of the house and Mother was at the front door waiting for me.

She said, "Well, Jack, have you made your last trip out of Texas, as you told father you would earlier this year?"

"Yes, Mother. I told Colonel Wheeler that I would not be coming back from this drive. He stayed at the ranch for this drive and let Grady Peterson handle the whole trip. He gave me a nice bonus and the papers to this sorrel, said if I ever change my mind I always have a home at his ranch."

As I walked into the house, Mother hugged me and told me how nice it was to have two of her sons home at the same time. She told me Jay was out helping Father shoe some horses for pick up tomorrow.

Mother said, "Grady Peterson. That is the same name your father is getting 12 horses shod for pick up tomorrow. Could that possibly be the same man you are talking about, Jack?"

I said, "Mother, the Colonel buys stock as he needs it and we had some older stock on this trip so I would not be surprised. Grady knows my uncle has this horse farm so I am wondering why he didn't say anything about getting horses from him." Mother was canning green beans and the kitchen smelled good since she has some cooked for supper in smoked hog's feet. She dished up a plate for me and I sat down for this wonderful treat that you don't get on a cattle drive.

Mary Alice came in from outside and jumped in my lap, almost spilling my plate of green beans.

I said, "Hey, girl you're getting too big for this lap. How come you are letting Thor get gray hair? He is just a pup, you know."

She said, "Jack, you're the one that made him old before his time. Making him follow all those wagons and then using him to round up cows in Texas. He has done more traveling by foot than any other dog in this country. And while we are on the subject of how you treat animals, Powder is a good example of a horse almost rode to death. I let him rest for six months before I put a saddle on him."

"Mother, get this girl off my back. I come to stay for awhile but if she keeps it up I can ride tomorrow. Come on Mary Alice, I need to get my horse put up and fed for the night."

We went to the front and she saw my new horse. "Jack that is the most beautiful sorrel mare I have ever seen. How did you get such a great horse in Texas?"

"She was bred by Colonel Wheeler. He is a real horse lover but this mare has no white on her lower legs only the white on her face and the Col. likes his horses to have white socks so he asked me if I would like to have her for my own. I said, 'yes' and she is mine to keep."

Mary Alice said, "She is too good for you. We need to breed her with Powder and then you would have a horse with more stamina and speed than any horse on this farm. Can I have her for a year to try that?"

"No, Mary Alice, you can't have her for a year. As of today, she is yours to keep and do what you want. I'll give you her papers too. She is a special breed and yep, she's yours. I won't need a horse where I'm going for a little while, so take good care of her. Her name is Beth, but don't tell mother until I'm out the gate."

As we walked Beth to the barn, Jay walked from behind Father's small shop and grabbed my hand.

Jay said, "Jack, my little brother. I have not seen you for over two years. What have you been doing with yourself?"

Mary Alice continued to the barn with her new mare and was singing something softly to the horse, inaudible to Jay and me.

"Well, Jay, I have been learning about cattle and have come to the conclusion that I am not cut out for ranching or playing cowboy. It is hard work and there are too many unknown factors that come up and get you just when you think all is well. So are you still driving stage for Ben Holladay?"

Jay said, "No, Jack. Ben sold out to Wells Fargo and I'm in charge of their fleet of coaches and the livestock. Big job, but I enjoy it. Never have two days the same. My office is in Denver, but I have to travel from Sacramento, California to St. Louis, Missouri. What do you have in mind, since you say you're through with being a cowboy and working cattle?"

"Well, Jay, I think I'll hang around here 'til my birthday. I will be 21 this December so I will have age to help my pursuit. I feel like I would like to try the railroad. Not sure where I can fit in yet, but I think it is an industry that is going to grow and I might as well be part of it."

Father came up the walk and hugged me as we headed for the house. He said, "Good to have both of you here. Mother is so happy that you both ended up here at the same time. She said supper would be ready about 5:30 so we better get cleaned up."

Mother had done buffalo stew with potatoes, carrots, and turnips along with more green beans and hot bread. She finished off with blackberry pie and whipped cream. Never ate this good on the trail.

After we ate, I said, "Father, would Uncle John have something for me to do until after Christmas? I don't need pay, just grub and a bed. When the New Year comes, I'm going to California and want to wait till I'm 21 to make the trip."

"Son, we need 30 some horses broke and trained for the Army by January 15th. I am sure John could use you for that job. He was asking around for help when we were in Salina, a couple of days ago. I would say yes tonight."

CHAPTER 56

Uncle John was receptive of my offer except I must take pay for my work. He said that was only fair because the farm would get paid for what I produce so hence, I would get paid or no deal. What can I say, but yes.

Jay spent two more days with the family and had to be on his way to St. Louis. He was riding a train and I told him he was a traitor to his livelihood.

Jay said, "Jack, the railroad is much faster and some of my situations call for more rapid response than I could accomplish by stagecoach. We use the railroad a lot. Our coaches are made in Concord, New Hampshire by Abbot-Downing Company and transported to the west by rail. Wells Fargo is also a banking firm and right now we have the largest mail contract in the country. We use the railroad for some of our deliveries. We also use steamers on some of the rivers, if the delivery is special or has great value like gold or silver transferring across the country. Wells Fargo is a very large company, Jack."

"Well, big brother, stick to it. You never know where you will end up in a company that size."

For the next couple of weeks, I broke horses to the bridle and saddle. November 11, 1869 was Mary Alice's 15th birthday. Since it fell on Thursday and she had to go to school, mother waited 'til evening meal to have her party. Aunt Ann, Uncle John, her cousins, Mary Lou and John Jr. came for supper and the surprise package opening. I had promised her the papers on the mare I gave her so I had the papers and the transfer to her name in an envelope. Father stepped out the back door and brought in a new silver studded saddle and bridle. This, he said, was from your mother and me. Uncle John stood and went out the back door. Soon he came in the door with a large chest, beautifully and ornately caved on the outside, with brass handles on each end.

Uncle John said, "Mary Alice, we had this made in New Mexico by a Mexican family we have known for many years. They make and sell these all over the west. We hope this will become your hope chest for your future."

Mary Alice was speechless and began to cry. She said, "This is beyond my dreams. Aunt Ann, Uncle John and you, my cousins, I am so happy to have this. I have a few things for it now but every time I open it my heart will come back to this night. Thank you. I love you all."

Mother said, "Alright everyone, enough of that for now, come into the kitchen and have some of the strawberry cake I made just for Mary Alice."

Late November and December were so cold we had to work the horses inside the barn. There was snow piled up all over the farm. All the animals had to be inside at night. The wind added to the temperature and Uncle John was glad he added a very large barn and stable to the ones he started with.

My birthday was on Friday, December 24, and Christmas was on Saturday. We fed the stock inside Friday morning and made sure there was water and salt for all the horses to help them during the cold spell.

Mother said, "Let's do like we used to do, celebrate your birthday on Christmas Day and just have a nice evening meal tonight. Tomorrow Aunt Ann and I are going to cook a turkey and some country ham with all the trimmings so we better eat light this evening. I want to finish my pies tonight and get some sleep so I can start the turkey early in the morning."

Father said, "Son, come in by the fire. I want to talk about your trip to the west coast. You say you have no idea what you are going to do but you will have no horse since you're going by railroad. You say you want to possibly work for the railroad but you don't know anybody that does. Are you sure you've thought this out enough to just run out there without a better plan?"

"Well, Father, all I really know is I have worked hard for the last four years and loved every minute of it. I have traveled many miles and met people from all walks of life except, maybe, politicians. I have found I don't want to drive wagons or cattle for a living so there has to be another field I can look into. Might not be the railroad but I thought I would start there. I have saved a lot of money since you left Denver and still have not touched what you gave me except to have Edwin invest it for me. I am frugal and if I don't find something to do for a year I will survive just fine. I know you have three successful sons and you and mother worry about me because I am still wandering the country with little to show for it. I am far from destitute and am fine with my life. I hope you and mother can understand where I am coming from on this continued venture I call my life."

"Son, today you are free, white, and 21. There are many people in this country that should be able to say that they are free but in our times we find that it is not true of many of our red and black friends. You are much blest to have the education, health, and background to accomplish whatever you want. You have my blessing and your mother's prayers following you wherever you go."

"Thank you, Father I accept your blessing and Mother's prayers as my 21st birthday present and wish you both a long and happy forever."

Christmas was a beautiful and cold day. Mother served hot cider with cinnamon sticks and the meal she and Aunt Ann put on the table was memorable.

Mary Alice and Thor were asleep in front of the big Christmas tree in mother's living room after the big dinner. Thor had his large head lying on her stomach and you could hear him snore just a little from where I was sitting. He had little to do with me since I came to the farm. I had been busy with the horses and he was with Mary Alice whenever she was not in school. He would be

10 years old next year so he needed to stay with her and live out his life with as little stress as possible.

I had missed him the last year and six months since leaving him with her, but the cattle drive and the quick trip to Texas we made when I started working for Colonel Wheeler was too much for him and also for Powder. Both of these animals saved my life more than once so I felt we were a great team once, but both deserve better than what my life had to offer them now.

I tapped Mary Alice on her leg and woke her so she could hear my proposal. "Mary Alice, I am leaving in two weeks. Thor is getting too old to travel with me on my escapades. Would you like to keep him from now on?"

She said, "I thought he was mine when you left him last time. I never gave it a thought he would go with you anymore. Yes, I'll keep him and give him good care."

CHAPTER 57

January 9, 1870 was a warm day compared to the last three weeks. It didn't get below 40 degrees as Father and Uncle John drove a buggy to Salina to drop me off to make the 10:00 a.m. train to Kansas City, Kansas, 175 miles away.

Ten hours later, I arrived in Kansas City. I think we stopped in every town in Kansas on the way. My seat mate said the Kansas Pacific line to Kansas City was called the stop and go to the big Mo., meaning the Missouri River. I can't say my first train ride was a thrill. More like if this was what the trip to California would be, maybe I should ride a horse. I found a hotel and got some sleep before having to board a steamer for the run up the Missouri River to the Union Pacific Depot in Omaha, Nebraska. From there I caught the train headed west.

I paid the $93.25 in coin for first class Pullman service even though I had no idea what that means. I paid another $15.00 for my saddle. Brother Jay said it was the only way to travel that distance.

To my surprise, the rail cars were larger than I expected with more leg room. Now, if they travel more than 20 miles without stopping, we might make it to California before my next birthday. When I saw the steam engine and the difference in size to the one on the Kansas Pacific line, I felt the four days and four hours, they said it would take, was possible. The car I was riding in was called a Silver Palace Sleeping car. The seats made into beds at night and it had a relief station, a heater for these cold winter days and nights. Better than a stagecoach. This 1,900 mile ride could be alright after all.

As I settled into my seat, I unbuckled my holster and bullwhip and laid them on the seat next to me. I had purchased a suit I felt would be good enough to wear to see my brother, Edwin, when I got to San Francisco. The cowboy rags could be embarrassing to him too much to be seen with me anywhere he might take me. I also bought a new pair of boots.

So when the gentleman in the seat across the aisle asked if I were a cowboy, I was surprised to find I had not covered my former type of work with new clothes.

"Yes sir. I spent the last two years working on a ranch in Texas and made several cattle drives from Texas to Kansas."

He reached across the aisle with his hand and said, "I'm John Omohundro. I ran cattle on the Chisholm Trail myself for a couple of trips out of Texas. I moved to Cotton Wood Springs, Nebraska last year. That's just a ways from Fort McPherson on the Platte River. I hunt buffalo for the Army when they run in that part of the country. I'm also an actor and am returning from working for the holidays in Chicago.

I said, "Hello, John, I'm Jack Knight. I'm on my way to San Francisco to see my brother and possibly stay in California."

He said, "Wait a minute. Did you live in Denver a few years ago?"

"Yes, I did. My family had a blacksmith shop and livery on Cherry Creek and my mother had a boarding house in the same area."

John got a big smile on his face and said, "Jack, we have a mutual friend. Bill Cody has spoken of you many times since I met him last year. The cross draw holster and bullwhip are just part of his stories about you. We hunted buffalo and scouted together for the army at Fort McPherson."

"Well, John, it is a small world. Do you know Bill's nephew Buddin Jeanette? He is a noted actor on the stage and writes plays too."

"Sure, we have been on the same bill together once or twice, I think. I didn't know his relationship with Bill though. He lives in another world as an actor and never comes out of it. Me, I have to have more excitement than just a stage right now in my life and that's why I love working with Bill. Never a dull day with him. By the way, people call me 'Texas Jack.' Picked up that handle up on a cattle drive into Tennessee a couple of years ago and it stuck."

Texas Jack and I talked about the theater, Buddin Jeanette, cowboys and both of our experiences with Bill Cody. After we ate in the dining car, Jack said he was in the Civil War with General J.E.B. Stuart as a scout and courier. He said he was 24 so he had seen a lot of life in a short time. We talked into the night and at 10:00 in the evening the porter came through to let Texas Jack know we were coming into North Platte and his station to get off the train.

While we are stopped in North Platte, Andy, the porter, made up my bed for the night.

I asked, "Andy, what is our next big stop?"

"Sir, after you have breakfast in the morning we will arrive in Cheyenne and stop for half an hour," he said. "You can get off and stretch your legs."

When we stop in Cheyenne, I looked out and saw 16th street. I had a friend from Denver that moved to Cheyenne to run the Ford and Durkee hotel. I walked up 16th street to the hotel but found Harry Sizemore had gone to Denver on business. I wrote him a note and left it for his return.

On my way back to the train, I passed the McDaniel's Theater and noticed that Saki was scheduled to play there in two weeks. As kids, our parents thought us inseparable; now as adults, we crossed one another's paths often but never at the same time. Andy was waiting for me with the handy step stool to help me on board.

"Laramie and Rawlins are ahead. Not much to look at on this part of the trip." I explained, "Andy, this whole area clear to Fort Bridger I walked and rode my horse while the road bed was being put down. It will look familiar in many places."

"Yes, sir, we pass Fort Bridger, but you will be asleep. When you wake up tomorrow you will be in Utah."

Andy continued, "Sir, after breakfast tomorrow you want to be awake to see the Wasatch Mountains and into Ogden, Utah. That is beautiful country."

Andy was right. The whole trip to Ogden and on to Promontory was great. The next day and a half was scenes of desert, bare mountains, tunnels, and bridges all the way to Reno, Nevada. When we left Reno and started down the west side of the mountains into California, we were in big trees, rolling valleys and the Sacramento River. Now I knew what I had been missing. I had had people try to tell me what this was like but until you see it, you had no idea about the expanse and lush green color.

CHAPTER 58

In Sacramento I had to change to the Western Pacific Railroad to San Francisco. It left at noon and, got into San Francisco at 6:30 in the evening. I hoped Edwin got my arrival time. I sent a Telegram from Ogden, Utah when I got the Western schedule. What a surprise. When I got to Oakland and they loaded the rail car on a ferry for a ride across the water to get to the San Francisco terminal.

Edwin was waiting at the arrival gate and showed me where to go to retrieve my luggage and saddle. Edwin said, "Well, little brother, you have grown taller and look very mature for only 21 years old. Let's get to my place and have supper. I have a buggy waiting on the street. What do you think of railroads after that trip?"

"I am still in shock as to how fast you can travel and the conveniences available to the traveler. We had good food, bed, heaters and relief stations all onboard the train. They even made my bed up for me at night."

"Well, Jack, what you have experienced is just starting on the west coast. We need to run rails north to Seattle and south to Mexico."

We headed for Edwin's home and I was amazed at the steep angles of the streets we have to go up and go down. People actually built homes on the hills and in the valleys of this town on the waterfront. When Edwin pulled the buggy into a small barn, he said it goes with the house. It had stalls for two horses and room for the buggy, besides room for hay and feed. As we entered his home there was a lady cooking in the kitchen and I ask if she came with the house.

Edwin said, "Jack, I am so busy I needed a housekeeper and a cook. And, yes, she lives here with me. This house has four bedrooms and plenty of room. She lives in the back of the house and we see very little of each other except at breakfast and supper. You take this room next to mine. Put your stuff in there and you can wash up to eat."

As we meet in the dining room, Edwin introduced me to Rose, an Indian girl, about 25 years old.

"Jack, Rose is Kiowa. She is from Oregon. She speaks English better than you and was educated by nuns at a Mission south of here. Her parents were killed when she was three years old and she was rescued by a Catholic priest after the raid on her village in northeastern Oregon. Later she was brought to California by the Catholic Church."

Rose said, "Jack, I am happy to meet Edwin's brother. Please have a chair and have supper of salmon and mashed potatoes with us."

I had heard of salmon, but never had tasted it. Now I had found a fish I liked better than mountain trout.

After supper, Edwin asked me into his home office and offered me a brandy. I asked for a sarsaparilla if he had it and sure enough he went to the kitchen and brought me one. I could hear Rose cleaning the kitchen but when she was finished she disappeared and I didn't see her for the rest of the evening.

Edwin said, "Jack, I have talked to a friend of both you and Father's. Ben Holladay has moved to Portland, Oregon. Ben sold his stage holdings to Wells Fargo Express a couple of years ago. The firm my firm bought, here in San Francisco, represented Ben and that is how we met. I saw Ben in November last year and I said you wanted to come out here to get farther west and that you were looking at railroading. Jack, he is in the railroad business and getting big in Oregon. He said he remembers you well and has a position for you if you want it. He needs people since he has a lumber mill and timber holdings to look after and I don't know what else. He might be a good starting point. He sure has a good impression of you."

Edwin continued, "Tell you a story of coincidence. December, last year, on your birthday, the 24th, Ben's company received the lucrative railroad land grants for Oregon when he completed 20 miles of rail out of east

Portland before his rival could complete his 20 miles on the west side of the Willamette River. He calls his company Portland Central Railroad."

I said, "Well, tomorrow I need to send Ben a telegram and let him know I am interested if he still is. I assume travel to Portland would be easier by ocean steamer than by stage if I were to go. By the way, you know Jay is working for Wells Fargo and is in charge of rolling stock and livestock?"

"Yes, we had a meal together in Sacramento back in the fall. He sent me a telegram about a trip he needed to make to Sacramento and wondered if I could have the time to come meet with him. We ate and talked for several hours. First time I had seen him since Charles got married. You know that he and Charles fish the river in front of the home Charles built there in Denver and then his wife Ida cooks the fish for their supper. Sometimes I think I live my life all wrong."

I said, "Edwin, looks like you have it pretty good. A very fine looking girl to cook and clean for you and she sure can cook salmon."

Edwin lit his pipe and said, "Rose is a very nice person. She is studying law and hopes to pass the California bar this year. She wants to help the Indians with their problems so when she passes the bar I guess I will have to find another cook. I will send a telegram to Ben tomorrow and see what he has on his mind as far as you are concerned. I get up early to go to the office but you can sleep in if you like. Rose will be glad to make you breakfast when you are ready. She studies in the dining room so she will see you when you are up and around."

"Thanks, Edwin. I am going to bed. It will be nice not to hear the train whistle blow every time it comes to a road crossing or into a town. But I will miss the clack of the wheels on the track since it kind of lulls you to sleep."

I awoke and sat straight up. I couldn't imagine what time it was so I grabbed my watch. It was 9:00 in the morning. It was so quiet I slept for 11 hours straight. I had never done that before. Must be the sea air and my body being worn out from the four days of riding the train from Omaha.

I washed my face and shaved before I dressed. As I walked into the dining room, Rose got up and headed for the kitchen.

She said, "Jack, sit at the table and I will bring your coffee. I have some fresh salmon roe to cook with your eggs if you would like? You said you liked the salmon last night. You will love eggs and roe with some toast and apple butter. Sound like something you could eat?"

"Might as well, Rose, if I'm to live around salmon I better learn to eat all of it. Do you get up early and fix Edwin his breakfast every morning?"

She said, "Every morning except Sunday. He takes me out on Sunday morning and we eat at the big hotel up that street. We talk about what I have studied all week and drink three cups of coffee sometimes. I think I learn more on Sundays with our talks than all the book work during the week. Edwin says I could be ready for my state test by the end of the year."

"Rose, tell me what are you going to do after you pass the bar? Edwin says you are leaving here and going to work with your people. I have some very fine friends from a Ute tribe in the Denver area and some good friends that are Arapaho. I have not thought about them needing the help of attorneys."

Rose replied, "As the country grows the Indian will need to be represented just as the white man. We will all be equal someday and to be equal the Indian will need to be represented just as everyone else, white, black or red skin. Your brother is my life now because we both need each other to survive. He works long hours and everyday I make it possible for him to have no worry about house or food and he gives me a fine home and teaches my mind for my later life. We are both winners."

I was not sure who was the winner but they seemed to need each other at this time in their lives. It looked like Edwin was taking advantage of her but after listening to Rose maybe she was receiving more than he was.

CHAPTER 59

Edwin was home by 7:00 and Rose had supper waiting. Edwin handed me a telegram from Ben Holladay. To Jack Knight. Stop Bring bullwhip. Stop Have position for you. Stop Just kidding about whip. Stop Ben Holladay.

"You know, Edwin, I don't have any idea why Ben would hire me. I know nothing about railroading and never learned to survey except what little bit father taught me. I know about wagons and mules and what they can do. I can fight Indians but I don't think Oregon has much trouble like that anymore. I can build barns and stables but never built a commerce building. He has no need for a gunsmith. I hope Ben is not putting me to work because of his respect for Father."

"Jack, believe me Ben Holladay is going to get the best you have to offer. Ben doesn't strike me as a man that doles out favors for anyone but him. He has a plan and you might as well take advantage of his knowledge and skills to further your own growth. He thinks highly of you for what you have accomplished and how you have handled your life. You need to walk with confidence when you meet him and he will see that confidence and respect it."

I said, "Well, I have come a long way for this. I just have to take the bull by the horns as they say in Texas and do it. I will make you proud and no matter what Ben has to give, I can take."

The next day, January 19th, Edwin came home at midday with a ticket for the three and half day trip to Portland on the steamship S. S. Yosemite leaving San Francisco Friday, the 21st, at 8:00 in the morning.

Edwin said, "A telegram that came to the office with this ticket said Ben would be at the dock in Portland late Monday to pick you up. You will enjoy this trip, Jack. The S. S. Yosemite is first class all the way. Get used to this life, Jack, because your new boss goes first class at whatever he does."

I had traveled on sternwheelers on the Missouri River and they took care of the passengers but never like on a side-wheeler steamship. There were over 100 passengers on this trip. Cabins were large and comfortable with food prepared like the fine hotels in St. Louis. For three days we ate three times a day and the cabin boy changed my sheets every day. They even had a bar and it was stocked with sarsaparilla along with anything else you could want. On the second day out, it was so smooth a ride everyone was out and sunning themselves on the decks. I had been cooped up for quite a while so I took my 12 foot bullwhip on deck and entertained the younger passengers for an hour or so to the delight of the parents who found relief for a little while from their children who had nothing to do.

Early on Monday we were crossing the bar into the Columbia River and this was the only rough part of the trip. When we got in the flow of the river and the ship was cruising on smooth water I was amazed at the large trees lining the river bank. Colorado had tall trees but nothing like what I saw in the forests of Oregon and Washington. It took most of the day to navigate the Columbia River. I saw the ship make its turn into the Willamette River and there, on the port side of the ship, were the docks and wharfs of Portland, Oregon. My new adventure was about to begin.

The dock side was full of buggies and wagons to pick up passengers and freight. My cabin boy told me where to go to receive my small trunk and saddle before leaving the ship. I had not spotted Ben yet but took my gear and disembark, as they say around ships.

Stepping on to the dock, Ben grabbed my saddle from my shoulder and greeted me with, "Hi, son. Good to see you after all these years."

I said, "I'm surprised you remember what I look like. It's been three or four years since we talked."

"Jack, you favor your father except for his mustache and you are almost as large a man as he. He might be a little taller and maybe better looking but the Knight blood is strong in you. Not sure where the red hair comes from but it looks good on you. Besides that, who else would bring a saddle on a steamship and have a bullwhip on his right hip?" Ben continued, "Jack, I need you to stay at my home tonight. Tomorrow we will go to Milwaukie and get you set up in my old house where we lived while they were building our home here in Portland. Milwaukie is only nine miles from Portland but we can talk about your mission and what I need from you and why I feel you are the right man to keep the wheels turning on this project."

Ben got his buggy out of the mass confusion on the waterfront and we headed uphill for about a mile. I saw what my brother meant about Ben's want and need for luxury. We drove through a gate onto a lane 200 yards long and approached a large three story white home that I would call a mansion. A man met us and took the buggy away as soon as we stepped down and grabbed my small trunk. Ben said to leave the saddle in the buggy and we would take that rig tomorrow.

We walked in the front door and a tall black man was waiting to take my trunk. "Jack, this is Orrin. Orrin, meet Jack Knight. He will become a frequent guest so you two need to get to know one another. When, and if, he ever tells you about cowboys and Indians or his escapades with Buffalo Bill Cody, probably he is not bragging because he lived those times. Orrin, take his trunk up to the front guest room and light a fire in his fireplace for the evening."

After supper, served by two servers, we retired to what Ben called his cigar room. He said his wife won't let him smoke anywhere else in the house. We both sat in large leather chairs as he lit up.

He said, "Well, Jack, it's time to let you know what you are getting into. Over two years ago I started to build a railroad 20 miles down the eastern side of the Willamette River. I had to finish ahead of another group working on the west side of the river in order to get the lucrative Oregon land grants from the government for further development of the railroad in Oregon. I did win that race December 24th last year. It was a close race only because of my people. We should have finished way back in June. I have timber and the mill to produce ties and wagons to move them where they need to be but no coordination between people. Jack, you have the skill to get my job done because you know how to coordinate and lead people."

"Ben, why do think I have these skills? I have never led any jobs or people in your field. For that matter I have never been in charge of anything like your talking about."

CHAPTER 60

"Jack, you have been in charge all your life. Your father could depend on you for anything and he did. I watched you grow when you were building the compound with your father and brothers. Your father told me how you handle yourself with the Indians and the respect they have for you. Jack, your people skills were born in you and you use them everyday and don't even realize it. What you can do for my companies could be done by your father but you are young and will succeed beyond your dreams. I need to expand the rails to Salem this year and on to Eugene by the end of next year. Don't get the wrong idea, Jack, I have people, and foremen. I have the Chinese laborers with Mr. Ping to run them, the mill, and timber with Albert Allen to run that operation. Warren Albrite is my surveyor. A big Irishman named Artimas York runs the bridge crew with an engineer, Gabe Turner. I have the right-of-ways and no one to make these people work in harmony with each other. Jack, I'm willing to pay you well for your efforts."

"Ok, Ben, show me your setup tomorrow and let's get started to wherever Salem is and on to California, if that's what you want. I am now a railroad conductor for whatever that is worth. By the way, where did this Artimas York come from?"

"That was the strangest meeting for me. Last year we were building a bridge over Johnson Creek when the engineer Gabe Turner, said the foreman had made a big mistake when he set the timbers on the second level above the creek. About the same time this big Irishman rode up from nowhere and asked who was in charge. Gabe pointed to me. The Irishman said you better stop and tear that second level off and start again. That bridge will collapse before you put a deck on it. Gabe looked at me and confirmed what the man said. I asked this guy how he knew so much about structures and bridges, he told me the army had taught him and he had built bridges in Nebraska and Colorado. Well, Jack, I fired my foreman on the spot and hired Artimas. We build the best bridges on the west coast, now."

As I headed upstairs for my room, Ben told me to be sure and look out my windows in the morning for the sights of Portland. It was nice and warm in my room with a fire glowing on one side of the room and the biggest bed I had ever seen on the other. As sleep over takes me, I wonder how Artimas York would receive my presences on the job. The next morning, I woke as Orrin was starting a fire in the fireplace.

He said, "Sorry I woke you, sir. It will be warm in here quite soon. It will be daylight in 15 minutes and you will have hot water to shave with by then. There are water and towels in this cubicle next to the fireplace. I will return in just a little while with the hot water."

What a way to wake up. Ben knew how to live. I remembered Edwin telling about the luxury, but I had no idea people lived this way.

After I shaved and dressed in a clean shirt, I looked west out the windows at the scene Ben told me about. What a sight high above the river. I could even see the Columbia River to the north. Ben said that Portland now has over 9,000 people living in its boundaries. Homes and buildings were being built all the way to the waterfront. I could see wharfs and building on the other side of the river under construction also. I understand when Ben says the populations will double this year.

We finished breakfast and Ben told me, "Orrin has brought your trunk down and we are ready to head for Milwaukie. The buggy is in front and we are burning daylight. An expression I heard your father use once. First we need to get you settled at the house and we can change to horses to go to the mill and out to the end of the tracks."

The eight mile trip to the house in Milwaukie was through beautiful unspoiled country. As we got to the house I asked how many of his people live in this two story white bungalow, as he called it.

Ben said, "You, Jack, this is your home as long as you work with me. I want you to hear what I said, Jack. You work with me not for me. There is a difference. We have a great responsibility to succeed in this venture since it means everything to me and also to the growth of Oregon. Don't take any part of this lightly, Jack. It means a lot to many people. You have to build about 40 miles of track this year and 60 miles each year after that. The Willamette Valley will be the bread basket of the west when you succeed. Our railroad will carry grains and products to ports you haven't even heard of, Jack." Ben pulled the buggy behind the house to where there was a barn almost as large as the house. There was a buckboard and four horses in the barn. I noticed a tack room off to the north side of the barn and asked what he kept in it.

"Oh, that's where Benny lives. He is your stable boy and sometime does the yard work if all your Chinese are busy. He is a little slow but he knows horses and mules very well. Treat him with respect and you have a loyal friend for life. Let's get your trunk and carpet bag in the house. By the way, Benny will saddle a horse for you with your saddle tomorrow morning while we are having breakfast. He somehow reads my mind and always has things ready for me at the right time. He will get so he is ahead of you too. Gets eerie at times but you will get used to it. Well, this is the house. You have a kitchen and dining room, plus a living room and office downstairs. Oh, yes, there is a small bedroom behind the kitchen for a maid. Upstairs there are four bedrooms. You can choose one tonight when we return."

The home was immaculate with lots of leather furniture. All the tables and cabinets were cherry, I believe. The office was complete with a drawing table and high chair to go with it. Father would have enjoyed this room.

We walked onto the back porch and Ben was right. Two horses are ready to go and my saddle was on one of them. I checked my cinch and saddled up. Ben said, walking his horse to the front yard, that it was about two miles to the mill. He saddled up and led the way south on a small creek that might be full of trout.

Ben pulled up after about 10 minutes and said, "Jack, I need to get straight on your pay before the day is out so we might as well do it now. I have told you what I need and what you have to accomplish. If it's alright with you, I will give a lot of extra things for your use like the house and horses and Benny, if you agree to work for 300.00 dollars a month for the first 3 months. Then we will talk again in April."

We shook hands and I said, "Sounds fair to me."

CHAPTER 61

For the next half mile, I could hear a saw cutting through wood. As we rode up to the mill, I saw a small office shack and we headed for it. When we dismounted, a short heavy set man walked from the shack and shook hands with Ben.

Ben said, "Al Allen, meet Jack Knight. Al, Jack is the fellow we talked about last week who is going to help bring harmony to our group."

Al said, "Nice to have you with us. We need someone to watch over this outfit. Ben is too busy with other projects to be here day after day. You're a welcome sight to me. Let me show you around."

The reception went well with Albert. His big problem seemed to be getting orders for ties and timber on a timely basis so he could react quickly for each crew as their demand came up. He told me he had to schedule the deliveries also.

Ben and I mounted up to continued on to meet Mr. Ping with the grading, tie, and rail setters. He was half-white and the half-Oriental, Ben told me as we ride the 10 miles to reach that crew. We were riding on a wagon trail next to the tracks that were used for delivery of product for both crews Ben explained.

We rode past several Chinese workmen and then on to meet Mr. Ping. He was twice as large as any of his workmen and was using a spike mall as we got off our horses near him. He handed the spike mall to the man next to him and came to shake hands with Ben. "Mr. Ping, this is Jack Knight."

Mr. Ping had my hand and was shaking it as he said, "Jack, please call me Ken. My name is Kenneth Ping. My people call me Mr. Ping because of my size, I guess." He continued, "Mr. Holladay has explained your function to me and I am looking forward to working with you. We really need your input and organizational skills to make this railroad run."

Ben grinned at me and said, "Jack, Kenneth has a college degree in geology. He talks very well for a half breed don't you think?"

I tried to ignore Ben's last statement and Ken said, "Jack, don't pay any attention to Ben. Wait till he introduces you to the big Irishman on the bridge crew. When he gets finished with Artimas you would think they don't like one another. But they respect and like each other deeply. We all get along well but need a person with spark and a flare for harmony."

As Ben and I started to mount up, a full bearded man with long hair rides up on the grade next to us.

"Jack, this is Warren Albright. He is our surveyor and all around ladies' man. Warren, this is Jack Knight."

Warren shook my hand and said, "Thanks for taking this job. I tried to get this crew in line, but failed. Good luck." Warren mounted his horse and rode off without another word.

Ben said, "Warren will warm to you within a week. Mark my word, Jack." Both Ben and I were quiet for several minutes as we rode for the bridge site. After a mile, Ben said we were headed for a bridge being built over the Molalla River and it would be a great bridge when finished.

As we rode toward a shack built at the end of the wagon trail, a tall man ducked his head to come through the door to meet us.

Ben shook his hand and said, "Gabe Turner, this is Jack Knight. Gabe is our line engineer and a good one. If you follow his design, you will have a great bridge that will last for years."

Gabe shook my hand and followed with, "Glad to have you with us. We have a long way to go so we need your input on a daily basis. The crew is working the north side footings today so they are hidden from sight. Let's walk over and I'll introduce you to Artimas, our foreman."

As we walked to the site, I saw Artimas standing with a wheelbarrow waiting for a load of rock. He was on level ground so I figured I wouldn't hurt him if I looped my whip around his knees. I pulled the whip out and saw

Ben look in wonder as to what I was doing. I cracked the whip and followed with a double loop around Artimas's knees. He dropped the wheelbarrow and turned with a mean look and immediately started laughing when he saw me. "Jack Knight, where the hell did you come from? Where's my big black dog? Ben, I didn't put this guy with the name when you told us about our new line super last week. Jack, it is good to see you survived the Indians in Denver."

Ben said, "You fellows know one another? Of all my crew I was concerned about you two hitting it off. I will sleep very well tonight. What does a big ugly Irishman have in common with a bullwhip, gun carrying cowboy from Denver?"

Artimas said, "A big black dog and a headless rat."

CHAPTER 62

On the ride back to my home in Milwaukie, Ben shook his head and said, "Jack, when you pulled that whip out you can't imagine the pictures that went through my head. I was not sure you were not going to whip Artimas before he figured out who you were and I wondered if you knew something about him that I didn't. You are quick as a flash with that thing. Ever use it for protection?"

"Yes, several times with Indians and a couple of times when I had to defend myself or a friend. It works better than a gun in some situations."

It was dark when we got to the house and Ben said he didn't want to make the buggy trip in the dark so he was staying the night. Benny had lit several lamps in the house and started a fire in the kitchen stove. Ben took a lamp and we went upstairs so he could show me the rooms up there. He suggested I take the front north bedroom as it was the largest and had a fireplace.

Benny had left six eggs and a loaf of bread on the table. Four apples were in a bowl in the center of the table next to the spoon cup. I scrambled the eggs and cut several slices of bread for our dinner. We were both tired and went to bed right after eating. The next morning, Ben headed for Portland just at daylight. I knocked on Benny's door and introduced myself and ask him to hook up the buckboard for me.

My first call would be to see Albert at the mill. He seemed to have a handle on the speed of the operation or lack thereof. I took a drawing off the table in my office that looked like the plans for track as far as the Molalla River.

The mill was just as loud as yesterday. Al was in his office and I brought the plans I picked up before I left and spread them out on his table.

"Al, tell me what I am looking at on this plan. It looks to me like the Molalla River is about five miles past the original 20 mile line Ben laid to get all the right-of-ways to build this line. I assume Warren has maps to Salem and has worked beyond the Molalla Bridge. I figure it's another 35 miles to Salem from the bridge. How is my guesswork for now?"

Al said, "You have a good start and have about the right mileage factors. We do have a problem with Warren. He tries to release just enough information to keep us going. If he would let us know his overall plotting we could plan much better and not have down time on any crew. We are expected to reach Salem by the end of this year. We need to get organized or it will take two years. I know that is why Ben hired you and I will help you all I can."

"Al, by tomorrow night, could I have a list of how many ties you can deliver a day and also how many board feet of bridge timber you can produce, a day. Those will be my first known factors and that gives me a start."

"I have a schedule, now, but, yes, give me time to go over my figures to make sure I am right. You know, the warehouse for cleats, spikes, gussets, fish joints and anything else used by the track crew is here, and I keep an inventory record up to date. It is here on the desk anytime you need information."

I asked Al, "Where is the blacksmith you use for the line?"

"Jack, I don't know. I give a list to Ben and tell him when we need the product and it is delivered by some delivery company."

"Ever have a problem with the product or delivery time?"

"Yes, Jack, several times last year we lost a couple of days of production due to late delivery. Never heard anyone complain about the product."

I said, "Al, thank you for the frank answers and I look forward to working with you. By the way, Ben has timber holdings. Are they sufficient for our needs?"

"Jack, when the railroad is finished we have timber enough to run this and another mill for 25 years. He made a real deal two years ago."

I needed to find Warren Albrite and have a heart-to-heart talk if this was going to work. I needed more information about him before I called on him. I wondered if I could worm information out of Kenneth Ping.

As I left, I ask Albert if he needed anything taken to Mr. Ping. "Yes, Jack, he wanted two dozen shovels, a dozen picks and a dozen new spike malls. If you take them I won't have to send a wagon up to him. Thanks a lot."

Glad I brought the buckboard. Gave me a great opening to talk to Mr. Ping and show I was contributing to our cause at the same time. The trip to the end of the line was uneventful so I had time to think of my discussion approach with Kenneth.

I saw Ken looking over a pile of rails and drove up close so he could see the hardware I had for him. He came over and climbed up on the buckboard with me and motioned for me to go to the end of the track. He got a couple of men to deliver the shovels, picks, and spike malls to the grade workers.

Ken said, "Jack, glad you came up here today. We need to talk. Warren and I had our once a week discussion this morning. My people can lay a grade within a half an inch of his request but when his figures change from one week to the next we all get upset. He has to get far enough ahead of us so that we only need him to come back and check our work once a week."

"Ok, Ken, the main reason I'm here is to figure out how to handle Warren. You two have worked together for a while. What is his problem? There seems to be a continued problem and Warren always seems to be part of it."

"Well, Jack, I feel Warren's problem is that we are not a Central Pacific or a Union Pacific laying ten miles of track a day. He used to work for the Central Pacific and that's what he compares us to. We have 75 Chinese laborers and they worked a thousand. And there were a thousand more to back them up when needed. We stock our production with wagons. He is used to a train dropping off 4,000 rails, and 20,000 ties every day. He thinks we are running a child's game instead of a railroad. We have a staff to lay three to four miles a month and our costs are scheduled to that goal. Warren just can't seem to work to our goals without making waves in scheduling and changes that are not necessary to accomplish them."

"To save time, how do I find Warren?"

Ken said, "Warren has a tent camp on the Molalla River. I don't think you can miss it when you get to the bridge site turn east for a ways. You should see him."

I noticed it was getting late to go there now and get home before dark so in the morning I would ride a horse to his camp. I wondered what I could say to this man to get him on board with the rest of us

CHAPTER 63

It was Friday morning the 28th of January. We only had 11 months to get the railroad rolling freight out of Salem. I went by the market yesterday on the way home and filled a bag with cans of fruit and salmon. Still had some of the bread Benny left on the table for Ben and me the first night in the house. I could last for a week now.

Benny had a horse saddled for me just as I had asked him to do last night. I rode for Warren's camp just after daylight. I still didn't know just how to handle him. I kept going over his background. I really didn't learn much about him from Ken. I wondered how old he was. You sure couldn't tell looking at his unkempt beard and hair. His voice didn't sound old and it had authority in it. I knew what father would tell him. Get your self cleaned up and we can talk. I could hear father now.

I had two hours to think of how to start with him, but was no closer to the answer when I saw his tent camp next to the river. I knew it was his place because I re-membered the horse hobbled close to the tent.

As I rode up he came out of the tent and says, "Well, I wondered how long it would take you to address the pain in everybody's neck?"

"Warren, let me start. Do you have enough information on paper for the crews to run all next week?"

He said, "Sure, passed it to Mr. Ping and Gabe Turner yesterday."

"Ok, Warren, tell you what we are going to do. You take a couple of days off and head into Portland and get cleaned up. Hair cut, get your beard cut off or trimmed if you want and buy some clothes that fit you. When that's all done come by the Milwaukie house and we can talk. By the way, how old are you?"

"Jack, I'm 34 and no one has talked to me like that in my life. Not sure I can accept your offer. You're just a kid."

"Tell you what, Warren, I might be just a kid to you, but this kid has a railroad to build and I need a surveyor that can get the job done. I hope it is you, but we do it the kid's way. If you can live with that I will see you Wednesday at the house in Milwaukie and we will talk."

With that I turned my horse and headed for the bridge site. Artimas and Gabe were on the far side of the river. I saw the small boat they used. My horse could swim but I didn't need to get wet in January. Artimas saw me and rowed across and picks me up.

Artimas said, "We saw you ride up the river earlier. Didn't hear any shots; must have been a good meeting. Warren is getting harder to work with every day. Don't think it is you, Jack. He has been impossible for some-time. Ben is soft with him and Warren takes advantage of that."

I said, "Let's give it a week. You might be surprised what happens. How are the anchors for your bridge coming? Bet Mr. Ping will be peeking at you by the end of February."

"We're a little behind. We had high water the first two weeks of this month so it was hard to work on our foundation but we had other preparation work on the grade so I think we will have the deck ready for rails when Ken gets to our site."

"Artimas, I'm going to ask you in three weeks if you will be ready for rails when Ken, gets here and I will need 'yes' or 'no' not 'I think.' Okay?"

"I'll have your answer, sir."

As I rode back to Milwaukie, I decided to swing by the market to pick up some vegetables and a few bottles of sarsaparilla. With the money I make now, I can afford some pleasures in life. I'm still in shock at the money Ben is willing to pay this cowboy. When Colonel Wheeler paid me $100 dollars a month to help Grady run that last herd into Kansas, I thought that was a lot.

It was Friday night and I knew the crews were only working half days on Saturday so I was not going to the job sites tomorrow. I asked Benny to eat super with me to find out about him and the fishing in the creek be-tween here and the saw mill.

Benny told me he went to school until he was 14. He was staying with an aunt in Portland, waiting for his parents to return from a missionary trip to Brazil. The steamer out of San Francisco bringing them home to Portland sank and they were lost. That was in July of 1865 and the steamer was called the Brother Jonathan he told me. His aunt died from grief over the loss of her only sister six weeks later. He was alone and had to find work to eat. He worked and begged around the waterfront and lived in abandoned shacks and hulls until two years ago. Ben caught him trying to steal food from a wagon he was loading to take supplies to a crew of workman.

Benny said, "Mr. Holladay grabbed me by my shirt and it was so old it tore and he just had cloth in his hands. He stuck a foot out and tripped me or I would have got away. Then he reached down and had me by the belt and I couldn't get away. He said if I was hungry I should ask for food, not try to steal it. I was 17 then and he wanted to know where my folks were. I said let me go; I don't have any folks. I started to hit him and he grabbed my arm and that's when he realized I was too weak to fight him. He sat me down and got on the ground next to me and asked why I didn't get a real job and try to live like other people instead of just trying to get by. I told him I tried to get a job but people just laughed at me and run me off. I am small now, but two years ago I was really small."

I had fried some potatoes and opened a can of salmon and heated it. With the bread and butter, it was a good meal and Benny ate until he was full.

Benny continued, "Mr. Holladay asked if I knew anything about horses. My father was a preacher and we had horses for him to get to his people and he taught me since I was very young to handle, feed and care for his horses since he didn't have time for that stuff. I said yes a little. Tell you what, he says, I need someone to handle my horses just like your father did. You can live in the barn and I will pay you with food and money. That's the way it's been now for over two years. I have a nice two room house to live in with a fine stove. I get my food at the market and just sign for it and Mr. Holladay gives me a twenty dollar gold piece every month."

"So, Benny, how long are you planning on living like this? Sounds like you will be 21 in a year or so."

"Well, I know I am slow thinking, but Mr. Holladay says I handle myself well enough to live on my own. But he likes me. I don't need anymore than I have here and he says I can stay till the cows come home. Mr. Holladay has no cows."

CHAPTER 64

The weekend and Monday slipped by rapidly. Tuesday morning there was a knock at the front door just as I was drinking my first cup of coffee. What a shock. I recognized the horse in front, but not the man standing on the front porch.

Warren Albrite stood in a brown suit, highly polished boots, and a new white hat. He was clean shaven with short hair and was grinning from ear to ear.

Warren said, "Jack, just let me talk for a minute. I have not felt so good for three years. When you left last Friday, I got to thinking about everything you said. I smelled myself and thought I would not want to be around me like this. I took my camp down and stored it at the mill. Rode to Portland and laid in a hot bath for an hour. Got me a room and on Saturday found my old barber and had a shave with a hair cut. Went down the street and bought new clothes, boots, and this hat. That night I went to a bar and had a drink of Scotch whiskey. Jack, I had forgotten what life was all about. My wife and two-year-old-son were killed in a Nez Pierce raid over three years ago and

I have not got over that yet. Your kick in the pants has not put that aside, but made me look at myself and I didn't like what I saw."

I said, "Well, Warren, come on in. How about some coffee? I make strong coffee but you can water it down if you want. By the way, you don't look 34 and I can see why Ben called you a ladies' man. You are one handsome devil. I understand a little bit better than last week. Sorry for your loss."

"Jack, while I sat in the hot bath, I thought about my life and considered why the men I work with have not shot me for the way I treated them lately. I used to love working with good people. Ben has some very fine men working for him. I do have trouble in my own mind thinking that we are a miniature Central Pacific railroad and expecting us to set more rails a day. I know now I have to scale my thinking to the job I am paid to perform. You want quality and safety from me. If you will let me, I know I can give this to our cause."

"Warren, this all sounds good today but remember the schedules and the speed we progress at are set by the size of the crew that Ben lets us have. You mentioned one thing that is important to me and that is safety. Remember we need to help the Chinese with safety just as much as all the others. Let's do this for a while and see how it works. Saturday mornings we meet here and go over your route and problems that you see coming up. If we need one of the other principles involved they can meet here too. If you need my office in there, the big table is yours. As you know, Ben expects to be hauling freight out of Salem by December of this year. Have you traveled the right-of-way into Salem yet?"

"No, and I should have."

"Ok, you and I are riding to Salem. I assume you know about where the right-of-way runs without all of your gear to guide us."

"Yes, all I need is a compass."

"All right, we can ride part way today and stop at a stage stop to eat and sleep. Did you buy some work clothes in Portland?"

"I did. Can I change before we leave? I have my other clothes in my saddle bags along with some canned goods."

"Warren, you can leave what you don't want to take. We will come back here and you can stay the night when we return, probably Friday, with luck."

Benny saddled my horse while I cooked off some bacon and stuffed it on some biscuits with cheese. This would be breakfast for Warren and me.

Over the next four days I got a lesson in surveying along with the story of a lonely man trying to forget the two people he loved and lost.

The Willamette Valley was green and the land was rolling. Small hills were scattered here and there. There were no mountains to have to find a pass. Several creeks that feed the Willamette River needed bridges, but other than a few cut and fill areas, our crews had little resistance. I saw what Ben was talking about when he said the valley could produce enough grain to export out of state.

The farmers were able to use steamboats now to transport their goods to Portland, but the area was growing so fast they needed the railroad to keep up. The costs would go down too, since the railroad rates are cheaper than the boats.

When we returned to Milwaukie late Friday, I asked Warren to stay the night before heading up the river to set up his camp.

"Ok, Jack. I appreciate your hospitality. I have enjoyed the time we spent together and you have helped me get back into the swing of life. I'm not sure where I was headed but it was not good. The life you have lived is far more exciting than mine has ever been. For a man your age to have had the experiences and mixed with the characters you have in such a short time is great. I enjoy your stories."

"Well, I started early and have had some good teachers. You heard some stories that I have never told anyone else. I just never spent time with any one person long enough to relate most of those stories."

"Warren, I think if we are going to run this construction on a timely basis and control everybody's efforts to the maximum, we need to project our progress in 10 stages or where we should be at the end of each of the next 10 months. I see less than 30 miles left. But what I see out there we can't just say we will do three miles per month. A couple of areas out there will take longer than a month for a crew our size to complete and I saw some level ground we should do much faster. Weather patterns have to be considered, too. Mr. Ping tells me he will cross Turners Bridge at the Molalla by the end of February, so we have only nine stages to worry about. Sound like something we can schedule by the end of this month?"

"That gives me three weeks, Jack. I'll have it if I have to work every weekend. My grunt might not get to chase women on the weekends but he should be with us to get it done on that timeline. He should be all worn out by now and ready to work. I told him to take this week off last Friday. Told him I had personal business to take care of. He will be shocked to see me clean shaven and hair cut. He has hinted I should do it but never pushed it. I think he was afraid I might fire him if he pushed too much. He is a good worker. I need to tell Donald that, because I have been very hard on him the last year."

CHAPTER 65

It was Monday, the last day of February. Rails were laid on the bridge over the Molalla River. I scheduled a meeting for Tuesday for all my top leaders: Warren Albrite, Kenneth Ping, Gabe Turner, Albert Allen, and Artimas York. This would be the first time I had them all together at the same site. My office walls were now covered with maps, schedules, and inventory levels for different sites.

"Gentlemen, around these walls are our future. All of you have been involved with the planning of the next nine months, so there should be no surprises. For the next two hours, I would like you all to look at what I have put together and tell me what needs a change if any. You will notice that the bridges, water towers, and stations are marked on the main map. We have one problem not discussed yet. That is a turn around at Salem. I've seen only one round house, beside the one in Portland. Gabe, do we need outside input on this or are you up for that challenge?"

Gabe answered, "I came to work for Holladay after the one in Portland was finished but I think I can improve on that one, given a chance."

I said, "My take on the Salem station and round house is that we need to start on that portion in August, no later than the first of September if it is to be open and operating by December. Gabe, can you have plans for both put together by the last week in March?"

Gabe grinned, "I'm one third done already. Thought maybe you would forget about it until too late. Should have known better."

I said, "I know this is early to start talking about, but remember we have to begin planning for next year and our assault on the rails to Eugene by October of this year. We are expected to run 60 some miles of rails next year not, less than 40 like this year. Warren tells me the terrain is a little tough compared to the level ground we have experienced up 'til now. I have talked with Ben and he figures we will have to expand the crews. He feels the Salem revenue will help that expansion,"

Artimas said, "When I rode up from California, I remember three large rivers we crossed after leaving Eugene. They were bigger rivers and deeper than the two we have to build over getting to Salem. Mr. Holladay is right when he says we will need more crew for that stretch of road."

No one seemed to have any problems with the schedules and drawings presented, so it was my turn.

"Gentlemen, we have left one thing out of our plans. That is a spur to the lumber mill. As we continue farther from the mill it is no longer reasonable to haul our rails, ties, and other needs by wagon. Every mile of track needs around 2,300 ties and 400 rails. Now that we have bridged the Molalla River we should start moving product by rail. I need to talk to Ben about this since he will have to schedule flat cars and engines as we need them. The bridge timbers will still have to go by wagon since that crew is always way ahead of Kenneth. Ken, you need to figure a way to split your crew for this job. Warren has finished his work on the spur so you and Gabe need to see what is necessary to start work." I continued, "I want to congratulate all of you for safety. There has been nothing but a few cuts and splinters for the month of February. No serious accidents help everyone's attitude and productivity."

On the 17th of March, Ben rode to Milwaukie to tell me we now work for the newly incorporated Oregon & California railroad. He told me he also acquired the West Side Company but was only having it go as far as McMinnville over the next two years. He asked me to make a pot of coffee and bring it into my office.

As we sat to talk he said, "Jack, in two months you have organized this rag tag group into a fine company. Albert has time now to expand the mill because of the way you schedule. Warren Albrite is a new man and just like he was two years ago when we worked closely together. You have done well. I need to do something for you. In

April, I am adding $200 to your salary. Just do one thing for me, help Albert Allen with his expansion. He is going to ask you for help."

Ben continued, "You are a very busy man. If you have no objections, I would like to add to your household staff. Orrin has a son that wants to become a porter on the railroad but is too young right now. Orrin has worked with him and says he would make you a fine gentleman's gentleman. James cooks, cleans, and will be at your call anytime you need him. I will pay him just like I do Benny."

I said, "Ben, I have a problem with that. I feel all men are equal, no matter their color, race, or religion."

"Jack, come on. Orrin and James are both free men. I pay them well and treat them as men, not slaves. They are employees just like all the Chinese, Irish, and Indians you have working on the railroad."

"All right, we will give it a go. But James needs to know I require training just like he does. We will learn together. My family would be appalled if they knew I had this kind of domestic help."

"You and James will be fine. Only thing he will ask is for, Sunday off to be with his family and also a horse and saddle to ride."

Friday, I rode to Aurora. Ken's crew had made the three miles from the bridge over the Molalla River to the first settlement past the bridge in 14 work days. Aurora area was all farm land worked predominately by German immigrants since before the 1860s. They welcomed the railroad and a way to get products to Portland without wagons and mules. On the south side of town we were building a spur to leave rail cars on for loading with a 50 foot dock for easy transfer. Artimas had a crew building the dock.

I rode up to Artimas, I said, "When will you be through here and on to French Prairie in the Gervais area?"

"Jack, we will finish this up tomorrow. Albert sent two loads of timbers by here Tuesday so we have plenty of wood to start Monday. We finished all the gussets on your bridge back there last Saturday. You can tell Ben he can use the bridge any time now."

I said, "Artimas, he has his hands full laying out his town called Canby back north of that bridge. He is naming the town for a friend, Brigadier-General Edward Richard Sprigg Canby. He has four surveyors working overtime to get the town laid out and find a spot for a depot."

CHAPTER 66

James was working out well. He cooked my meals and kept the house in good shape. I wouldn't let him work in my office because when he finished in there I couldn't find anything. He and Benny got along great. I hadn't got James to eat with me yet but I was still working on it. I offered him a large bedroom upstairs but he liked the maid or butler quarters behind the kitchen just fine. After the dishes were washed at night, I never saw him. I found he reads any time he has nothing else pressing. I was getting used to having the clothes I asked for the night before ready next to my shaving cubical every morning. On Thursday, September 1st, I rode to Salem for a meeting with Warren, Gabe, and Artimas. We needed to start moving dirt if we were to have the round house ready when Mr. Ping got his rails here in November. Gabe Turner had all of his drawings and Warren had stakes all over the area. Donald, Warren's assistant, was digging a ditch around some of the stakes.

"Donald is marking the circumference for our hole." Gabe said, "It will be three feet deep and lined with brick. Warren and I both feel we should hire a crew led by Artimas to dig and line the sump because his bridge crew is tied up for the rest of this month. We also have to figure for the drainage on this sump and plan for its run off. Warren and Donald need to be here so I will bird dog Artimas's crew for a couple of weeks."

"Let me wire Ben and get his ok to spend that kind of money. I'm sure he will ok it but I have never spent that much above our normal budget," I said.

In downtown Salem, I sent a wire to Ben. I returned to Warren's camp and got a miserable night's sleep. The next morning I got a wire. I should have known he would want an estimate. I rode back to the site and had a conference.

Gabe said, "Sorry, Jack. I had a figure yesterday and could have saved time. I know how Ben is. It's my fault I didn't give it to you."

"It's still early. Maybe we can still get this done today so we can start hiring on Monday. I will stay in Salem 'til you're set up, Artimas." I rode back to the telegraph office and sent the estimate telling the telegrapher that I will return before he closes hoping I get an answer today.

By 5:00 p.m., my answer arrived. Ben said go ahead with the plan and Oregon Iron Works in Oswego would have round house castings ready September 19. On my ride back, I saw the Bennett House on State Street and stopped to make reservations for the next three days. I told Artimas I would stay until he had a crew. When I got back, I told the guys, "Ben says OK to our plan. From what he says, I can load the castings from Oregon Iron on the 20th. I'll borrow three wagons from the mill and have that stuff on site here by Thursday, the 22nd."

We did not finish the round house by September 29th, but on Thursday September 29, 1870 the first Oregon & California steam train whistled south through the Willamette Valley from Portland to Salem.

We completed the line to Albany in December, another 18 miles past Salem and we had freight running from Albany to Portland by my 22nd birthday on Saturday, December 24, 1870.

The next 49 miles to Eugene took over 11 months. We had bigger and longer bridges and a few more cut and fill areas to contend with. We continued to move our crews with trains carrying supplies to a moving site. As sidings were built, the crews had sleeping and eating quarters built into rail cars and were moved closer to the site every week. We expanded the bridge crew by two as the McKenzie and Willamette Rivers had to be bridged. We were over the McKenzie River and into Eugene by November 1871. We finished the Depot and round house by mid-December. December 1871 was a cold and wet month. We left the crew quarters with wood and food for the crew members who don't want to go home. I took Gabe, Warren, Artimas, and Donald McBride, who became the second bridge crew foreman, to my home in Milwaukie for the last two weeks of December to rest and relax after a tough year. Mr. Ping came around during the day as his family lived in Oswego, a couple of miles down the road. Albert had his logging crew out of the woods so he had time to join us also during the day. James was a very busy fellow. He was in his element with all of us to take care of. Five of us were at breakfast, seven at lunch and sometimes eight for dinner as Ben Holladay came by to talk several times during our planning meetings for the coming year's assault on the next 70 miles to Roseburg, Oregon.

We celebrated my 23rd birthday, December 24, 1871 and Christmas as one holiday. We set up a tree in the large drawing room and had the Ping and Allen children in for gift distribution by Benny and to all in the house.

CHAPTER 67

1872 was not only a leap year and we had one extra day to build a railroad, but I was now old enough to vote this year.

My crew had returned to Eugene, and by the end of January, had completed the line to Cottage Grove, spanning the Willamette River twice with bridges.

Rail service to Eugene from Portland was now on a daily schedule. The same engine pulled a Pullman car with freight cars and returned to Portland the same evening except for Sundays.

On Thursday, February 1, I was riding to Eugene and read in the Oregonian newspaper that Bill Cody during January had taken Grand Duke Alexandrovich of Russia on a highly publicized royal hunt in Kansas and Nebraska.

It had been over two years since I had seen a buffalo. You would think that with all the good fishing I did, my mind would not wander to the wide open spaces of Kansas and Colorado. I knew if I ever left Ben Holladay's employment, I would not live the pampered lifestyle I had here in Oregon. I had a nice home. Benny took care of my livestock. James cooked, cleaned, and had my clothes taken care of on a daily basis. And the money, where do you make the kind of money Ben paid me?

The terrain south of Cottage Grove became very hilly and Warren had to run the right-of-way in an easterly direction and then westerly to continue south toward Roseburg to avoid large cuts. As he continued south, we were forced to make large cuts and fills as the Cascade Mountains on the east and the Coast range on the west seemed to come together and we were no longer working in a more or less level valley like the Willamette to Eugene. We were blasting on a daily basis and had to increase our labor force to keep the rails moving south. I had temporary quarters in Cottage Grove and spent at least three days a week on site. Kenneth Ping was doing well in my point of view but Ben was down here at least once every other week pushing for more track. Fortunately, Ben went through me to push the crews. On Wednesday, March 20, we were laying rails and it was raining making the ground slippery. Near dark I was trying to help and slipped on a slick tie and fell just as the rail setters place two rails end to end. My right index finger was between the ends of the rails as they came together. When I pulled my hand away, I had no index finger clear to the knuckle joint. The amputation was so quick the pain did not hit for several seconds. Some of the crew helped me to the engine at the end of the line and we rode back to Cottage Grove and a doctor.

As the doctor sewed the skin together over the knuckle, he remarked that there went my trigger finger. I had to correct him and let him know the next finger was my trigger finger and that the index just lied above to steady the aim. I'm sure there would have to be some practice to regain my accuracy. The handle on the whip could take time to get used to, also.

April and May were dry and our progress was good, even by Ben's watchful eye. The swelling in my hand had left and I was regaining the full use of it. Still tender, but I could draw my weapon now, if needed. The whip was another story. I never realized the strength needed in your hand to use the whip. I would be patient and work the hand back to its original strength in time.

It was Monday, June 3, and I was riding the Pullman to Eugene. As I scan the news from the east in the Oregonian, the name Buffalo Bill Cody catches my eye. The news story tells of an Indian fight back on April 26 in Nebraska where Billy, as a civilian scout with the Fifth Cavalry, with bravery and tenacity beyond the norm, helped Captain Charles Meinhold. Meinhold made the recommendation for the Congressional Medal of Honor because Billy saved several troopers' lives and killed one Indian to recover their horses. President Ulysses S. Grant made the presentation, by mail, on May 22, 1872. That must have been a fight and a half. Billy was only three years older than I am and he had won the Medal of Honor. The world was passing me by out here in Oregon.

The more whites that moved in on Indian Territory, the harder the Indians were to keep calm. Our government made treaties and broke them as soon as it is to their advantage. Edwin's housekeeper, Rose, was right. The Indian needed to be represented by council it could trust.

As August and September were upon us, Ben was not his usual self. He was argumentative and downright surly to the men and would spit a cuss word out at the drop of a hat. Considering the terrain and the number of bridges we had to build, we were making good time and laid rails every day.

I realized I had to have a talk with Ben before our company started falling apart.

CHAPTER 68

It was the end of the first week in October and as I rode the Pullman toward Milwaukie; I had a strange feeling that something was wrong. The newspaper was full of bad news about the economy. The Republican Party had split and Horace Greely, a liberal Republican, was running on the Liberal Republican Party's ticket for President. Ulysses S. Grant was running for a second term and was expected to win. Crops were good here in the Willamette Valley and prices seemed stable but there seemed to be a lot of nervous people in Portland. On Saturday morning, I had Benny saddle a horse for a ride to Portland and a talk with Ben.

As I knocked on the door, Orrin opens it and said, "Jack, glad to see you!" Then he dropped his voice and said, "Ben needs your help, Jack; he's in trouble."

What a way to start my day. I came here to get my head on straight and now Ben needed my help. Orrin led me into Ben's home office and offered me a cup of coffee that I needed badly.

Ben Holladay walked into the room unshaven and in slippers. "Jack, we need to talk. I am having some problems and they are big ones. You have been like my own son so I will find a place for you. I have to tell you that we are going to put the Oregon & California Railroad into bankruptcy. What gets finished by the end of this month is as far as she goes. Your part of the company will be shut down until further notice." Ben got himself a cup of coffee and continued, "I have to protect my timber and the mill. I have the steamships to operate also. The railroad will keep running, but by the direction of the bank, a judge puts in control. I have over-extended myself but will come back when the economy surges back. Benny will come to my home here in Portland. James is old enough to get the porter's job he has wanted. Your crews will be let go October 31. Hopefully, the line will be in Roseburg by then."

"Ben, I felt something was wrong. You have not been yourself for a month or so. I will stay till October 31. But as soon as I vote, November 5, I will head to San Francisco, California. I love you and respect you but you don't need me around to worry about. We have had a good ride for almost three years and what you have taught me and given me will remain with me the rest of my life. If I were to stay I would feel like extra baggage and you don't need that. I feel I was a very productive part of your railroad and let's leave it that way. And, yes, the line will be in Roseburg when we shut down."

"Son, I have worried about this conversation for a month. You are quite a man. And I respect your wishes. I hope you saved some money over the last few months. It is a bad economy out there."

"I'm fine, Ben. I will have three or four 20 dollar gold pieces when I hit San Francisco."

Over the next four weeks, the crews worked wonders as they finished the round house and depot. All the workers were being phased out as we completed projects. All of the management team was aware of what was to happen at the end of the month. Warren and Donald were teaming up again and moving to central California for a railroad job. Gabe said he would retire with a job he had in Seattle. Kenneth Ping was going to build a road from Portland to The Dalles alongside the Columbia River. Artimas York said a brother in Jacksonville, Oregon had a saloon and wanted him to come help him run it. My whole company had someplace to go except me. That's all right. If Edwin had not spent the $12,000 that I had sent him to invest over the last two or so years, I might not work for a little while.

As we completed the company's withdrawal from Roseburg, Gabe and Artimas were the last two beside me to ride the rails back to Milwaukie.

Benny had moved the stock except one horse to the Portland barn. James had gone to San Francisco on a steamer and would end up in Atchison, Kansas working for the Atchison, Topeka & Santa Fe railroad as a porter.

I had my ticket on the S. S. Yosemite that left Portland on November 7, 1872. I had a steamer trunk now to worry about and two more pieces of luggage, beside my saddle. I had no idea where I will wear the clothes that I had accumulated but they were too good to throw away.

The house in Milwaukie was cold and I had cleaned all the food out of the house so I had to eat in town.

On Tuesday, November 5, I voted for the first time and felt good about it. Now if we get enough votes for Ulysses S. Grant maybe the country would prosper.

On November 7, Orrin took me to the dock in a buckboard and I boarded the side wheeler for my trip to San Francisco, and the rest of my life.

ABOUT THE AUTHOR

To start at the beginning, I was born May 27, 1936 in southern Oregon. My father and maternal grandfather were both outdoorsmen so I naturally migrated to the adventures of the area laid before me. Fishing, hunting and camping at the high lakes in the Cascade Mountains and following several rivers in the area for steel-head and trout became my passion.

Spending a lot of time with both of these gentlemen from about age 10, I listened to stories of my paternal grandfather's adventures and escapades from men who knew him very well and liked to pass these stories on. Sometimes the three of us with an uncle would spend four or five days hiking and fishing the lakes and rivers of southern Oregon. At night at the campfire, the stories would start.

As I grew up, many of these stories of adventure my grandfather endured and lived through kept returning to my memory and I began saying I am going to write a book someday so others would know how one man coped with the American West. In school all of the English teachers that I had would probably roll over in their graves if they knew I would someday write a novel as English was one of my worst subjects. History and science got me through with the help of geography and arithmetic.

My education included a major in forestry at Oregon State, now a University, but marriage to my high school sweetheart redirected my path and later continued education at San Diego State to study engineering. During the following years I owned and managed several businesses, leaving little time for writing other than technical and trade reports. Growing up and raising a family of three boys and three girls and spending the time to make a living curtailed my writing a novel; however, I would not change the challenge of watching them grow up and having grand-kids for anything.

Finally retiring for the third time in 2001, my thoughts returned to the desire of writing about my grandfather. My wife, Yvonne, and I moved to Arizona and I started my novel and wrote chapter one about five times before I was able to start chapter two. At 70 years old, I enrolled in a writing class at Pima Community College and my teacher explained to me that we all have a story to tell and we just have to start putting it on paper.

I have enjoyed writing West by Bullwhip mostly because of the memories that returned when recalling the stories by the many campfires and miles traveled with my father.